One Smoking Hot Fairy Tail

KEVIN JAMES BREAUX

Write Makes Might!

ONE SMOKING HOT FAIRY TAIL

Dedication

One Smoking Hot Fairy Tail is dedicated to cosplayers, gamers, and anime lovers worldwide.

ISBN, Rights, Credits

Write Makes Might!
ISBN: 9798868959219

Copyright © 2016 Kevin James Breaux
New 2024 Edition
All rights reserved.

Editor: Gretchen Stelter of Cogitate Studios
Cover Artwork: Shawn Ignatius Tan
Cover Design: Kevin James Breaux
Layouts: Kevin James Breaux

Copyright © 2016 by Kevin James Breaux

All rights reserved. No part of this book may be reproduced in any manner whatsoever without written permission except in the case of brief quotations embodied in critical articles and reviews.

New Printing, 2024 - Write Makes Might!

Chapter One

The Past is Not Always the Past

Sabrina dreamt about that night all the time. Sometimes tiny details were changed—the kind of car she was driving, the name of the corporation she targeted, the number of animals she saved—but it always ended the same. After so much excitement, so much thrill and pleasure, she always forgot to pick up Cade's camera. *That stupid fucking camera.*

She remembered every detail about it: its brand, its resolution, the lens size, that it was made in Japan. It haunted her so much that she had bought several cameras identical to it since, just to smash them to bits. Her first therapist said that it might help, but except for giving her a brief moment of delight when the tiny circuit boards and chips spilled from the cameras like a slasher-film victim's guts, it really did nothing to alleviate the pain of the past.

The dream came tonight shortly after she'd collapsed in bed half-naked and fully drunk—at least she was alone and not making another mistake like the one she had made with the new host of *American Idol Replay*.

Sabrina had wanted to touch herself, but her hand only made it as far as her lower stomach, her long, pink and white fingernails just inside her panties, before she passed out. However, there could still be satisfaction to come. The dream was not entirely bad, after all. It may have featured the catalyst to the worst night of her life, but it also contained some of the best sex she'd ever had.

Sabrina dashed across the parking lot, looking between the mesmerizing flicker of a dying streetlamp and the building behind her. The emptiness of the parking lot, the stillness of the air—it all seemed surreal, like something out of an old horror film. But she was not afraid of movie monsters—not when she knew real ones existed.

Sabrina was out of breath, both panicked and energized. She coughed harshly for a moment, irritated to have the exhilaration of the moment ruined by her hack. *I really need to fucking quit smoking.* She took one last glance behind her at the pharmaceutical corporation's lab. There was no alarm blaring, no flashing security lights; they had succeeded. Those poor lab animals were finally going to be safe.

"Tell me again, Cade, why you made me park so freaking far away?"

"I destroyed the surveillance cameras on the east side of the building where the loading docks are, but that pink car of yours... it's like a damned billboard advertising America's sweetheart, Sabrina London, is here," her boyfriend replied.

It had only been six months since they'd met, but it felt like longer. As much as she hated the term "whirlwind romance," it applied to the two of them. It had been the best six months of her life. She was in love, but she wasn't sure if he knew that yet or felt the same. The undead—their emotions could be nearly impossible to read, even for someone as empathic as her.

"Slow down!"

Cade pointed his tiny HD camera at her feet and grimaced. "I wouldn't have to slow down if your boots didn't have heels. What are those, five inches tall?"

"Three and a quarter inch, actually, and very sturdy. I mean, they better fucking be for eight hundred bucks."

"When I told you to wear boots tonight, I meant combat boots or work boots."

"Jimmy Choo doesn't make combat boots."

"Who?" Cade snickered. "Never mind. Keep running, my sweet sunshine. We don't want to be here when the authorities arrive."

Sabrina smiled; she loved it when he called her that.

"Wait," Cade said, suddenly serious.

"What? Did we forget something?" Sabrina nearly choked on her fear.

"You wore combat boots with the camouflage bikini in that one magazine protesting the war in the Middle East." Cade smirked, running his tongue over his teeth. "I remember that photograph very well. It was my favorite to—"

"I remember that one too," Sabrina interrupted. "Good pay. I kept the bikini but not the boots. I hated those boots—heavy things, made my toes all yucky and sweaty."

"They *gave* you the bikini?"

"Well, I *normally* get to keep what I wear."

"You stole it."

"I didn't *steal it*, Cade. That would be wrong."

"You say that now," he laughed.

A truck roared nearby as they reached her car, a pink Lamborghini Gallardo with opalescent rims. The sound assured them their accomplice was making his escape, speeding down the main road, away from the building. Both tracked the vehicle until it was well past the two traffic lights and out of sight.

"Good. He's clear." Cade nodded. "Let's make haste."

Sabrina jumped in and floored it—racing out of the parking lot in the opposite direction of the delivery truck. Not a minute later, Sabrina caught Cade's eyes on her legs as they worked the pedals. His lustful stare reminded her of the promise she had made: his help with this excursion for a night full of passion—a night that, even in his long life, he would not soon forget.

"Are you sure he'll do what we asked? I mean, can he be trusted not to, you know, eat any of the animals?"

Cade lifted his eyes from where they had been glued to her inner thigh and answered, "You know Nicodemus."

"Sure, I've seen him out a few times these past two weeks, but the guy just creeps me the hell out."

Cade laughed.

"Shut up." Sabrina smacked his leg. "You know I've waited a very long time to do this."

"I know."

She paused to catch her breath; the adrenaline that had burned inside her moments ago had begun to wear off, and with its absence came the urge to yawn.

"You and Nico have talked a few times. You should already know he's honorable," Cade said.

"Honestly, Cade, the old man can be a little hard to communicate with. I swear, when I talk to him, he just looks straight through me."

"Well, he still has trouble with English... especially its modern incarnation."

"Still?" Sabrina replied. "I just don't want to find out tomorrow that he ate them all."

"He promised me all the animals would be distributed, safely, among the five pet rescues you provided addresses for. The colonel takes *all* his jobs seriously. You have nothing to worry about, my love."

"Good."

"Regardless, I made sure he ate before the mission."

She looked at Cade's smiling face and laughed. "Thanks."

Sabrina shifted gears and the engine growled in that way that always made her feel more... *alive*. When the speedometer hit sixty-five, she pretended to look for cars behind them while she checked her makeup in the rearview.

"I still don't understand why, after all this time, you two are besties. I mean you guys are so... different."

Cade shook his head. "You and Moselle are different."

"I know..." Sabrina wanted to have a better comeback. "But he's like sixty. You guys look like you could be father and son."

"We are father and son—well, as near as our kind can come. You know Nico is the closest thing I'll ever have to a—"

"I don't like when you say that."

"Sabrina, I told you when we first started dating that our love, no matter how grand, would never create a child."

"I know. I know." Sabrina pushed the thought out of her head. "Can you honestly say people have never thought you two were maybe—"

"Sabrina, if it was you who had spent the entire winter with Nicodemus in Stalingrad..." Cade trailed off.

"Are you okay?"

"Stalingrad." Cade shivered. "It brings back a flood of memories. Gun fire, explosions, screams, death, blood. So much blood."

"I'm sorry." Sabrina patted Cade's knee.

"Don't be."

"Let's talk about something else."

"The more I think of it, there's no one I would rather share a foxhole with than Nicodemus."

"Gross," Sabrina let slip.

"Mother Russia," Cade sighed.

"Someday, you'll have to take me there."

"Perhaps. I haven't returned since World War Two." Cade pondered a moment. "I hear the Cold War ruined much of its history and splendor."

Sabrina glanced over at Cade. She still had to remind herself he was centuries old, regardless of how young he looked. When a twitch crawled across his handsome, clean-shaven face, and ended in a wince, Sabrina knew something was wrong.

"Hey, you okay?"

"Pull over."

"Why? What's wrong?"

"Sabrina, please, pull the vehicle over."

Sabrina turned down a side street and parked behind an abandoned building. The surrounding area was filled with shadows, but with her high beams on, enough of the place could be seen that she felt safe. As soon as she put the car in park, Cade was out the door so fast a pile of receipts she had stuffed in her cup holder were knocked loose.

"Cade?"

He was gone for a moment but reappeared several feet in front of the car. Awash in the bright headlights, he fell to his hands and knees, the look of pain on his face clear in the harsh glare.

"What is it?" Sabrina asked as she stepped out of the car.

"The pull. The pull is too strong."

"The what? Cade, stop fooling around." She approached him cautiously.

By the strain on his face and the way the lean muscles in his arms bulged, she would have sworn he was in the midst of a heart attack or a stroke. When he did not answer her pleas, Sabrina shouted, "What the fuck is wrong?"

"Too long. I cannot fight it much longer..."

Sabrina wrapped her hands around his arm and tried to help him up. Cade was heavier than he looked, but she tugged until he was finally standing.

"What the hell do you have in your pockets, Cade? Lead?"

"Bullets."

"Bullets?"

Sabrina reached into his jacket pocket and withdrew a handful of bullets. "You weren't fucking kidding."

"Gun's worthless without ammo," he grunted.

"Cade..."

Sabrina didn't know whether to yell at him or hug him. She had no idea what was going on and he was being his normal, stubborn, uninformative self.

"I'm sorry, my love, all this excitement, and I haven't eaten all day. I'm just hungry."

"You scared me. I thought something was seriously wrong, like you were having a stroke or something." She slapped his shoulder.

"You know how I get if I don't eat."

Sabrina frowned, but a sly grin was forming on Cade's face—one she had come to know meant trouble.

"I love you."

"I love you." Sabrina finally relaxed. "Cade, I think I've had my fill of excitement tonight."

"Are you sure? Because I do recall you saying something about going back to your place to—"

She stopped him before he could say it. "Yes, I did. Let's hurry, okay?"

"Why wait?"

Sabrina tilted her head back and moaned into his lips; the sensation of her breath being stolen was as pleasurable as it was painful. The blue-black sky was all she could see, and she fixed her eyes on the brightest star. *Don't focus on the coming pain*, she told herself. *Don't focus on the pain.*

With a yank, Sabrina's hoodie and shirt came off. She hoped he hadn't torn the hoodie; it was one of her favorites—given to her by the owner and head designer of Rebel Spirit Clothing.

"Cade..." her voice softly faded away.

He gently slid his hands up her back but then yanked again, ripping her bra off as well, leaving her hardened nipples open to the cool night air.

Sabrina's body tensed up as Cade's cold tongue worked the tight buds. She anticipated the first bite, knowing it would hurt. She tried to think of anything else, to concentrate on his flicking tongue, but was still jolted with irrepressible fear when his long fangs brushed her flesh. The first bite was always the hardest. Cade did his best to control his nature, but his hunger for her love was often outweighed by his hunger for blood. Sabrina gazed down at her breasts in his hands as he massaged them, running his tongue up her quivering chest to the base of her neck.

"Fuck, Cade!" Sabrina yelped as he penetrated her breast where it met her armpit—one of his favorite spots.

"Sorry."

Sabrina blinked her tearing eyes and whispered, "Someone might see us."

Cade smiled and revealed the tiny video camera clutched in his hand. When he pointed it at them both, he chuckled. "Smile, my love."

"You've got to be fucking kidding me, Cade," Sabrina grumbled on.

"Not at all."

She swatted the camera out of his hand, the small electronic thing, no larger than a credit card, landing on the ground beside them.

Sabrina thought to grab it and turn it off, but in the blink of an eye, Cade had spun her around and bent her over, her hands the only things at rest on the hood of the car.

Running his fingertips down her bare back, he leaned in and whispered, "I want you to release—"

"Not here," Sabrina replied over her shoulder, her long blonde hair shielding her embarrassment.

"Why not?"

"I don't want anyone to see me—us."

Sabrina heard his frustrated sigh; it was deafening to her. She did not want to disappoint him, not after all he had done for her tonight, so she peeled her tight leather pants off slow and steady.

"What are you waiting for?" Sabrina asked huskily. "Aren't you going to fuck me?"

"Yes."

Sabrina jumped when she felt something cold slide up her inner thigh, to the softness of her folds, and then scrape up her back, to her right hip. When her panties began to move, she realized exactly what she was feeling.

"Don't cut them," she said sternly.

It was too late; a simple flick of Cade's hand severed the elastic band. Now completely naked, Sabrina spun around to face him and poked him in the chest.

"I don't think you realize how many pairs of my panties you ruin, Cade."

"Maybe I do."

"You know what I mean!"

"Should I buy you some new bloomers, sweetie?"

Sabrina wanted to say something witty back, but all of a sudden his icy hand was cupping her, caressing the very area the small article of clothing had just been covering. Cade began to spread her open, soothing the ache that had been building between her legs since the night started.

"Do you remember our first time?"

"Yes."

His fingers, although chilly, were welcome inside her and she guided them in deeper. Cade moved, slowly at first, gliding gracefully in and out, making her quiver.

"What do you remember most?"

As one hand fondled the warm, soft space between her legs, the other cupped her breast, giving it a squeeze while lifting it to his mouth.

"I remember how much it hurt, how the pain suddenly shifted to pleasure."

A long kiss stole away time. She only felt Cade; the rest was nothingness. Sabrina's eyes fluttered open when she felt his hard length brush against her wetness. Their eyes locked as he entered her. Sabrina smiled. With each push inside her, he brought her closer to the edge, blocking out thoughts of anything but their physical connection.

"What else?"

"What else do I remember?" she asked.

He did not answer. By the look on his face, he was in ecstasy. Sabrina took great pride in knowing how good she could make him feel. The notion amazed her. It had such beautiful meaning—she was everything her man needed: body, soul, and...

"I remember the blood."

With that, Cade bit her again, sinking his teeth into her shoulder as he increased the tempo of his thrusts.

She wrapped her arms around him and whispered, "Never let me go."

Waking up in her bedroom after the dream again, Sabrina screamed. *The camera, the fucking camera.* Grunting in anger, she reached down the front of her underwear. Tonight, the dream was unsatisfying in every way. Tonight, Sabrina needed to take control.

Chapter Two

Fame

Something seemed wrong. Sabrina had always been sensitive to the world around her as well as its minute changes, and her whole body was telling her: something was off.

Dressed in her pink Agent Provocateur bikini, Sabrina stared down into the buzzing city of Beverly Hills from the balcony of her Rodeo Drive penthouse apartment, twisting her jeweled silver bangle. It had become a habit over the past few years, one that normally surfaced when she was anxious.

The wind fluttered the pages of an old *People* magazine beside her. Startled out of thought, she listened to the tips of the glossy paper as they struck the white wood of the French bistro table.

That magazine—she would never forget the day it was given to her. One year ago, Sabrina had stood on that very spot—set to end her life. Her wealth, her family, her job—everything was at risk, with the exception of her fame. Fame was like a highway, and one year ago, like it or not, Sabrina was traveling in the fast lane.

"I swear, Mira, I feel like there's something big happening out there, you know? Something that requires my attention."

Mira, her best friend, was treading water in their small, indoor pool. Mira lived to swim, and together the girls did a hundred laps in the thirty-foot indoor pool each day. Though Sabrina credited her tight, athletic form to swimming, Mira did it simply for pure enjoyment. On days the pair were not busy, she would stay in the pool as long as Sabrina would allow it.

A gust of wind whipped Sabrina's pale blonde hair around her face. A helicopter's spinning blades thumped louder as it drew near. It had been months since a desperate photographer tried to make a buck off a photo of her in a skimpy bikini, if that were the case today, she would give him exactly what he wanted.

Sabrina placed her hands on the railing of the balcony, spread her legs shoulder-width apart, and bent over slightly at the waist. Chest pushed out, she quickly adjusted the bra's sailor's knot detail at the center of her cleavage. She wanted to make sure that if this photo showed up on the tabloids and social-networking sites, it was a damn good one.

Surprisingly, the helicopter passed by, it's red and white blades a blur of motion as it sped off in the direction of the highway. *Fuck me, probably another car accident*, she thought while relaxing her stance.

"Isn't today the day?" Mira called from inside the penthouse.

"Yes, the funds I transferred into your account should be good now. You know what to do."

"I already found a no-kill animal shelter in Nacogdoches, Texas, which could use the money desperately."

"Great."

"Are you sure you don't want to donate it yourself, Sabrina? The press you would get from it would be incredible."

"No, Mira. It has to be completely anonymous, untraceable to me. I seriously don't want to read on some asshole's blog that I'm trying to buy back my celebrity status."

Mira nodded; Sabrina knew she understood.

A sudden chord of music from Sabrina's favorite heavy metal song alerted her to an incoming call. Snatching her cell phone from the table where it sat next to the weathered *People* magazine, she pressed accept with a quick glance at the unknown caller ID.

"Sabrina, at your service."

"Greetings, Sabrina," a sultry voice licked at her ear.

"Moselle!" Sabrina cheered. "I didn't recognize your number."

"I had to change it again, my friend. It has a way of falling into the wrong hands."

"I understand." Sabrina rolled her eyes; she too had been the victim of such annoyances. "What's up, babe?"

"Do you recall the texts I sent you last month, telling you my father would be opening a new Club Afterlife? Well, forgive me for not calling sooner, but the red carpet grand opening is this Friday."

"Really?" Sabrina bounced with excitement. "When and where?"

"I will text you all the details."

"Great. I'm there."

"Will you be bringing a date?" Moselle inquired.

"I'm kinda single at the moment, so Mira will be my date for the evening. How about you, sexy? Still eating men alive?"

"I *have* found someone special." Moselle replied. "I will introduce him to you at the club."

"Oh, no juicy details?"

"All I will say is that he has beautiful eyes and smells so delicious, my mouth waters at the mere thought of him."

Sabrina laughed. "I can't wait to meet him. See you there, babe."

With the *People* magazine rolled tightly in her hand, she marched inside to tell Mira the news.

"What's today's date?" Mira asked when she saw the rolled-up magazine in Sabrina's hand.

"You know what day it is."

"Then it's time you got rid of that stupid thing." Mira pointed from the water where she bobbed up and down.

"I know."

Sabrina took one last look at the cover: *Sabrina London, People Magazine's Most Beautiful Woman.*

"Sabrina..." Mira prompted again.

"Yeah, I know."

Sabrina pictured herself a year ago—weak and disheveled, with wind-scattered hair sticking to her tear-stained makeup. It was the night the video of her freeing the test animals went viral. CNN called it a crime—her father called it unforgivable.

Sabrina's heart seized as the painful memory played out further—her mind burned with the hurtful words that filled her ears that night.

The same old, dangerous thoughts echoed in her head as she watched her past self climb the slippery railing and slide her bare feet to the edge. *If only the pharmaceutical corporation would have accepted my bribes. If only Cade wouldn't have filmed us. If only he hadn't left his camera lying in that fucking parking lot where anyone could find it.* It had been a long time since Sabrina considered just how close she was to giving up and jumping.

Cade is gone. Those days are gone. Sabrina couldn't think about it another second. She swallowed her sorrow and, with all the strength she could muster, pitched the magazine over the balcony, out into the empty sky.

"Done," she said.

"Done," Mira repeated.

Sabrina took a deep breath and pulled back her shoulders. "Well, we better get dressed; Moselle invited us to her father's new club opening."

"Where?" Mira asked as she climbed from the pool.

"Back east."

"Not tonight?"

"No, Friday." Sabrina dashed by her friend.

"Oh, then what's the rush?"

"I want to hit the Christian Dior sale before noon, and if that skinny bitch from *The New Hills* is there buying up all the embroidered platforms, I *will* punch her in her newly sculpted nose!" Sabrina shouted from her room.

"Sabrina, must I remind you that you're trying to clean up your image before you launch your career as a pop star? Fighting reality show stars will only lower your q-rating."

Mira wrapped a towel around herself and tucked a corner over the top edge. She shuffled carefully across the marble floor of the pool room, through the hallway, to the main living room. Mira always squinted when she passed through the living room, which was the center of the radial design of Sabrina's apartment. She worried that the bright pink, white, and black color scheme would burn her corneas when the sun shone through all four skylights. Sabrina's furniture had been specially ordered from overseas, before Mira knew her, and she often wondered where she found a company that made couches with such vivid pink leather upholstery.

Who am I to complain? Mira thought, crossing the tall, white shag carpet to the hall where her bedroom was.

"What shoes should I wear?" Sabrina yelled from her room.

"Not sure," Mira responded, uncertain about anything to do with fashion, as usual.

"Well, I can't just go to buy new shoes wearing old ones!" Sabrina yelled from her walk-in closet where Mira knew she was rummaging about on the floor.

"If you say so."

Mira took a long look at herself in the full-length mirror. The mirror was exquisitely crafted, covered with ornate designs, but Mira rarely saw anything other than the plain girl reflected before her.

Mira tossed her hair from one side to the other, sighing loudly. Although her hair was long, it was dull and stringy, not voluminous like her friend's. And her eyes matched her hair: brown—entirely unremarkable. Mira drew her shoulders back and pushed her less-than-ample chest out.

One characteristic Mira could not hide was her body's clear strength. She was trim to the extent of having nearly zero body fat; her muscles, although lean, were cut at such tight angles their presence was emphasized.

"They'll probably compliment you if you wear the ones you bought there last month," Mira suggested, changing out of her competitive swimmer's one-piece bathing suit.

"Nah, you can wear them. I wore them that one time out with that quarterback. He said they made my feet look scrumptious and he wanted to lick them. Gods, it was gross."

"That is gross. Professional athletes are too cocky. The things they say."

Sabrina entered Mira's room holding the shoes by their straps; she had on a pleated miniskirt and bouclé keyhole-front sweater—together the price tags totaled over a grand, Mira guessed.

"No, silly Mira, I mean him licking my feet was gross."

Mira looked up at Sabrina as she fastened her bra. She knew her friend was joking. Sabrina had been careful not to create any scandals recently.

"You're wearing a miniskirt to buy shoes? I bet you're not even wearing underwear," Mira accused.

"Maybe... maybe not." Sabrina shrugged.

"You slut!" Mira joked.

"I'm almost twenty-three years old now, Mira."

"So?"

"So, I prefer harlot, it sounds more..." Sabrina shrugged again. "I don't know... classy."

Chapter Three

Spoiled Contentment

Later that night, as the sun was setting on Beverly Hills, Sabrina sat on one of her large, leather loveseats, her legs dangling over the arm. She wiggled her toes while she admired the swirling crystal design on her new, black pumps. Music so loud it seemed like it would be impossible to think vibrated the room. Sabrina loved music and always said the only way to listen was to feel it. Although she wanted to become a pop star like the ones that were played all over satellite radio, she loved nineties heavy metal.

Mira paced the room. Sabrina had bought her a new pair of high heels, fuck-me pumps really. Sabrina peeked up from her feet to the spectacle of Mira marching back and forth. It made her smile; Mira was truly an awkward sight. It seemed as if Mira was testing the heels' stability with every other step.

Although Sabrina wore a look of contentment after a long day spent shopping and hanging out with her best friend, she was far from happy. Under her smile was a maelstrom of emotion, one that Sabrina had spent months burying and disguising. Her smile, like the rest of her façade, was mostly for show.

Once the nucleus of a close and loving family, Sabrina had been excommunicated by her mother and father, not only for breaking into the pharmaceutical company and freeing the animals, but also for what happened with Cade afterward—they found it inexcusable, embarrassing, and lewd. He may have been one of the world's most respected businessmen, but to Sabrina he was simply Daddy.

Sabrina had hoped the loud music would pound the thoughts from her head, but it didn't work; no matter how hard she tried to forget, her father's enraged voice seeped into her mind. *Not now. I can't.* His words echoed in her head, flashing and flickering like a neon sign that burned on her mind's eye. Sabrina screamed inside, her anger drowning out her father's venomous lecture before she had to hear it all over again.

Sabrina refocused on the music and thought of a time, not so many months ago, when, during moments of such introspective angst, she would have done drugs to get through the heavy emotions. Now when she felt her pain was showing through her mask, Sabrina deflected any suspicion with a well-timed snarky remark.

"When did you learn to walk, Mira? Last week?" Sabrina yelled over the roaring guitars.

"Ha ha!" Mira wrinkled her nose at Sabrina.

A sudden vibration in the seat of Sabrina's skirt alerted her to an incoming call.

Every time her phone rang, she prayed it was her father, finally calling to apologize after a year of silence. A wave of relief began to wash over her. She would be part of her family again. She knew it; all she had to do was answer her phone.

"Mira, shut the music off," Sabrina yelled as she freed the tiny phone from where she was sitting on it.

Mira stumbled to the remote, nearly tripping over her own feet. She mashed several buttons at once until the music shut off, just in time for Sabrina to look at the incoming call number. Her smile faded, Sabrina turned away from Mira, she did not want the disappointment on her face seen. This was not the call she had prayed for, but she answered it anyway, nerves braced, but dying inside.

"Sabrina at your service."

Chapter Four

The Calling

Sitting in her shadow-soaked bedroom, Moselle Abdul Aziz Al Ghurair repeatedly glanced at her smartphone, eager for it to ring. A candelabrum burned seven small red flames, illuminating her room just enough for her to not only spy two of her Abyssinian cats as they chased each other across the marble floor, but to also see what she was mixing.

Moselle poured jojoba oil from a large container into a small, dark glass bottle with a glass rod applicator. Ten drops of jasmine oil from the flowers she had handpicked in her garden the night before splashed into the bottle as she pondered how much ylang-ylang oil she should add to the mix, desiring nothing but the most erotic scent to seduce the man she had been dating.

At the chime of her smartphone, Moselle set the bottles aside and pressed the answer button with the tip of her index finger's nail.

"Greetings, Father."

"You sound disappointed, my daughter." Moselle's father's voice was deep and steeped with his strong Egyptian accent.

"No, no, no... not at all." Moselle cleared her throat and presented him with the respect he was due. "How may I serve you, Father?"

"I am pleased to inform you that everything has gone as designed with the new Club Afterlife," he said. "This opening is already being touted as a once-in-a-lifetime, red-carpet event."

"Blessings be, Father."

"Have you made travel arrangements yet, Moselle?"

She took a second to compose her words before speaking.

"I have not. Father, it is a great honor to attend, not only as the subject of all of the advertisements in your recent campaign, but as your loving daughter, still I have a request." She sat up.

"You know full well your mother is currently unable to entertain," he stated, clearly assuming she was going to ask if her mother could be at the opening.

"Oh, yes that. I haven't broken bread with Mother since last year's birthday party. I do miss her."

"Birthdays?" She heard her father's dissatisfied tone. "Moselle, you know I find them a foolish distraction."

"Yes, I know."

"Good," he replied quickly. "I will send the private jet to Los Angeles in two days. It will transport you to New York City for the event."

"Father, my request," she reminded him. "I have met someone very special, a young man whom I have been dating. He works at the advertising agency you hired for the new club."

"Tell me again, Moselle, why do you find them so interesting?" Her father's tone was filled with frustration and annoyance. "What could you possibly have in common with this... this American?"

"He is strong, handsome, and funny, Father."

"He is *not* one of us."

"I do not care about that. He warms my soul with his humor and kindness. When we work together preparing your advertisements, I find myself inexplicably drawn to him. I have not felt this way in ten or more years."

"Moselle!"

Her father's raised voice startled her so badly her body froze. She had not angered her him in many, many years, not since long before she had moved out of his home into her own.

"Why do you tell me this?"

"I would like him to accompany me to the grand opening as my date," Moselle answered timidly.

The phone went silent, and Moselle waited patiently.

"So be it," he conceded. "Invite him, but he will need to find his own means of travel to New York. Understood?"

"Yes." Moselle beamed.

"Did you pass along my request to your other friend?"

"I spoke to Sabrina earlier; she accepted the invitation already."

"She is well now, you say?"

"As well as can be," Moselle admitted.

"Good, then, regardless, this will be an opening night for all to remember. Safe journey, my daughter."

"Safe journey to you too, Father."

Moselle watched the slender metal hands on her wall clock tick forward another notch as she hung up. The hand's movement boomed in her ears like the footsteps of a titan. It was nearing nine o'clock at night; she had hoped her new boyfriend would have called by now. She unconsciously tapped the bottom corner of her smartphone on the table, harder and harder until... *Snap.* The protective case broke.

"Curse this devil's game." Moselle ran her finger over the jagged crack. "My phone, a sacrifice to you, Hathor. See it not wasted."

Moselle pressed the speed-dial graphic, a tiny photo associated with his name: Jackson Abernathy.

"Hello."

"Jackson, darling, it is Moselle Abdul Aziz Al Ghurair."

"Hey, Moselle..." He paused a moment before finishing. "What's happening?"

Jackson's voice did not ring with the excitement she had yearned for, and she had a clear guess why.

"Are you still at work?"

"Yeah, I'm putting the finishing touches on that freelance project I did with Candice Swanepoel."

Moselle finally heard a hint of excitement in his voice, but it was not for her.

"You work too hard and play too little." Moselle stood feeling suddenly jealous; she was more driven than ever to see Jackson now.

"To be honest, I need the extra money. I lost a few bucks on the game last night."

Moselle admired herself in the full-length mirror attached to the inside of her closet door as she listened. She examined her eye makeup, which included a coat of sparkling purple mascara that complemented her dark eyes.

"All I am suggesting is that you take a short break."

"I took a break earlier when you sent me that one text message. The one with the picture attached. What did it say again?"

"It said that tomorrow marks a full month on the calendar since you asked me out. It said to prepare for a night filled with earthly delights."

Jackson laughed. "Moselle, you are unlike any other girl I've ever known."

"You are right, Jackson. All you have known are girls, scatterbrained models with apathy toward most things. I am a woman, one who knows what she wants."

"Well... I wanted to finish this project and then get a jumpstart touching up that advertisement of you in the silver bikini with the—"

"Jackson." Moselle's voice rose in frustration. "Such labor should be done during the hours our beloved sun is high above us."

"You're right, but wouldn't your father be even more impressed with me if I handed him extra work?"

"While I find it pleasing that you strive to win my father's approval, Jackson, I must ask you this: would you have me spend the next few hours alone while you stare at my likeness, or would you gaze upon me in person over a few drinks?"

"Would you like to go out for coffee, Moselle?"

"I would love to."

Chapter Five

Walk Like an Egyptian

Jackson sat across from Moselle in the packed, trendy coffeehouse. A popular local folk singer was performing and had drawn a large enough crowd to fill the tiny establishment. Although the music was loud, Jackson only heard the woman he was with. All his senses drank in Moselle. He felt as if he was living a dream—one that he would savor every second of. He was mesmerized by her beauty but couldn't bring himself to fully admit it.

Beauty had become his drug of choice ever since he had met his first model on a photo shoot for *Allure*. At that moment, years ago, he would have sworn she was the most gorgeous girl he had ever encountered, a true natural beauty in all aspects. Even the act of breathing felt like a show put on to entice him. She was a twenty-year-old from Czechoslovakia and had flawless, milky white skin that looked almost like porcelain in photographs, and he had fiercely desired her, but never asked her out.

Jackson had regretted his mistake for a long time and tried to make up for it by dating other models he met, but no one compared until he met Moselle. She was different—as she had said, she was a *woman* compared to the girls he was so accustomed to. She was no coked-up model he could easily seduce with a mere mention of his position in a leading advertising agency in Los Angeles; she had wealth and power, not to mention a brain. With Moselle, Jackson had to constantly remind himself to stay cool.

Moselle had the most amazing caramel skin he had ever seen. Unlike other models whose photos he had worked with, Moselle had that complexion naturally, a result of her Middle Eastern heritage. Jackson could not identify exactly what it was about her, and he thought about it a lot.

"Thanks for meeting me here tonight, Moselle."

"No, thank you," she replied with a slight bow of her head. "Please, tell me something about you that I do not know."

"Like what?" Jackson shrugged.

"You have never told me how you came to do this line of work."

"Well," Jackson exhaled, "by accident, I guess. I never imagined I would end up on this path, you know?"

"Please continue."

"Right, well, I guess I thought I'd be playing professional hockey by now. I mean, I never saw myself as an artist, not like the other guys in the studio."

"Please, your talent far supersedes theirs." Moselle warmed him with another smile.

"Thanks." Jackson smiled back. "I don't like to brag, but I am—*was* a natural on the ice. I could outskate everyone in my college. And as fast as I was, I was equally hard to knock down, which is why my buddies called me Stonewall. Get it, Stonewall Jackson?"

"Why did you stop?"

"I didn't stop. I was stopped." He shook his head. "A really bad collision during my senior year shattered my left wrist."

Jackson pointed at the horizontal scars which, although faded, still decorated his arm.

"I had not noticed your scars before, darling."

"I've found creative ways to hide them. I don't like being reminded of my failures."

He watched Moselle slowly reach for his arm, and when her hand glided over his scars, he flexed his muscles.

"It's been five years now. I'm all healed, but... yeah, it took forever to recover from such a bad break. It was really depressing at first. Hockey was my life, and that life was suddenly over. All I could do was sit and watch as my friends, my teammates, moved on without me."

"Change can be a very difficult thing." Moselle cradled his arm in her hands.

"One day, I was extremely bored, so I sat down at my laptop and started pasting photos of my head on the bodies of pro players. After a few weeks, I got good enough to make them blend in. Oh, there was this one shot—man, I had really worked long on it, and it ended up pretty good. It was a photo of my favorite San Jose Shark on a breakaway, but it was my head in his helmet. I ended up e-mailing the picture to all my friends, family, and old teammates. You know, as a joke. I even sent it to the National Hockey League."

"Silly Jackson."

"Oddly enough, a week later, the NHL emailed me back... with a job offer. The years go by and the next thing you know, I'm here doing graphic art and photography work for your father."

"In all our conversations, you never mentioned your past. Do you miss your sport?"

Jackson nodded, combed the loose strands of his curly hair back over his ears with his fingers, and said, "Not a day goes by that I don't miss playing hockey."

"I am sure, had you been able to play, you would have become a champion."

As they shared a smile, Jackson sat silently, staring at his date as she pinched the tip of the straw in her latte, slowly placing it in her mouth. Her full lips closed down on the straw gently and her cheeks sunk in as she drew the warm liquid into her mouth. Never had he witnessed such a mundane act become one so filled with sensuality.

"Tonight marks our fourth date, Jackson." Moselle licked her lips. "Very exciting."

Jackson was unsure what she meant and did not want to make any assumptions. "It's hard to believe that just a month ago, I was afraid to ask you out."

"You feared me?"

"Well, you are the daughter of my company's biggest client, and yeah, that felt dangerous." Jackson laughed. "What if we had gone out on our first date and you totally hated me? Your father could've had me fired."

"You should not worry about him."

"Trust me, I wanted to ask you out the first day we met, but I figured you would've just thought I was another man helplessly spellbound by your beauty," Jackson teased, but there was truth in his words. "You must be tired of men bothering you."

"Women never grow tired of worship."

And she was worthy of worship. Moselle had dressed to impress this evening, wearing a tight black skirt and a golden colored top that appeared to be a single piece of fabric wrapped a million times around her chest. Black straps from her flat sandals wrapped all the way to her knee, accentuating her lean calf muscles. She wore her shiny raven-colored hair down, long, and straight, with several strands tied together with highly polished golden beads on the sides and back.

"Do you like what you see?"

Although Jackson had seen Moselle in various stages of dress and undress, especially the elaborate costumes the advertising agency had her wear, he was always most impressed with her style out in public, especially tonight. Jackson had never seen her wear any kind of dress or shirt with sleeves. Moselle's arms were always bare apart from the shiny golden armbands she wore right below the deltoids. Tonight, those bands lacked detail yet bent with a fluidity that reminded him of coiling snakes.

"I do. You look stunning, Moselle."

"Care to take a closer look?" Moselle leaned across the tiny table.

As her face moved closer to his, Moselle inhaled deeply, not surprised that he smelled as delicious as the last time she had been in his presence.

"What is that scent, Jackson?" she whispered. "I need to know."

"Okay, you caught me. I use this fancy mint shampoo. It costs like thirty-five bucks, but I think I'm worth it," Jackson joked.

"It is such a yummy scent," she whispered, her eyes telling him yes—make the move.

Jackson caressed the side of her face, careful not to smear her dramatic makeup. His skin on hers was electric. His hand moved slowly but surely as he reached behind her and hooked her neck to pull her in for a kiss. His lips pressed lightly against hers; they tasted as she had imagined they would: sugary with the sweet promise of more to come.

Jackson's blue eyes sparked, as if they had only been partially lit before. "You have no idea how bad I want you right now."

"Come home with me, Jackson," Moselle breathed.

"Are you sure?"

"Please, I need—"

The waitress interrupted them before she could finish, and Moselle ordered another drink to go, her eyes locked on Jackson's soft lips as she imagined all the places on her body she would like them.

"Two grande lattés in one night? Moselle, that much caffeine is going to keep you up all night," Jackson teased.

"Would that be so bad?" Moselle lustfully eyed his lap as she spoke.

"Not at all."

"Leave your car here. I want you to ride with me." Moselle stood, straightened her skirt and blouse, and walked off.

When Moselle's driver called for clearance at the front gate of her home, Jackson tied back his nearly shoulder-length, light brown, messy hair and took his first look out the window. He had never seen such a large home before in his life; he suddenly understood the term *estate*. Moselle's home was not only sprawling, but it was also the tallest house he had ever seen, with dozens of stone columns stretching high into the dark sky above. They were so tall that even after leaning back, he couldn't see the tops of them. Jackson shivered. The open arches and windows gave an appearance of airiness that made his skin chill even though he had not left his seat in the warm car.

The limo came to a stop in the crescent-shaped driveway where a marble pathway, lit in golden light, led to two large stone pylons. At this distance, he could detail the building's dusty sandstone façade—everything felt so suddenly grand and intimidating.

Jackson wanted nothing more than to get out of the car and begin a night he knew would be one to remember. But when he tried to get out, the door wouldn't open. He turned to Moselle for an answer and found only complacence.

"The door won't open."

"No, Jackson, it will not."

"Why not?"

"Because my guards have not arrived..."

Jackson looked up just as the large front door of her home opened. Four tall African men stepped from the shadows. Dressed in dark red suits and matching red berets, the armed men looked more like third-world militants than security guards. Each man wore a leather shoulder holster that even from his distance appeared heavy with its contents: a handgun that glimmered when stroked by the bright outdoor lights.

Jackson's heart sped up at the sight of the long, curved swords the guards also wore. Why Moselle needed such security, or even allowed these men to be armed like that, boggled his mind.

"Jackson?"

Her voice startled him. "What?"

"The guards will want me to exit the limousine first."

"Oh. Okay."

Before Moselle could answer, the car door opened and a large, dark-skinned hand reached in. Moselle placed her tiny hand inside it, and with a quick, fluid motion, she exited the limousine.

Jackson poked his head out first and assessed the situation before he stepped out. Moselle waited for him with a smile painted across her face but also an anxiousness in her eyes that made him wonder if there was something she was not telling him. Jackson straightened and gazed up at one of the guards who was glaring down at him. A tall man himself at six foot three, he had never felt small until that very moment. The guard must have been over seven feet tall and covered with muscles so that he appeared as thick as a tree trunk.

"Come, Jackson, let us go inside before the cool night air nips at our flesh."

She took Jackson by the hand and led him down the golden path to the shadows that stood at the threshold.

"My God your house is tall. How many floors are there?"

"There are three floors aboveground."

"Only three? Wait, what do you mean aboveground?"

Jackson lost track of her comment the moment he stepped into the vestibule of Moselle's mansion. Her home, which seemed so cold and lifeless on the outside, came alive as soon as he entered. Although minimally lit by candlelight, he caught the sparkle of precious metals in every direction he looked. A handcrafted staircase ascended into the darkness in front of him. To the left and right of where he stood were large stone statues, two each flanking the massive archways to other rooms. Moselle led Jackson directly to the stairs, but his curiosity kept him looking around, catching the glimmering outline of something large in the room to his left. He squinted to get a better look, but before he could make out the shape, two of Moselle's guards blocked the way.

"Do you live here alone?" he asked.

"Not at all."

"Wait, your parents live here too?"

"No. No. No. I have not lived with my parents for quite some time now, Jackson."

"Then who lives here with you? A roommate?"

"Twenty-five guards."

Jackson would have stopped in his tracks if it were not for the constant tug on his arm.

"Twenty-five? Where do they all stay?" he questioned, tinged with frustration.

"Jackson, let us not forget why we came to my home. How do you Americans say it? Keep your eyes on the prize?"

Moselle had defused him—it was a trick she had used before when he got tense at work, and she was becoming quite skilled at it. He shifted his attention back to Moselle as they ascended the stairs. "You're right," he answered.

"Of course I am."

As they reached the landing, something small dashed before them, from one room to another.

"Is that one of your cats?"

Moselle lit up; Jackson knew she cherished her cats and loved being asked about them. Although he had only seen a streak of pale fur, she knew exactly which it had been.

"Yes, Imhotep likes to sneak about at night. He plays seek and find better than any human."

Jackson laughed. He had read interviews where Moselle talked about her cats. She never revealed exactly how many she had, but it was rumored to be more than a dozen, all exotic breeds.

"Please, Jackson, join me in my bedroom," Moselle stated as she entered the dark room.

Instinctively, Jackson reached up, brushing the wall where he thought a light switch would be. When he did not find one, he turned to the opposite side of the door.

"Where are your light switches?"

"Oh, I forgot, I never told you about my home. No, Jackson, all light *inside* my home is natural and pure."

Left to stand just inside the doorway, Jackson watched Moselle maneuver through the room in near darkness until she reached for what appeared to be a long rope that hung from the ceiling. She grasped and pulled it hard, suddenly separating two large, wool covers from a skylight. Bright moonlight illuminated the room, giving Jackson his first real look at it. The space was enormous, easily three times the size of his entire apartment. Moonlight reflected off the dozens of mirrors that decorated the walls. What limited furniture she had was lavish beyond imagination and peculiarly oversized, especially the focal point: the bed.

The enormous canopy bed sat centered in the room, surrounded by four stone pillars. Elevated atop a marble platform, with a set of wide stairs on each side, it had the appearance of being more than a place to sleep—a piece of art in a museum.

"The moonlight really spotlights your bed."

"The skylight was designed to perform such a task," Moselle said as she passed in front of him, her eyes fixed on something on the ground. "Do you like it?"

"It's amazing." Jackson gazed up to the cloudless sky, then back to the bed. "I've never seen a bed so artistically framed by a room."

"You may take a closer look."

As Jackson approached the bed, Moselle bent over and snatched something from the ground, dumping the object into the closest of the four large wicker baskets that filled each corner.

"What was that?"

"What was what, Jackson?" she replied coyly as she walked back to him.

"I swear I saw something... wiggling."

"Then you must have been looking at my hips, because they are the only thing doing so."

He took a long look at Moselle. *But I saw something... Oh, it doesn't matter. Look at her. Damn. I'm way out of my element and way out of my league here.*

"To be honest, I was not prepared for... all this," Jackson admitted.

"I share your nervousness, Jackson. I have not invited a man into my bedroom in many, many years. This is my innermost sanctum, a place that holds my most precious secrets."

"Then perhaps I should go."

Turning around, Moselle presented him with her backside. "Would you please untie me?" she asked, pulling her hair forward over her shoulder.

Suddenly, Jackson remembered his objective. Relying on a talent he had picked up on the ice, he blocked out the white noise inside his mind: the doubts, concerns and fears were all suddenly gone, and his focus was solely on the amazing woman who had invited him to her bed. Jackson untied the knot of her wrap with ease.

"I am going to freshen up, my love."

His eyes locked on her backside as she sauntered across the room to her bathroom. *Is this truly about to happen?*

He looked around; her abundant wealth was equal to her beauty. There was more to Moselle, he knew it, and he was very much looking forward to discovering those secrets, inch-by-inch.

As he pulled his shirt over his head, a rattling emerged from the wicker basket Moselle had stood near only a moment ago. He approached the basket with caution, walking on the tips of his toes, until Moselle startled him—her voice cutting the silence like a knife.

"All you will find are undergarments in that basket, Jackson."

Moselle stood in a contrapposto stance only a few feet from the open door to her bathroom. Retracing his steps back toward the bed, Jackson got a clearer look at what Moselle was wearing. Her hands held a long, black silk shawl around her shoulders that hinted at the voluptuous curves of her body.

She stepped closer to him, into the moonlight.

"Unfortunately, if it is undergarments you seek, Jackson, you will find no such things adorning my body."

She placed her hands at her sides and the shawl opened, creating a triangle of bare skin beginning between her breasts.

He brushed his palm against the soft flesh of her lower stomach only to stop centimeters before her bared pelvis.

"Your skin is so smooth."

"Thank you."

He lifted his eyes slowly, mapping her body from bottom to top. With his eyes finally settled on hers, he said softly, "Incredible."

She exhaled suddenly—he had hit the mark. He placed the palm of his hand just below her belly button and slowly smoothed it up. When he reached her chest, Jackson turned his hand fingers up and glided between her breasts. At her collarbone, his other hand joined in and together they dove underneath the silk shawl.

Moselle moaned quietly and nodded—her skin tingled under his palms. With a flick of his hand, Jackson removed the silk wrapping, it dropping like a feather to the ground behind her.

"You're a goddess, Moselle," he declared, gazing down at her, his heart throbbing.

She smiled slowly. "Not yet, perhaps one day."

Moselle stepped around him and sat on the bed. Her eyes still locked with his, she leaned back onto her elbows and drew her left leg up, her toes pointed sharply. Jackson took in her beauty, unsure where to begin. In one graceful motion, Moselle tilted her hips up, slid herself toward him, and spread her legs.

"Kissing you, during the ride here, I asked myself how could this night get any better. Now, I see how." Jackson smiled.

"I have waited..." Moselle trailed off when he touched her. "I have waited... so very long for this moment," she finished breathlessly.

Jackson traced a wavy line from her right hip to her left with his hand. Moving slowly, his fingertips barely pressing her skin, gliding atop it smoothly. When they reached the finely trimmed hair of her pubis, Moselle shuddered and when they slipped between her legs, her head dropped back, and she moaned.

Jackson gently stroked her, teasing but not entering her until her wetness soaked his fingers, gripping his own hard bulge in his other hand.

"I am ready," she whispered. "Are you?"

He peeled his boxers off and showed her just how ready he was. Grasping her ankles, he raised her legs, and smoothly entered her as far as his body would permit. She was tight and wet, and he seemed to fill her perfectly.

Thrusting faster and faster, Jackson's excitement built quickly. He'd wanted to explore her curves desperately from the moment they met, and now that he could, his hands frantically worked her body from top to bottom—wherever he sensed she needed them—as Moselle moaned, her fingers clawing the sheets.

When he slowed, he was surprised that she opened her eyes and cried, "Harder!"

"Roll over," he delivered his reply in a confident and commanding tone—there was no way he would deny her request. "I'll show you harder."

Chapter Six

Doubts

Later that night, Moselle lay comfortably atop her disarranged sheets, her eyes staring up into the lavender night sky. She didn't need a clock to know that dawn was nearly there. Moist with sweat, her body ached. She had never been so satiated by a man in all her life. Jackson had devoured her flesh—fed upon her like a starved man. His fervor had unlocked an undiscovered primal desire inside her. Moselle had growled with arousal and spoken filthy words that had never passed her lips before—words that challenged him, seduced him, and empowered him. Jackson may have been a simple man—but Moselle now saw him as much more: a champion.

The distant static of the guest room's shower was calming, further lulling her into tranquility. When it stopped, she knew her savoring time was drawing to an end. She wanted nothing more than to lay still the remainder of the night, side-by-side with the man who had just filled her with such pleasure that she had released twice. She wished she could bask in his scent, the one that she found so deviously arousing, but her ancient traditions would not allow it.

Jackson exited the bathroom of the guest bedroom with a towel wrapped around his waist while he worked another through his hair.

"Real swift, Jacks." He shook his head. "Showering in the guestroom... so lame. Why be shy now?"

The guest bedroom was decorated rather normally, nowhere near as eccentric as Moselle's bedroom. An old-fashioned sleigh bed sat in the middle of the room with a bureau positioned directly across from it. Two matching armoires bookended the bureau, and a small yet ornately carved curio filled with tiny stone statues sat against the wall next to the bathroom.

The closest armoire caught his eye. The old piece of furniture stood out in the sea of splendor that surrounded it. The armoire, obviously handcrafted, may have been old and worn, but it held a sense of warmth, as if its owner once took great care of it.

"You sure do have some old taste for a girl your age," Jackson said, as if Moselle were sitting there with him. "Damn, I don't even know how old you are... thirty, maybe? Yeah, better not ask."

Across the hall, Moselle sat up; the inevitable was upon her. She did not want to move but forced herself. With the sheet wrapped around her, she glided across the room to her perfume bottle-cluttered bureau. Next to a pair of tall, glass flasks was a quill and ink. Moselle slipped a tiny piece of paper out of one of her smaller drawers. She knew her actions would create many questions in Jackson's mind, but she had no choice; it was late, and she had to perform her nightly rituals or risk the consequences.

Jackson exited the guest bedroom with an extra spring in his step. He felt like the luckiest man on earth. Moselle was incredible—sexy, smart, and unpredictably fascinating. Jackson could not wait to join her again; who knew what the remainder of the night would bring? To his dismay, standing before her closed door was one of the armed guards he had seen earlier. As Jackson approached the door, the man's glare shifted into a sneer, as though he smelled something rancid.

"Excuse me, Moselle's probably waiting for me."

The guard pitched Jackson's crumpled up pile of clothes right at him, striking his bare chest dead center.

"What the hell?"

Rage filled Jackson's chest. His instincts said to throw down, an old response to having hockey gloves tossed at him before a fight.

"Lady Moselle will no longer be entertaining guests tonight." The tall man spoke in a thick African accent that was barely comprehensible.

"What?"

"The mistress gave me this note to give to you."

The guard stretched out his arm, a rolled-up piece of paper bound with ribbon clenched tightly in hand. As Jackson reached for the paper, the guard opened his hand, letting it fall to the ground.

"What the hell's your problem?" Jackson asked as he stepped up to the big man.

"Lady Moselle's limousine will return you to your vehicle."

The guard pointed over Jackson's shoulder to the stairs, a clear sign that he was being asked to leave. *But why?* he wondered. *What have I done wrong?*

After dressing as fast as he could, Jackson tore off the ribbon and unraveled the paper as he descended the stairs. Moselle's message was short and simple:

Jackson, my love,
The night has grown very late, and I require a little sleep before an appointment I must attend in the early morning hours. I fear if you stay, there would be no rest for either of us. I will speak with you soon, darling.
Moselle

Her note reeked of sweet perfume—a strange juxtaposition to its sour message. *Am I nothing more than her toy?*

Chapter Seven

Grand Opening

"You want me to get out first, Sabrina?" Mira offered timidly. "That way, I can turn around and make sure your dress is not too far up when you step out. We might be able to avoid another spread of tasteless photos."

The crowd outside the limousine roared with excitement. Moselle's family knew how to draw a crowd, but this was the biggest opening yet. Sabrina knew since she had attended the last one just over a year ago.

The young starlet wanted to believe the ruckus outside was, at least in part, because she was there, but she knew better. Recent events had humbled her, if only slightly.

"Are you trying to say I have an ugly pussy?" Sabrina cocked her head and smirked.

"I would never," Mira replied with a fake sneer, then poked out her tongue.

Sabrina's heart skipped in anticipation; in a moment the door would open, and the world would welcome her again.

"I appreciate your concern, but, nah, I got this, Mira," Sabrina declared.

"Wait. No... you're wearing underwear, aren't you?" Mira's question sounded like an accusation.

"There's a first time for everything, right?"

Both of the girls heard the heavy footfalls of the limo driver as he approached the door. Soon, Sabrina would be reunited with her fans through the raving madness that was the paparazzi. As the spotlight spilled in through the crack of the slowly opening car door, Sabrina hoped to be greeted by fans screaming her name, but it was not her fans who called out for her. It was Mira.

"Sabrina, your wings are showing!"

Painted across the young starlet's back was a large, colorful tattoo of fairy wings. The body art stretched from the far tips of her shoulder blades to the small of her back, an intricate piece of artwork with countless layers of colorful depth. The tattoo, considered by many to be one of the best pieces of art adorning a celebrity's skin, was all a ruse that covered up her most precious secret; Sabrina actually was a fairy.

A flicker of multicolored light over her shoulder confirmed Mira's statement; something had caused her wings to unfurl. Years of evolution had allowed the fairy-kind to merge their energy-based wings with their skin, where they would lie hidden until called for. Sabrina had practiced for years to keep her wings atop her skin, only partially melded, an action that disguised them as an elaborate tattoo.

The ability to hide her wings took little more effort or concentration than holding a tightened fist. It was something that was natural for her kind. Few things triggered the unconscious release of a fairy's wings, and those things both excited and terrified Sabrina.

Mira acted fast. She pushed off the seat to the open door, past her friend, and out into the night air first. The blinding flash of camera lights was the last thing Sabrina saw as Mira waved her hands to distract the paparazzi.

Sabrina held her breath as she focused, her wings sliding back into their hiding place. In a moment's time, the disaster was averted. Still, Sabrina needed tactile proof that her wings were disguised as they should be, so she reached over her shoulder and ran her hand across her skin, finding only soft, warm flesh. She sighed with relief. *Relax, Sabrina. You got this*, she told herself.

Sabrina adjusted her breasts, straightened her dress, and ran her fingers through her hair. Her spaghetti-strap, red dress made it appear as if she were wearing a baby-doll nightie. Sabrina knew she looked like sex and nourished the feeling; there was nothing she would let ruin this night.

The paparazzi yelled and those caught behind the velvet rope cheered, while Sabrina basked in the light of the camera flashes.

"Are you okay?" Mira asked, deep concern lacing her question.

"I'm fine. See, Mira? They missed me," she whispered to her friend. "Let's go."

Inside, the spacious club shook with the pounding of loud techno music. The multiple stacks of speakers created a wave of sound that made Sabrina's skin quiver and reverberated in her stomach. She loved it. She danced her way into the club, swaying her hips and raising her arms over her head. This was going to be a night to remember.

Mira trailed not far behind. She knew the drill; she was there to keep an eye open for other celebrities, producers, directors, anyone Sabrina may want to "accidentally" bump into. Scanning the crowded club, Mira saw lots of familiar faces, including the one that belonged to their hostess, Moselle.

Moselle was dressed as an ancient Egyptian queen, following the theme of Club Afterlife. She stood on the smaller of two stages and was flanked by two giant, onyx statues of the Egyptian God Anubis. Mira stared at her enviously. Mira would never tell Sabrina, but Moselle was the image of perfect femininity to her. In time, Mira pushed through the crowd toward her to get a closer look.

Moselle's queen outfit was so skimpy that Mira wondered if Moselle could truly feel comfortable with so much flesh bared. Moselle's breasts and ribcage were the only parts of her body completely covered, enclosed by a golden breastplate in the rough shape of a heart. A stretch of skin glimmered with sparkling body oil from just above her belly button all the way down to the smallest beaded bikini bottom Mira had ever seen. Hanging from the thong's sides and back were long, white, transparent veils. Although hard to pull her eyes away, Mira turned her gaze to Moselle's face, which was painted heavily with violet makeup. Upon her head was the stereotypical Cleopatra-style headdress, complete with the solid golden shape of a cobra.

"I wish I..." Mira's words trailed off as she panned over a collection of tables and noticed a man whose eyes were glued to Moselle just as hers had been.

Jackson lifted his beer to his lips and took a sip. It was the bitterest oatmeal stout he had ever tasted. He looked at the label for the fifth time in as many minutes—he knew this since he followed each glance at the bottle with a look at his watch.

It had been two days since he had left Moselle's home in the middle of the night. She had canceled their date at the last minute, to go to the club a day early to prepare, she claimed.

It's been two days. Two fucking days since I've seen you, two days since I've spoken to you. Two very fucking long days since we had sex, he thought.

The only substantial contact since had been several texts, like the one he received last night in which he had been instructed by Moselle to fly to New York City. Jackson had not been asked, but instead told that he was to be her date for the club's opening.

Sipping at his beer again, he continued to stare at Moselle; she was gorgeous. The lowness of her bikini bottom made his mind drift places he wished it would not in such a public spot. Like it or not, Jackson had to adjust his pants; the crowd was not the only thing growing larger by the minute. As he looked away from Moselle and glanced over the mob, he made awkward eye contact with a woman who seemed just as out of place as he was, just as lost.

Mira blushed. She knew the man she watched was getting aroused at the mere sight of Moselle—a power she wished she had over the opposite sex. Behind her, Sabrina cheered, she was having fun—a sign that it was time for Mira to return to task. Hundreds of faces faded in and out of view in the strobe lights. Mira identified a few actors from cable television shows, but one person stood out.

Mira recognized Alexander Kintner, the CEO of Kintner Co. the moment she laid eyes on him. An advocate of all the new anti-smoking laws which had just been enforced last calendar year, Mira was proud to have been the person who got Sabrina London to quit smoking and followed all of Kintner's tobacco research. Mira detested smoking and had been a supporter of Kintner's since his first announcement that he'd found a cure for nicotine addiction. Mira considered his appearance at the grand opening a wonderful surprise. Equally exciting was his date, the singer Riley Dalton.

Mira turned to seek out her friend and found her standing next to her, having just left the dance floor.

"Five-hundred-dollar high heels may match my red dress well, but they weren't made for dancing." Sabrina fanned her glistening neckline. "Woo, sweating."

"Want me to cool you off?" Mira asked.

"No, no, no," Sabrina said as she looked around. "I'm okay."

"Need a drink or—"

"Who have you seen, Mira?" Sabrina interrupted.

"Most of the cast of that horror series on MAX you like are over there." Mira pointed.

"Really?" Sabrina sounded interested.

"And Moselle's up on stage, greeting people."

"Cool, we need to go say hello to her." Sabrina nodded to a young man close to her own age who stared longingly at her as he passed.

"You know who else I spotted? I also saw Alexander Kintner."

"Who? Is he one of those soap stars you like?" Sabrina guessed.

"No, he's the man who's going to cure nicotine addiction."

"Never heard of him."

"Sabrina! He's been all over the media for the past couple years."

"If you say so."

"Kintner is only a few weeks away from releasing his cure. I tweeted the article to you twice."

"Really? Well, you know I hate watching the news ever since... actually, I guess the last name does sound a little familiar."

"It should, we listened to him give a speech on satellite radio this morning on the way to the airport. Remember?"

"Oh, right! Who's he here with?"

Mira sighed and shook her head. "Riley Dalton."

"What?" Sabrina straightened up, suddenly interested.

"Yes, Riley and Alexander are together. It'll be great to meet them both."

"We need to let Moselle know we've arrived first." Sabrina said tracing the outlines of the inlaid pink sapphires on her silver bangle. "Maybe get a drink too."

"You are right," Mira nodded. "It would be rude if we didn't go see Moselle first."

"No need to rush tonight, Mira."

Chapter Eight

United

    Moselle remained under the spotlights of the smaller stage in the club. The bright lights made her costume and her skin shimmer. Her father had disappeared into the crowd with three of his business associates. He didn't have time for small talk so he had quickly wished his daughter well and thanked her for her hard work with the advertising campaign. Moselle thought he seemed in high spirits, less stressed than normal—that was until she had mentioned her date had arrived. Perhaps it was her wicked smile when she pointed in Jackson's direction that her father found inappropriate; regardless, he did not even glance at Jackson. It was clear to Moselle that her father did not care about meeting him.

    Although bothered by her father's actions, Moselle did not show it in front of the scores of men who came up to meet her. Moselle had become well known from the club's advertisements and using the excuse that her signature would one day be worth something, a group of her father's investors had lined up in front of her. She enjoyed every moment of it.

    Moselle finally spotted a friendly face. Not only did Sabrina's slinky, red dress scream for attention, but also the air around her smelled of a scent Moselle found exclusive to her friend.

"You must have waxed yourself all the way down to your—" Sabrina shouted from the dance floor; her words drowned out by the music.

"Sabrina, my dear, such vulgar words in front of my father's associates," Moselle said, glaring at her friend.

Sabrina smiled as the group of men excused themselves and walked off. Moselle knew Sabrina loved to shock people.

"Many thanks for chasing them away. The shortest man smelled rotten of cigars and cheap cologne."

Sabrina nodded.

"Look at you Moselle, you're almost naked, babe! And under these lights, you must be sweating your tits off."

"I assure you, my breasts are not sweating. You know me better than that." Moselle smirked. "Is this Mira?"

"Ms. Moselle Abdul Aziz Al Ghurair, it is a true pleasure to finally meet you." Mira bowed.

"Quit your bowing, lame ass." Sabrina nudged her friend in the ribs.

Two of Moselle's guards rushed to her side to help her step carefully down from the stage the moment she approached the stairs. Once on the club's floor, she embraced Sabrina and then Mira.

"Tell me, do you like my new perfume?"

"I do, but it does not cover up your normal citrus-laden scent," Moselle stated nonchalantly.

"I'll never understand that." Sabrina shook her head.

"Understand what?" Mira asked, inserting herself into the conversation.

"Moselle has the most sensitive nose around, and she swears I smell like oranges all the time. I would think she's teasing me, but—"

"I don't tease."

"She doesn't tease." Sabrina laughed.

"So, what do I smell like?" Mira stood up straighter.

Placing her hands on Mira's shoulders, Moselle leaned in to sniff her neck, and Mira blushed shyly.

"The ocean. Of course, you smell of the ocean, my new friend."

"Ha! I thought she was going to say chlorine," Sabrina said. "Mira loves to swim."

After another laugh, Moselle excused herself; she wanted to change out of her ridiculous costume before introducing her friends to Jackson.

"I promise I will return soon, and when I do, we will share a meal. Until then, please enjoy all that my father's club has to offer."

The club filled up, yet when Jackson spotted Moselle crossing the floor, the churning masses split like Moses parting the red sea. A guard on each side of her, Moselle walked toward Jackson, the way she moved telegraphed her class and poise. Jackson wondered if she had practiced this march across the club earlier in the day.

When the three of them reached Jackson, Moselle waved off her guards and took the final steps to him alone.

"Your Majesty." Jackson bowed his head as he greeted her.

"Silly Jackson."

"You look... you look too good for words."

"Thank you," Moselle replied, patting his chest. "I am glad you came; we are going to have such a splendid night."

"Moselle, look, first thing's first. The other night—" he began.

"You have nothing to worry about, Jackson."

"Well, the silent treatment the past few days didn't make me feel like things were all good."

"I am sorry."

"Seriously, Moselle, what happened? Why haven't you answered my calls? What—"

"Jackson, calm yourself," she interrupted. "All is fine."

"I didn't know if I pissed you off or... wait, Moselle, did I hurt you?" he inquired, reaching out to touch her exposed thigh.

"No, you gave me pleasure more intense than I ever dreamed of, my king," she whispered inches from his face before she planted a quick kiss on his lips. "You may have left me numb for a day, but I assure you, I am unharmed."

Jackson smiled; *Moselle sure did have a way with words.*

"I am very thirsty. Would you mind getting me a drink, darling?"

"Wine?"

"No, a bottle of water will be superb."

Jackson gave her a long, smoldering look that made her quiver with excitement, nodded, and walked to one of the bars in the club. Between him and the bar were several of Moselle's guards. He glanced at them; each had their eyes locked on him, a look a disdain on their faces. Jackson wanted to avoid talking to any of them, so he weaved in and out of the empty stools in front of him. Just as he was nearly clear of the maze, Moselle shouted, "Jackson, two bottles please?"

Turning to acknowledge her, his foot hooked the corner of the last stool between him and the open dance floor. Pushed forward, Jackson collided with the stool, nearly falling over it. Straightening up, he kicked the stool out of the way with a grunt then glanced back at Moselle with hopes she had not witnessed his clumsiness. She hadn't.

It took but a moment to procure two bottles of water and a tall glass of lemon-lime soda for himself. Stuffing five dollars into the bartender's tip jar, he nodded thanks to her and made his way back to Moselle.

On his return trip, Jackson walked around the stools that had tripped him. Since he was still carefully watching his feet as he went, he did not notice two of Moselle's guards as they moved to intercept him, and he bumped directly into them. His soda splashed, and he bobbled one of the water bottles as he peered up and into the eyes of the wall of muscle that blocked him. It was the guard who had given him the note at Moselle's home, and the large man had something Jackson's father would have called a shit-eating grin on his face. Just as Jackson balanced the loose water bottle, Moselle's guard reached out and swatted the drink out of his hand.

"What the fuck is your problem?" Jackson asked.

"You are, boy. Stick to your own kind."

Straightening up to his full height, Jackson tightened every muscle in his body. Had he been wearing his hockey gloves; he would have thrown them to the floor.

"Or what, big guy?" Jackson grumbled.

"You'll get hurt."

"No, you will."

"Jackson?" Moselle called out from the other side of her guards.

After scooping up the bottle he had dropped, Jackson walked around the guards. His face had gone a shade of blood red. Heated, he wanted to shout.

"Your guards are assholes."

"Although under my service, my father's influence is hard for them to ignore; these men are, after all, on his... payroll." Moselle said. "Please, ignore them."

"Yeah, that's a little hard."

"All that matters is me, Jackson." Moselle placed the first bottle of water to her crimson lips and proceeded to empty it.

"Wow, you *were* thirsty." Jackson thought back to his college years, the days of watching his friends chug a beer in one go.

After the last drops of the water bubbled from the bottle into her mouth, Moselle looked at Jackson with an eyebrow raised. Resealing the empty bottle, she reached for the second one.

"Have I done something embarrassing?"

"Not at all."

"Good then." Moselle smiled. "Jackson, be a dear and stay here while I change. I would like you to meet my friend, Sabrina London, when I return."

"America's favorite daughter turned felon, turned party girl, Sabrina London?" Jackson asked.

"One and the same."

Jackson couldn't help but grin; she had always been one of his favorite pop-tarts, as the bloggers called her.

"Damn, I thought I recognized her dancing."

"Oh my, you've seen that dreadful film, haven't you?"

Jackson quickly lied. "No, I mean I've heard of it and all, but never seen it."

"You have no doubt seen some of the paparazzi photos taken of her, read about how she nearly jumped off her penthouse balcony?" Moselle asked.

"Who hasn't? Is it true a spying neighbor called the cops when he spotted her getting ready to jump? That the police tasered her off the railing?"

"Yes and no."

"Wait, how are you two friends, Moselle?"

"We modeled together several times years ago, before her incident."

"Really? I need to find those photos. I bet they're amazing." Jackson's smile turned to a devilish smirk. "Tell me, where's she been for the last—what, six or seven months? I haven't seen or read anything about her in forever."

"In hiding, Jackson, waiting for the storm to pass."

"Wow. I never would've expected to meet her tonight."

As Moselle and Jackson talked, Mira and Sabrina entered the VIP-only rooms. Divided into six semiprivate rooms, each with a wall of golden beads covering their entry, the VIP area held a vibrant energy that leaked out into the common area. A dozen or more starlets passed Sabrina and Mira as they moved. Giggling and clearly lit from drinking, the girls laughed about something that Sabrina couldn't quite hear. Hooking the last girl's arm with her hand, she asked what was up.

"Riley's doin' her thang."

With a yank of her arm, the girl pulled herself free. Left to wonder what the partygoer meant, Sabrina stood motionless until she saw the beads spread open to one of the VIP rooms, and another girl stumble out.

Mira gasped. "That's Alexander Kintner..." She pointed.

Seated on a large leather couch, the man had leaned back, at ease. His white teeth gleamed as he cupped the back of the head of the thin girl who knelt down between his legs and pleasured him. Dressed only in a tiny white thong, the girl would have been anonymous if not for the infinity tattoo on her shoulder and the streaks of pink and green in her long hair. Sabrina cringed; it was Riley Dalton, using her mouth to satisfy the man Mira kept talking about.

Sabrina watched as Riley brought the man to climax. When done, she stood wobbling slightly atop her knee-high boots. One of Alexander's guards threw Riley's tank top and skirt to her, while he told her to put them on. As Riley dressed, Alexander's eyes shifted from his most recent conquest to Sabrina. Sabrina was no stranger to having men gawk at her, but something about his gaze made her feel like food—like a steak he wanted to carve up and consume.

"I think he's looking at you."

"Mira." Sabrina shushed her friend, too afraid to do much else.

As Alexander stood, he waved his hand at Riley, as if to dismiss her, and she exited the room without a word. As she shuffled by, Sabrina realized her idol must have been stoned, which was not a surprise, as the tabloids said Riley was battling a serious drug addiction.

"Riley?" Sabrina softly called as she passed.

Suddenly in front of her, Alexander produced a wad of cash from his front pocket and peeled off several bills.

"I have not had the pleasure of being introduced to you, Miss...?"

Sabrina, as disturbed as she was, could not deny that, even at twice her age, possibly even older than her father, Alexander was ruggedly handsome. His thick, dark blonde hair was styled in something her hairstylist would call a fashionable mess. For Sabrina, most remarkable were his eyes—a shade of amber so dark they seemed to burn like molten lava.

"London, Sabrina London," Mira answered for her.

"Y-yes, my name is Sabrina. This is my friend, Mira," she stammered.

"You *are* a special treat aren't you, Miss London?" Alexander's fiery eyes traveled up and down her body as he spoke.

"Mira, be a good girl and run to the bar and get us two bottles of Cristal," Alexander said, slapping a large sum of money into Mira's palm. "I would like to take this moment to get to know the lovely Miss London more."

"I—" Sabrina began to say.

"You know what? I think you are exactly what I've been looking for, Sabrina, exactly what I need." Alexander pointed his index and middle fingers at her, making a firing motion with the flick of his wrist.

"Don't go, Mira." Sabrina took her friend's hand in hers.

A tingling sensation tickled Sabrina's back. She could feel her grip on her wings loosen. At any moment, they would spring out in front of everyone.

"Bathroom," Sabrina whispered to her friend.

"Now?"

"Now!"

"Wait," Alexander said in an arrogant tone. "Don't leave me, Sabrina, not when I've just found you. Stay. I have so much to show you."

"Like your cock? Sorry, pal, no thanks. Seen it, not interested!" Sabrina spit out.

She rushed to the VIP bathrooms, which were blessedly close by, and stepped into the closest stall; Mira, right on her tail, shoved the door shut.

Moaning in pain-tinged pleasure, Sabrina finally released her wings. A flash of red, yellow, and green light, like the twinkling of Christmas bulbs, emanated from the stall top and bottom.

"What is that?" a girl at the sink choked out.

Sabrina's wings sparked into existence like colorful static electricity, stretching past her butt and above her head yet, to her relief, still hidden by the stall.

"Fuck me!" Sabrina pounding the stall door with her fist.

"What the hell?" the girl asked, louder this time.

"It's nothing, really, just a costume malfunction," Mira answered.

"Fucking freaks!"

While the girl stormed out, Sabrina heard Mira checking the other stalls.

"What happened back there?" Mira called over the door.

"Fuck if I know!" Sabrina blurted out. "Same damned thing that happened earlier, but this time I felt it coming. Shit, did I feel it coming!"

"You going to be okay?"

"Nothing a few good drinks and a hard screw wouldn't fix," Sabrina joked, but she was shaking all over.

"I could—" Mira began.

"Just watch the door, okay?" Sabrina interrupted. "I need a minute."

Chapter Nine

Things Change

Jackson felt like an ox; he was that incredibly awkward on the dance floor. At least it was a relief that Moselle was the center of attention. Jackson could not blame the people who stared. He too was enticed by Moselle's body, especially by the way she slithered around and undulated like a belly dancer.

When the DJ unexpectedly played something fast, Moselle kept the crowd's attention as she bounced up and down and swung her long hair in circles. Eventually, Jackson stood back and watched her just like everyone else.

But watching her wasn't an option for long—not when he knew he could touch her—so Jackson returned to her, placed his hands on her hips and his mouth on hers. His hands slid up her back and drew her into his arms, until her body was pressed hard against his and their hips were touching.

"The things you make me want to do to you, Jackson." Moselle whispered.

"Get a room, tramp!"

Sabrina stood with her arms crossed. It appeared to Jackson like Sabrina was trying to give Moselle a disappointed-parent look, one he now wondered if Moselle had seen many times before.

"My friends, there you are," Moselle cheered, wiping any smeared lipstick that may have been there from below her bottom lip.

"Do you have cameras in your VIP rooms?" Sabrina twisted the silver bangle around her wrist.

"I have no idea. I would have to ask my father."

"Well, if he doesn't, tell him he should consider it." Sabrina peered over her shoulder.

A sudden surge in volume made it nearly impossible to speak over the music. Leaving the dance floor, the group moved to a quieter corner of the club that was roped off for privacy. Once seated, Moselle formally introduced Jackson to Sabrina and Mira.

"Nice to meet you, Jackson." Sabrina smiled as they shook hands.

"Hey, strong grip you got there, Sabrina. Nice to meet you too."

"Moselle has told us nothing about you. How did you crazy kids meet?" She raised her hand to stage whisper the next question. "You two have sex yet?"

"Sabrina!" Mira admonished.

"She does that just to shock people." Moselle slapped the top of Sabrina's hand. "She means no disrespect."

"Advertising company," he coughed out. "I'm in charge of the new ads for her father's clubs."

"Really? Are you a graphic designer?" Mira lit up with the information. "I love art."

"One of the best," Moselle said.

"Thank you."

"My friend, I am so glad to see you again. It has been ages since we attended a party together or sat down for a meal." Moselle held Sabrina's hand as she spoke.

"Well, you know how things have been." Sabrina's head titled and she shrugged. "To be honest, I'm a little surprised your dad *let* you invite me, especially after what happened last time I saw him."

Moselle giggled in a way Jackson had never seen before. Something about her tone hid something truly sinister.

"What happened last time?" he asked.

"Moselle got caught up in my lifestyle for a few days; there was this huge party, an epic one, and—"

"Please, such a story is in poor taste at the dinner table." Moselle shot Sabrina a glance.

"I puked on her dad's shoes."

"Oh, no." Jackson smiled at Sabrina, and she smiled back. "That's horrible and kinda funny."

"It was."

"Yes. Well," Moselle hurried the conversation on. "That being said, it is truly good seeing that the fog that once settled upon you has finally blown away."

"Well, I kicked smoking and cocaine, so, yeah, I feel much better, thanks to Mira." Sabrina patted her friend's shoulder. "I just woke up one morning, on some rock star's tour bus, covered in whipped cream, and I realized... it was all so lame. I want to be a musician, you know, a pop superstar."

Sabrina's story made Jackson's heart nearly stop. Not allowing his brain enough time to fully calculate his response, he blurted, "Covered in whipped cream, like head to toe or just the good parts?"

"What do you think, big guy?" Sabrina sat up straight, arching her back as she spoke.

"You sure did know how to party," Jackson said shaking his head.

"She's teasing you, darling." Moselle pinched the back of his arm.

"Seriously though, if it wasn't for all those shitty scandal rags, I would never have realized how bad my problem had become. Those pictures..." Sabrina cringed. "I didn't like who I was, and my life was all being documented right there in front of me."

"My father always says you are the butterfly that returned to its cocoon," Moselle added.

"Yeah, well, I mean, it's weird. That freaking video started everything. The media and the paparazzi are to blame for nearly killing me, yet at the same time, all those hateful pictures... in a lot of ways they helped lift me up, out of the hell I was putting myself through."

Jackson had never looked at the flipside of Sabrina's history. All he saw was a hot mess, a "celebutard," even a slut, but that was beginning to change.

"What was it your German philosopher said, Jackson? That which does not kill us makes us stronger." Moselle smiled.

"Good one, but I'm not sure I'd call him *my* German philosopher?" Jackson smiled.

"That should be the slogan for the next sale at Christian Dior." Sabrina laughed and tapped Mira on the shoulder. "It was hella bad there."

"Oh! Did you see the shoes Sabrina bought me?" Mira lifted one of her feet off the ground to show.

Jackson sat back and watched as the three girls chatted and laughed at one another's stories. He gazed out into the crowd to find dozens of jealous eyes on him. The scent of filet mignon, no doubt cooked to mouth-watering perfection, overwhelmed his senses as six members of the waitstaff approached their table. *Fine food, beautiful women; this club may have been called Afterlife for the right reasons*, he thought. Jackson felt like he was in heaven.

Chapter Ten

Media Release

"Sabrina!" Mira shrieked. "Wake up!"

Sabrina yawned wearily; her body felt heavy. She could have slept well past noon. There was no reason to wake up so early. What had it been, only three or four hours since she'd passed out after mixing two Clonazepam with a full bottle of wine? Sabrina's cloudy, swimming head could not remember.

Sabrina knew her rehab doctors would not approve of such behavior, but she justified it with two facts: one, it was the only way to get any rest after the night she had, and two, at least it wasn't vodka and cocaine.

Fairy-kind blood was much more resistant to the effects of alcohol. In order to feel drunk, she had to put away twice as much to feel half the effect. Sabrina had learned to skillfully disguise her consumption over the past few years. Had she not acted drunk from time to time, people surely would have suspected something was amiss when the skinny girl in her twenties put away more than the average beer-craving frat boy.

"Sabrina!" Mira yelled again; this time the sound of her voice was followed by thunderous footfalls.

"What?" Sabrina yawned. "I heard you the first time."

Running into Sabrina's large hotel room, Mira carried her tablet.

"It's bad. Look."

Mira dropped her tablet onto the bed for Sabrina. In the center of the display was TMZ's website. Under his colorful, animated banner and a flashing advertisement for a new reality show, sat a blurry photograph of Sabrina. There she was, last night, inside her limo—her wings out and partially visible—the heading: "What the #!@$! has Sabrina London been hiding?"

Sabrina felt sick; it was happening all over again. Her personal life would be smeared all over the web, her secrets revealed, yet this time the potential fallout was much worse.

"I expect the Assembly will need to be alerted—"

"Fuck that!" Sabrina exclaimed as her mind searched for a way out of this trouble. "Turn on the TV."

Mira switched on the TV and it buzzed into existence in the middle of a news brief. The newscaster reiterated that Kintner Co. had decided to move up its release of the nicotine addiction-curing drug DUST. DUST would be available next Monday in limited quantities in select states on the West Coast and Southwest. They aired a clip of the field correspondent for the show interviewing Kintner as he arrived at Club Afterlife last night. The images of his limousine outside the club made Sabrina hold her breath in a prayer that her folly would not been shown next.

"Mr. Kintner, rumor has it your drug DUST will have a limited release soon. Was the recent alleged setback all a hoax? What can you tell us?"

"The demand for a cure has been great, and so the demand for DUST is great. Yes, we faced a small setback last month, but production will go back into full swing soon, I promise. It may take a little longer than I had expected to reach every city, but trust me, all of America will have the cure very soon." Kintner sounded like a campaigning politician.

As the newscaster ended her report, Sabrina and Mira stared at each other, both relieved that the big news of the day was the release of DUST and not the discovery of Sabrina's fairy wings. As the news rattled on in the background, Sabrina searched Google for her name. It seemed only TMZ had posted a picture of her from last night; maybe there was no reason to panic at all. TMZ was known for doodling on the photos of celebrities; maybe people would think the fuzzy wing-shaped glow behind her in the dark limousine was just one of his silly drawings. Suddenly, an idea came to her.

"Shit! Moselle's boyfriend! Quick, call Moselle!"

"Where's your phone?" Mira scampered off to a pile of dirty clothes, the most likely location of Sabrina's phone.

Suddenly, another familiar name caught her attention. A picture of Riley Dalton on screen accompanied the terrible news; Riley Dalton had been found dead.

"Riley Dalton apparently committed suicide last night when she jumped from the rooftop of the hotel she was staying in. Her body was identified by her close friend and manager early this morning. Seen last night partying at the new Club Afterlife, eyewitness reports say she left the venue alone and severely intoxicated. The doorman of the club has said she stumbled away in a stupor, half naked and completely drunk."

"Gods no!" Sabrina gasped.

"An investigation is underway, but it is no secret the Grammy Award-winning musician had drug issues and many demons."

The loss of her idol pushed Sabrina over the edge she had teetered on since waking up and she began to cry.

"I need a minute."

Sabrina's attention was split between the images of Riley's music career as they flashed on the TV and her own image on TMZ. Sobbing, she shut out the sounds of the room and let her emotions have free rein.

Sabrina rolled onto her side and her wings fluttered as they freed themselves, illuminating the window behind her.

Sabrina thought about her life, her family, and her history. It was times like now that she wished she were just a simple human, and her wings would just vanish under her skin forever. *But that is not possible...*

Time to man up, Sabrina. No more feeling weak.

"Hand me the phone."

By the time the last digit of Moselle's number was pressed, Sabrina's eyes were dry.

"Moselle. It's me."

"Sabrina, how are you? You did not say goodbye last night; you left much earlier than I imagined you would." Moselle's disappointment was clear.

"It was late. Too many soul suckers around, if ya know what I mean."

"I do. So how may I be of service?"

"Where's your man? He still alive?" Sabrina joked.

"Yes!" Moselle let a chuckle slip before she continued. "He is alive and well, in his room packing as we speak. Sadly, my stay is a brief one; we fly home shortly."

"Moselle, I need his help. My fucking wings popped in the limo last night and some asshole snapped a photo of them."

"Someone took a photo of your wings? That is as unfortunate as it is—"

"I know and to think Mira was afraid someone might get another shot of my lady parts," Sabrina interrupted, sneering at Mira. "Fuck, I wish it was my coochie in this damn picture!"

"You need Jackson to work his magic? To make an alteration to this nefarious photo?"

"Yes."

"I will ask Jackson to begin the moment we get home. I am sure he will gladly do it. Fear not, your father—"

"Please don't even mention him, okay?"

"Very well."

Moselle's steady calmness had filled her with so much relief that Sabrina's mind drifted to other things, and after a long yawn, she asked, "So, did you two screw last night?"

"Sabrina, my friend..." Moselle paused, and Sabrina figured she was going to get reprimanded for the use of such language. "How many orgasms have you had in one night, because I can now say I have had ten."

Chapter Eleven

Hit and Run

The sun was high in the sky as Sabrina and Mira stood at the cash register of a swanky, outdoor New York eatery. Sabrina fumbled through her handbag in search of her Dubai First Royale MasterCard—she felt much better now—the warm sun helped, and so did Mira.

"Tiffany's was such a good idea, Mira. This tanzanite drop pendant was a total steal."

"It's a beautiful piece."

"Here it is!" Sabrina handed the black credit card to the young girl who operated the cash register.

As Sabrina waited for the receipt, she looked around, her eyes settling on none other than Alexander Kintner. The man sat at the far end of the restaurant with two other men who appeared to be bodyguards. His eyes had locked on her and stayed that way until she and Mira sat down.

Sabrina ducked her head, so that Mira's body blocked her. "That drug guy is here."

"What drug dealer?"

"No, the guy Riley blew at the club." Sabrina nodded forward so Mira would turn and look over her shoulder.

Sabrina watched Mira twist around and stare directly at Alexander Kintner; she completely lacked any subtlety.

"He *is* undeniably attractive."

"Mira!" Sabrina snapped.

Sabrina peeked again. Dressed casually in a Nike tracksuit and wearing dark glasses, Sabrina assumed he was attempting to keep a low profile, although he had already attracted a few onlookers.

"Is that jerk signing napkins? What the hell do they think he is—a rock star?" Sabrina asked sarcastically.

"He might be a jerk, but he's going to be a very famous, very wealthy jerk in a few weeks."

"Whatever. I mean look at that one lady; she's flirting with him with a cigarette hanging from her mouth! Would you look at that... he's signing an empty cigarette carton?" Sabrina huffed angrily. "Stupid much?"

Stabbing her salad with a fork, Sabrina sneered. Although relieved that DUST had trumped any potential story related to her wings, she still felt Alexander Kintner was creepy and probably the reason Riley was dead.

"I have to pee."

"Want me to join you?" Mira offered

"No, I'm a big girl now. You sit; enjoy your lunch."

Sabrina walked with an extra swing in her hips as she passed the other patrons. She had considered telling Mira to call out her name, as if to ask her a question, just to get everyone to look at her, but at the last second, she decided against it. Maybe today had seen enough turmoil.

Sabrina straightened her skirt as the automatic flusher roared behind her. She looked down at her feet and kicked a bit of toilet paper away. She hated walking in public bathrooms in her expensive shoes. With a handful of toilet paper, she opened the door and, to her surprise, came eye to eye with the last person she would have expected in the women's bathroom.

"We meet again, Sabrina London." Alexander Kintner's booming voice filled the entire bathroom.

Startled, she jumped.

"What the hell are you doing in here?" Sabrina asked. "You know the little boy's room is next door, right?"

"A woman like you—such a prize, and one that does not often fall in a man's lap, but yet here you are in mine."

Kintner stepped closer to Sabrina, digging for something in his pants pocket. When he found it, a smile stretched across his face from ear to ear.

"All these months spent searching for more fairy-kind, hunting them in Alaska, France, Canada..."

Sabrina gasped. No human should know what he did; it was forbidden. But that was only the start of her problems. Disbelief washed over her as she watched the man produce a shiny knife from his pocket.

"Come here!"

Kintner lunged forward, seizing her by the arm so he could spin her around. Stumbling over her heels, Sabrina was powerless to get away from him, and when the cold metal of his blade brushed against the bare skin of her lower back, she froze.

"All this time I knew about you. I mean, it's virtually impossible to not know of Sabrina London and her many sides: the socialite, the famous model"—Kintner drew a deep breath—"and my personal favorite, the substance abusing whore."

He shoved her hard, and Sabrina fell forward into the countertop between two of the bathroom's three sinks. Kintner moved quick and pinned her in place with his hips. The air vanished from her lungs, and her chest felt hollow. Sabrina tried to free herself, but the fight in her was not enough. Back and forth, she teetered on a snapped heel, unable to get good enough footing to even attempt an escape.

"Get the fuck off me!" Sabrina screamed the moment she caught her breath. "Mira! Help!"

Kintner chuckled and slid his hand up the back of her tank top. When he reached her shoulders, he pressed heavily with his palm until her chest was pushed firmly against the cold, stone counter.

"Let's see those wings!"

With one swipe of his razor-sharp blade, her top was cleaved in two, and her tattoo fully revealed. Kintner gasped at the splendor of Sabrina's skin art.

"Magnificent." He ran the back of a hand across the multi-colored flesh.

"You haven't seen anything yet, you bastard!"

Sabrina released them, rapidly—and fully into his face. The flash of vibrant light knocked him off balance, freeing Sabrina. With a flutter of her butterfly-shaped wings, Sabrina lifted herself several inches from the ground and pivoted to face her assailant.

"You like that? That's nothing! I can make these puppies glow so bright, your fucking eyes will sizzle!"

"Bitch!"

Alexander Kintner was fast—faster than Sabrina would have imagined. The small knife in his hand scored her tanned stomach, leaving a line of blood in its wake. She dropped to the floor in shock—the heel of her other shoe snapping under her weight. Bent over at the waist, Sabrina grabbed her stomach, her fingers reading the depth of the laceration.

"Asshole, you cut me!" she spit.

In response, Kintner backhanded her. The impact of his knuckles knocked her backward and spun her, so she was once again facing the countertop. As the room swayed back and forth, Sabrina glanced up at the mirror, seeing the glow from her wings sparkle off his blade like fireworks on the Fourth of July.

"I was only going to sever your wings, but now I'm going to cut your throat too!"

"Back away from her!" Mira shouted as she entered the bathroom.

"What the hell are you going to do to stop me?" Kintner yelled back.

"This!" Sabrina screamed as she waved her hands in front of the sink sensors.

The stream of water from each spigot grew larger and stronger as Mira raised her hands, palm up. In no time, the water was flooding the sinks, and it was then that Mira redirected it at him. When the two streams, now twisting together like a waterspout, struck the man, they intensified again, this time building to the force of water released from a fire hose. Facing Kintner, arms out, Mira controlled the steady blast until it knocked him off his feet and through the door of one of the bathroom stalls.

Sabrina pushed herself off the counter gingerly. Her cheek tingled with the pain of Kintner's strike, yet that discomfort was no match for the anger she held in her fluttering chest.

"Fuck you!" she screamed at Kintner, who laid crumpled in a pile beside the toilet, knocked unconscious by the force of Mira's attack.

As Sabrina stumbled toward Mira, her eyes overflowed with tears.

"Let's get out of here, Sabrina." Mira took her friend in a tight hug. "Let's go home."

Chapter Twelve

Going Home

Twenty thousand miles above Ohio, cruising at 400 mph, Moselle sat holding hands with Jackson across a small table in the cabin of one of her father's private jets.

Moselle had planned to take a short nap, but she and Jackson had started talking and hadn't stopped yet. Jackson told a story about a flight he had been on that got grounded, because a famous action-adventure star was sloppy drunk and took a swing at a Federal Air Marshal. He reenacted the actor's slurred ramblings with such precision that Moselle was laughing uncontrollably.

"Honestly, this is a lot cooler than flying commercial," Jackson observed.

"I think so too." Moselle smiled.

"Too bad we aren't alone," he whispered, nodding at the three guards traveling with them.

"Oh, do you have something wicked in mind, Jackson?"

"Maybe."

"Well, could you be a dear and get the lotion out of my bag?"

"Lotion?" He raised his eyebrows.

"My skin feels dry," Moselle announced, running her hand over her forearm.

As he opened her purse, Jackson realized it was filled with all sorts of make-up.

"It's in the bottom, darling."

Jackson dug through her purse, until he spotted the screen of her smartphone glowing with a missed call alert. Lifting the phone up revealed the location of the lotion.

"I think you missed a call, Moselle."

"No worries." She smiled. "Could you help me?"

Moselle lifted her sweater over her head, and her black lace bra filled Jackson's vision.

"Damn..." he said. "What about the guards?"

"They are forbidden to look at me in such state at risk of my father killing them."

Jackson laughed. "Oh, I can imagine him using an old double-barreled shotgun."

"You doubt my seriousness?" Moselle asked as she pulled her long black hair over her shoulder and turned her back to him.

"What? No, not at all."

Jackson applied a modest amount of lotion to her back and rubbed it in. While he massaged her shoulders, he listened to Moselle moan; the sound was deliciously arousing.

In a matter of seconds, his desire overwhelmed him. With a deep breath caught in his chest, his heart racing, Jackson allowed his lust to control his actions. With the straps pinched between his thumb and index fingers, he peeled them down until the lace cups were about to reveal her nipples. When he expected Moselle to stop him, she instead she reached up, over her shoulder, grabbed Jackson's neck, and guided him into a kiss.

"Remove your pants," Moselle breathed.

"Are you sure?" He stepped around in front of her, his arousal evident. "Maybe we should stop."

Her phone rang again as Jackson stared down at her, her breasts spilling from her bra.

"You smell good enough to eat. Would you deny your lover her meal?" Moselle pushed her forehead against his stomach and then inhaled his sweet scent again.

"No."

"Then feed me," she whispered while stroking him over his jeans.

Before he could unbutton his pants, the smartphone rang again.

"I hope that's not important," Jackson joked, his focus divided.

Sighing, she put out her hand and left it out until Jackson placed her phone in it.

"Hello?" Moselle's said, sounding exasperated.

Sabrina's panic-stricken voice roared through the phone, so loud that Jackson could tell it was her but couldn't make out the words.

"Sabrina, what is wrong?"

Moselle flinched and held the phone off her ear at Sabrina's yelling. "Sabrina, darling, please relax. I can't understand when you yell."

With her thumb, Moselle lowered the volume.

"Tell me... are you okay? Where's Mira?" Moselle motioned to Jackson for her sweater, covering her chest with her other arm. "Put Mira on."

Moselle put her top on as she listened. Whatever had happened must have terrified her, as she looked as if she had been told someone had died.

"This does not bode well, Mira. I have read about a few attacks similar to this. I never dreamt that they would be tied to one man. You better take refuge at my home when you return to the West Coast."

Moselle rubbed the bridge of her nose and closed her eyes. "No, no, no. We are all family, after all."

When Moselle ended the call, she let the phone slip through her hands, to the floor. *Someone attacked Sabrina for her wings.* Mira's words had a frightening context. *Could a human actually know that fairies exist? If so, what else did he know?*

This man, Alexander Kintner, he was on the brink of becoming a hero, and now had suddenly become a very dangerous person. Every ounce of Moselle's being screamed that she should quickly retrieve her phone and dial the one number she prayed she would never have to use: the Otherworldly Assembly. To dial it meant to alter the world she knew and had grown comfortable in; it also meant losing Jackson.

"What's wrong?" Jackson's voice was full of concern. "Is everyone okay?"

"Sabrina was attacked."

"Holy shit! What happened?"

"Some guy tried to... tried to rape her in a bathroom back in New York City," Moselle lied.

"Christ, is she okay?"

"Yes, but I have invited her to stay with me a few days."

"Good idea."

Moselle had not felt such fear in ages; not since she still lived with her parents, in a much different land than this one. The answer then was to escape, to run away and hide. Although the problem scared her, the solution terrified her all the more.

"Jackson, my love, when we get back to Los Angeles, would you stay with me at my home too?" Moselle asked timidly. "It would be a great comfort to have you with me."

"Sure," Jackson answered, his eyes glued to one of her many armed guards. "Absolutely."

Chapter Thirteen

DUST

Alexander Roosevelt Kintner, the CEO of Kintner Co., stood on a catwalk above his workers in his main processing plant located in central Los Angeles. Had his employees paused in their work, they would have seen their boss's grin, a mouthful of shining pearls stretching ear to ear.

After years of efficient and successful clinical trials, the FDA had finally approved his drug: Dentrohydrate Ultriniumpyrilene Sisotryphate. More commonly referred to as DUST, it was the first proven cure for nicotine addiction.

Two months ago, production had begun; all was going as planned. Nearly a quarter of the preorders for DUST had already been manufactured, packaged, and prepared to ship to sellers. Alexander Kintner was on the threshold of becoming a billionaire on the first day of the pill's sale, which medical journals were already calling a prime solution to the nicotine addiction epidemic that was responsible for the population dip in 2018.

Soon, Kintner Co. facilities in Los Angeles would complete production of the drug, making it ready for wide-scale release. Soon, everyone in America would know the name Alexander Roosevelt Kintner; he would become their savior.

In order to complete the batches produced today, his personal attention would be required. Alexander withdrew a long, slender glass vial from his Armani suit's pocket. The contents of the bottle made his hand glow a dull yellow-green, like that of a dozen lightning bugs. Alexander poured the flakes from within the vial into his open left hand, sure to prevent the slight overflow from spilling to the floor. He carefully placed the bottle back into his pocket and cupped his hands together, moving them in a motion similar to that of packing a snowball.

The flakes emitted a new shine as the power within them gradually intensified. The burning light soon encompassed both his hands but did not harm him.

Alexander slowly separated his palms. The glowing light had transformed into a form of floating energy and when released it slowly drifted in the direction of the DUST that was still being processed in two large, stirring vats. The energy stretched out from Alexander's hands, down past his employees, who, dressed in their hazardous material suits, continued to do their work completely undisturbed by its existence.

When the glowing energy reached the vats of medicine, it was instantly absorbed. He mumbled a few words to himself, summoning several orbs of dark purple magical light, which shot from his arms, pulsating down the beam of energy, into the vat. The spell was complete. A new batch of DUST was ready.

"Sir!"

One of Alexander's managers busted through a pair of double doors into the production area. Sweat poured down the young man's head and the moisture from his armpits created two large circles.

"What is it, Mr. Buhner? You know I am never to be disturbed when working with the DUST." Alexander asked as he watched his employee suck in air as fast as his lungs would take it.

"I know, sir. It's just…" The man gulped down a breath before continuing. "The warehouse in San Diego… it's been destroyed. It's all gone."

"What?"

"It's all gone, sir. The police—"

Gritting his teeth, Alexander shoved his rage back down. "Was it them again?"

"All signs point to yes."

Although deeply concerned, Alexander would not show it.

"How long is this going to set me back?"

"Depending on how extensive our search becomes locating key replacement ingredients, I imagine another month… two tops."

"Two more months."

"Sir, the logistics department has run a new disaster-recovery report each week since last month, when the first warehouse was destroyed. I'll have them run another one tonight with the new data but I'm afraid to say, well, I-I fear our inventory is…" The young manager tried to provide more details but trailed off.

"Rome was not built in a day, Mr. Buhner."

"I'm sorry, Mr. Kintner." He continued, "We can spin this, sir. I know we can. *And* we still have one large shipment of materials inbound from our facility in Washington."

Alexander quickly eliminated his concern, after all, in his mind, he had already won.

"Don't stress yourself. We stand in the eye of the hurricane; a full-scale addiction epidemic swirls around us on all sides. Just imagine what this announced setback will do. It will cause an even greater frenzy. Do you remember what the government reports stated would occur by 2025 if a cure was not on track?"

"Sir?"

"Predictions for January 2025 show the population of the United States of America to be well under the two-hundred-

and-eighty-million mark. As a result, a nationwide recession is feared. Supply and demand, Mr. Buhner. Prepare the press releases, and by tomorrow afternoon, we'll watch the preorders for DUST quadruple."

"I wish I had your confidence, sir, I'd probably worry less."

Rubbing his left shoulder, where it was still sore, Alexander thought back on his encounter with Sabrina in the bathroom as he asked, "Do you believe in fate, Mr. Buhner?"

"I do, sir."

"Good, then you may find some relief when I tell you this," Alexander smiled. "I know exactly where to find what we need. *What I need.*"

"You-you do?"

"Yes, so I hope Thrasher and his gang enjoy watching the entire country beg me to save them. Because their efforts have been wasted."

Chapter Fourteen

Sacked

While she searched Sabrina's pockets for the keys to their apartment, Mira listened to her friend repeat a single phrase over and over again. Mira had become virtually mute since boarding the plane home. She kept thinking about Alexander Kintner and the one thing that stood out in all this chaos.

Not once in the time between Sabrina leaving and hearing her cry for help did Alexander leave her view—yet somehow he managed to attack her friend in the bathroom.

"He wanted my wings..." Sabrina whispered. "He wanted my wings..."

"I know. Here's the key. Let's go inside and gather some clothes quickly." Mira sighed. "In an hour or so, we'll be at Moselle's, and everything will be fine."

When Mira opened the door, she was greeted by an unexpected scene: the place had been ransacked. Tattered clothes cluttered the entryway along with broken wine bottles and scattered kitchenware.

"Fucking robbed? Again?" Sabrina screeched in anger.

"Maybe not. Stay here, Sabrina; let me check this out."

"Fuck!" Sabrina stomped her foot.

Mira tiptoed through the debris toward the central room, careful not to make a sound. Everything her eyes took in had some degree of damage, from rips in the couch's fabric to wires severed and pulled free from the audio system. Mira could tell this was no robbery, as the things worth any money were still there.

By the howl of the wind through the apartment, Mira assumed the sliding door on the balcony was open. While Mira crept toward it, someone entered the center room from the kitchen. Frozen, Mira watched the skinny young man walk aimlessly around the couch until he stopped and stabbed at it with a large butcher knife. Before she could decide what to do, there was a crash on the balcony. She was right: this was no break-in; this was an attack. It was time for her to do her job.

Mira sprinted across the room at the knife-wielding young man. She tried to grab the man's shoulders but lost her grip on his loose clothing, and he spun suddenly around, lodging his knife deep in her belly.

Face to face with her foe, Mira saw nothing in his eyes; they were a black void. The motion of his stab was meant to disembowel her. Mira should have screamed in pain when the man twisted the knife in her gut, but such a physical attack meant little to her people. Mira was a water spirit, an entity entirely made of H_2O, with complete control over the element. In her natural form, she could reshape herself, even increase her mass or volume with access to additional water. She could move at the speed of the ocean's tides or merge with them.

Pinned by the man's knife, Mira had no other option.

"Surprise," she said as her body popped like a water balloon, spilling to the floor at the man's feet, only to re-form instantly behind him.

Unfazed, the young man swiped his blade at Mira as she rose from the ground, returning to her human form. When the metal struck her, it passed through, splattering a watery mess across the wall behind her. Unharmed, she placed her hand into the man's open mouth and extended herself into his throat, funneling the ambient moisture in the air through herself. In a matter of seconds, Mira filled the man's lungs with water, and although he choked, he showed no fear of dying.

After the man dropped to the ground dead, Mira steadily crossed the room toward the pool where two more people were slinking about in the shadows. Young, like the one she had already dispatched, Mira wondered what their motives were until Sabrina entered the room.

"Wings!"

Mira summoned the water from the pool into the shape of a funnel, and with just a thought, the waterspout launched across the room, striking one of the new attackers and spinning him around until he lifted off the ground and slammed into the ceiling.

"Get out of here!" Mira shouted at Sabrina as she drew more of the pool water into her own being, doubling her size.

But Sabrina found her way blocked by two girls, also with knives. Chanting "wings" like a mantra, the pair lunged at Sabrina.

Sabrina released her wings, catapulting herself safely away from the young women, as Mira created two waves that spread out before her and raced toward the two girls. When they struck the girls, the rushing water swept them up and slammed them against the wall.

"Who are these people?" Sabrina yelled to her friend, who had engaged the last man standing.

"I don't know. Check the girls' pockets," Mira suggested.

"Fuck! They aren't breathing! Did you have to kill them?"

"To protect you, to guard the secret, yes."

"These two look like they're barely in their teens. What the hell are they doing here?"

Mira extended her arm, ramming directly into the chest of the last assailant.

Sabrina cringed, "Did his rib cage just snap?"

"His breastbone," Mira corrected. "Yes, it did."

"Gross, Mira."

Sabrina landed then knelt beside the girls. "Look." She pointed.

Sticking out of the pocket of one of the girl's tight, dirty jeans dangled a packet labeled DUST. Sabrina pulled the package from the girl's pocket, but before Mira could examine it, another attacker stepped from around the corner and swung at her with a baseball bat. The wooden bat passed through Mira's head, diminishing its size slightly but still causing her no harm.

"Pathetic." Mira created another wave that knocked the man directly over the couch.

Undaunted, the man pushed himself up from the floor picking something up as he rose. At first the lamp's long black electrical cord looked harmless, but when he cut it, the cable came to life like a wiggling snake.

"No!" Mira said as she realized what he was doing. "Fly, Sabrina, fly!"

"Fly, damn you!" Desperation filled Mira's voice as the man knelt and placed the cord in the water.

Electricity sparked from the end, jolting the man's body only a second before lighting up Mira's.

"Holy shit!" Sabrina rose as quickly as she could until she bumped her head on the ceiling, staring below in disbelief. "No..."

Sabrina could not believe her eyes. Mira was gone, vanished into a puff of sizzling vapor.

How long did she hover there—five minutes? Ten? Fifteen? Sabrina was unsure. The penthouse had fallen silent and entirely dark. *The power must be out—a breaker tripped.* Sabrina called out to her friend, but she received no reply. Not knowing what else to do, she fluttered her wings and sailed out the broken balcony door into the Beverly Hills night sky.

Chapter Fifteen

Radical Behavior

Darkness swallowed the edges of the Golden State Freeway —the moonlight wrestled against the endless rows of trees to wash the road in its pale sheen.

Four bikers blazed down the highway, headlights off, their speed well exceeding the limit as they shattered the silence.

It took them forty-five minutes, but the group finally found what they were searching for: a lone tractor-trailer. They slowed down and fanned out, taking up both of the dark highway's lanes as they approached the truck from behind. The biggest of the four men rode the biggest Harley with its tires on the double yellow lines and motioned with his fist, an unspoken command for his men to attack.

The other three howled with excitement as they raced ahead of their leader. In no time, their speeding motorcycles pulled up alongside the tractor-trailer, and one by one, they flipped on their lights and passed the cab, cutting it off. The trailer slowed and swerved to avoid a collision yet held steady within the confines of his lane.

"What the hell is wrong with you?" the driver shouted out the window as the bikers passed.

When they pulled ahead of the truck, they lined up, creating a barricade in the middle of the road, and reduced their speed, forcing the truck driver to slam on his brakes. When the sound of tires sliding across asphalt signaled the bikers, they sped away.

The leader of the bikers, who had stayed behind the truck, finally made his approach from the shadows, decelerating just long enough to aim and toss the burning Molotov cocktail that he held at the trailer's back tire, before vanishing into the darkness.

Swerving during a sharp bend in the road, the front right corner panel of the cab struck the guardrail with a glancing blow that rattled the truck end to end. In seconds, the remainder of the large vehicle slammed against the guardrail, filling the quiet roadside with the sound of tearing metal.

With the loss of the back tires, the trailer bounced, sliding against the guardrail and tilting until the weight of its contents shifted. Metal bent, tires shredded, and the inevitability of gravity took over. Falling to the side, the heavy vehicle slid against the pavement, sparks flying high into the air.

The three bikers who had ridden ahead were stopped in the middle of the highway, facing the oncoming truck. Each man bigger than the next, they held themselves like posturing professional wrestlers. Their weather-beaten faces were covered in unkempt, thick beards, making it hard to get a pulse on their ages, though it was obvious they were two dozen or more years out of fashion. Sitting atop their cycles, the trio waited as the semi came to a slow, grinding stop a hundred feet from them.

Their leader joined them, revving his engine so it sounded like a roaring lion celebrating a kill. His pale blonde beard stretched far enough up his face to reach the edge of his thick plastic sunglasses. His dense, long hair matched his beard and flowed halfway down his back.

"Good work." He nodded to his men as he turned off his engine. "Barton, go see if the driver's still alive. Clayton, pry open that back gate. Rex, go lay out the police flares."

His men jumped into action. As Clayton walked around the side of the trailer to its gate, Barton effortlessly climbed up the nose of the tractor, toward the passenger door. A man of little patience, Clayton un-holstered a revolver, pointed the gun at the padlock that held the gate shut, and squeezed off two shots.

"What've we got, Clayton?" the leader asked coolly as he watched the lights from Rex's flares pop into existence.

"Exactly what you said would be in here, boss. It's fucking perfect."

"Good. Torch it. I'll feel better when everything of his is ash."

Thrasher was what their leader called himself and with good reason. Each man in his crew knew his story, a journey so stained with blood it was black. Once a family man, married with a son and two daughters, Thrasher had witnessed the one thing that could break any man: the slaughter of his loved ones.

He had only been able to watch, helplessly, in horror as his wife and children dropped before his eyes when a bank robber fired into a crowd of pedestrians with a pair of six shooters. A sun-kissed morning in the spring of 1887 gave birth to his unquenchable thirst for revenge.

Thrasher had taken the law into his own hands when the sheriff and deputies gave up. Using his skills as a hunter and poacher, he had tracked the bank robber deep into the forest. After three days with nothing to eat but what he could scavenge from the land during the scant moments he was willing to waste, Thrasher had found the robber's campsite and ambushed his family's murderer with a Bowie knife.

The thick blade had become an extension of Thrasher's body, a focal point of his rage. No matter how many times he had swung it, no matter how many times Thrasher had carved tiny chunks of flesh from the robber's body, he had not felt any better; his pain was not relieved.

What Thrasher did next would label him as an ungodly cannibal in the eyes of all who heard the story. To him it was a resurrection of sorts. His humanity gone, swallowed whole by rage, Thrasher consumed the robber's flesh. The act made him feel whole again, returned his lost sanity. There were many sights, sounds, and smells that Thrasher would never forget about those days, but the most powerful was the odd symbol branded into the bank robber's satchel...

Thrasher stared at the logo on the side of the trailer, a red, runic, wolf symbol: Kintner Co.'s logo. It may have evolved through the years, but there was no denying its similarity to the one burnt into his mind's eye. This company, and the man who ran it, were undoubtedly connected to the robber who had killed his family so many years ago.

"You mother fucking ecoterrorists!" the driver screamed at the top of his lungs, jarring Thrasher back to the present.

He had pulled himself out of the passenger door's broken window and aimed a double-barreled shotgun at Barton's chest with his shaky hands. As Barton turned, the driver squeezed the trigger. The impact knocked Barton off the side of the downed cab.

Thrasher saw the driver was shaken by the act of shooting another man—his hands trembled so badly he dropped the shotgun, which bounced its way from the windshield to the nose of the cab.

"Barton!" Clayton screamed as he ran around the corner of the trailer.

Thrasher stretched out his arm, stopping Clayton as though he had run into a locked turnstile.

"Hold off." Thrasher took off his coat between deep, measured breaths. "I'll... handle... this."

"Get out of here, you fucking assholes, before I call the cops!"

In the blink of an eye, Thrasher's skin turned black as coal and a deep, jagged crack formed down the center of his spine, slowly splitting his body in two. Akin to a caterpillar shedding its cocoon, a new being emerged from the dry, hard shell. While newly born to its environment, the beast that Thrasher had become was neither naked nor defenseless. Covered from head to toe in thick, brown fur, the creature shook its body like a dog shaking off rain and then pointed its snout to the stars and released a reverberating snort.

"What the fuck... what the fuck is that?" the driver screamed.

Thrasher growled, baring two rows of sharp, canine teeth, and then effortlessly leapt up to the side of the trailer.

"Get 'em, boss!" Clayton yelled.

Thrasher stood with a significant hunch; his massive shoulders as wide as anvils. His crown was remarkably bear-like, almost as if God had combined a timber wolf and a grizzly, then placed the head on a human's torso. Thrasher knew he looked like something straight out of hell, and he was fine with that.

"Please d-don't hurt me," the driver begged, his arms raised in defense.

Thrasher's yellow moon eyes were the only relief from the shadows of his face. Though bright and alive, he had been told many times that his eyes held no compassion, no forgiveness, only rage—cold, dark, bottomless rage. When he opened his fists, he showed the driver the weapons of his deliverance—his shimmering, long, black, sharp claws.

"No!" the driver screamed.

Thrasher's attack was quick—a downward swipe of his right claws that cut from the driver's neck to his stomach with such speed it tore his vest and shirt off. The man stood gawking for a second before his blood spilled and he screamed in pain. Thrasher watched him grasp his wounds uselessly as he sobbed —he was already dead but his mind had not yet processed it.

"No, please-please, oh God, please."

Thrasher growled as he clamped down on his prey's neck, where the blood was already pooling. Lifting the driver back to his feet, the man-beast shook his head violently, like an alligator, closing his vice-like jaws steadily.

The driver's gargling screams filled the night air until Thrasher's teeth sunk deep enough to collapse his windpipe. The taste of blood flowed down Thrasher's throat as the man gripped in his teeth went limp.

Thrasher swung his head side to side until the tractor trailer driver's head came free, his body falling to the pavement below.

"All yours."

The words left Thrasher's slavering mouth in a tone hardly recognizable as human.

"What the bloody hell happened here?" Rex asked as he stared at Thrasher, only now rejoining the group.

"Green light," Clayton replied in a cheery tone.

Rex stood back as his friend shed his dried skin casing like a corn snake molting. After Clayton dropped to all fours, he launched himself forward. The beast Clayton had become pounced on the corpse, tearing into its flesh with razor-sharp teeth.

"Thrasher?" Rex called out to his boss. "Can I?"

"Torch the truck first, pup," Thrasher grumbled after he jumped down to the ground.

Barton sat up suddenly, coughing. He gazed at his chest, where the shotgun blast had not only destroyed his leather jacket and shirt, but also scored his flesh with finger-deep lacerations. After a long sigh he let out a roar.

"Barton," Thrasher growled. "Eat. Heal."

Chapter Sixteen

Delivery

The tires of Sabrina's custom-pink Ferrari GTB Fiorano squealed as she turned sharply into Moselle's crescent-shaped driveway. She had called not five minutes ago, so Moselle had left the gate open. That was not the only preparations she had made; Moselle knew the state Sabrina would arrive in and took the necessary precautions.

She mixed some crushed Valeriana officinalis with some chamomile, and she boiled some water. Earlier that evening, she had readied a guest bedroom and sprinkled lemon oil around the room. The scent of lemon had always calmed Moselle's nerves, and she hoped it would help her friend as well.

Moselle knew that in Sabrina's frantic state, she could say or do anything, so having Jackson present at the first moment she arrived was too risky. After she suggested he take advantage of the peaceful moment to take a shower, Moselle waited at the front door. Her mind flashed with the recent events. When Sabrina had first called, roughly an hour ago, she was in a deep panic. She had said that Mira was gone but she was too upset to explain further than "evaporated." Two attempts on Sabrina's life in just over a day. But if this villain intended to try again, Moselle considered, he would face dire consequences invading her home.

She saw the glow of Sabrina's brightened wings glistening through the glass windowpanes and ordered one of her guards to let her friend in.

Sabrina stood in the open doorway a shade of her former self, disheveled from head to toe. Her top had been torn from the abrupt release of her wings and hung like a mascara-stained bib. Her hair, windblown and greasy, was tangled and pulled back into a loose ponytail. It was clear that Sabrina's mind was fractured. Barefoot, she padded into Moselle's home and straight into her friend's open arms.

"You are safe now, my friend. No one can harm you here."

"Mira... I'm not sure if she's dead or not," Sabrina sobbed. "I-I should've gone back for her."

"Mira is your bodyguard, correct? She did what she was employed to do."

"You don't understand! Mira was—is, was my friend!" Sabrina yelled before she lowered her voice to a whisper. "Mira saved my life twice today. I should've gone back."

"Please let me help you up to your room. You are weak; you need rest."

"Thank you, Moselle," Sabrina said, giving Moselle a peck on her cheek.

"You may thank me by withdrawing your wings; they're a bit bright and burn my eyes."

"I didn't even realize..."

Later that night, Moselle flopped backward on her bed, mentally exhausted. Jackson sat beside her shirtless, in a pair of pajama pants he had packed for the trip to New York City. Moselle assumed he would want to have sex tonight, but after she collapsed on the bed, it was obvious from the concern on his face that he wasn't thinking about sex at all.

"I've never seen you so worried, Moselle. You, okay?"

"It has been a long day."

"Maybe a shower would help. Helped me."

Moselle had detected the scent of her body oils on his freshly cleaned skin; it aroused her hunger, but her worn out muscles would not respond. Glancing slyly at Jackson's watch, she noted the time. It was late, and she knew it would be best to send Jackson to a different room, but deep down she did not want to be alone.

"Jackson, I am torn," Moselle started, but she did not continue as she weighed the consequences of saying more.

"Torn?"

"What happened to Sabrina today has left me thinking... Life is much more fragile than I like to admit. Happiness can come to a sudden end, and I fear—"

"Moselle, I'm here," he said, taking her hand.

"Jackson, my culture... I have certain responsibilities. I have traditions I must follow, or I will suffer great consequences," Moselle explained as best she could.

"I think I understand. If you need me to sleep in the other room, I can." Jackson stroked Moselle's hair as he spoke.

"God of the heavens, Jackson, that feels nice," she breathed. "No, I am just afraid of what you might think of me if you knew of my traditions."

"I can't think of anything you could do that would make me like you any less, Moselle." He leaned over and gave her a gentle kiss on the lips.

"I could eat you; you know."

"I hope so."

"I pray this is not a mistake, my love." Moselle steeled herself. "Each night, before sunrise, I wrap my body from neck to toe in lotion-soaked strips of linen. It takes me nearly an hour, but I do this so my skin will stay youthful and soft."

"Really?"

"Yes," she replied with her eyes closed.

"Every night before you go to bed?"

"I knew you would be disturbed," she moaned, rolling away from him.

"No, I'm just surprised by what women put themselves through to look good. You know, if you wanted, I could wrap you up tonight."

Moselle breathed a sigh of relief.

"You would do that for me? And stay the night in my bed?"

"Of course."

Moselle beamed as she stood. It had been many years since anyone wrapped her; in fact, the last person to do so was her mother.

While she undressed, Moselle gazed over her shoulder and smiled. As she did, she saw something move. Under the bed, near where his feet dangled, was a small red and black snake. Having seen thousands of snakes in her lifetime, she knew exactly what kind this one was—more, she knew the poison it carried in its fangs.

As her bra dropped to the floor, Moselle asked Jackson to close his eyes. When he complied, she walked over and knelt between his legs, snatching the snake off the floor.

"Keep those eyes closed," Moselle said when she caught him peeking. "I only wish to help you relax before bed."

"I'm fine, Moselle, you're the one who needs—"

"Shush, my love, you are my guest, and I take great pride in pleasing my guests."

When Jackson closed his eyes again, she pulled his pants all the way down to his ankles with her one hand while holding the coiling snake in the other.

"I hope you don't please *all* your guests this way."

Carefully watching the snake, she was startled when it struck at, but missed, Jackson's thigh.

"Only the ones I want never to leave."

Moselle knew that placing this snake in one of her wicker baskets would only arouse Jackson's suspicions, so she thought of another plan. While she rubbed her breasts against his lap and then up his stomach to his chest, Moselle eyed the open bedroom window—a long throw, but she thought she could make it.

Now above Jackson's head, the snake squirmed, its tail dropping down only centimeters from his nose.

"Your hair is tickling my nose."

"Just keep your eyes closed, my love."

Slowly, she slunk down his body, cocked her arm back and quickly pitched the snake out the open window.

Moselle guessed that the breeze created by her sudden movement might make Jackson open his eyes, so she quickly slid her body up his lap again, brushing her long hair over his chest and up into his face.

Relief would have filled her thoughts had Jackson's fingers around her waist not felt so good—his warm skin underneath hers, his muscles tight and strong—his hard-on pressed to her belly. With her hands on his solid chest, Moselle leaned closer —his scent drew her in.

"Jackson..." She lowered her nose until it was touching his. "Tell me what you want," she said before placing a gentle kiss on his lips.

Jackson sat up. His hands still gripped tightly around Moselle's waist; he guided her body and positioned her hips so she was seated atop his lap.

"I want you, Moselle. All of you."

"Then this... this is going to be a night to remember... for all eternity."

Chapter Seventeen

Cry Wolf

Sabrina awoke suddenly, less than an hour before sunrise. Her heart pounded as if it were desperate to escape the confines of her chest and she knew why. Over years of evolution, fairy-kind had developed two very powerful abilities.

While one was a purposeful means to heal themselves, the other feature was more of a defense mechanism. It allowed fairy-kind to sense dangerous otherworldly entities. For Sabrina, the sensation always began with a sudden increase in her heartbeat.

Adorned only in pink gym shorts and a tank top—ones she had left behind that last time she slept over at Moselle's—and a pair of matching slippers, Sabrina paced the hallway trying to make sense of what she felt. By the time she reached Moselle's room, the sensation began to peak.

"Moss? You awake?" she called out. "Moss? Moselle?"

------⚭------

Jackson heard Sabrina's voice through the door; weary from their late night, he tried to ignore it, but soon realized it might wake Moselle.

It felt like only a few hours ago that Jackson had wrapped Moselle in her lotion-soaked strips of linen after he helped her apply a cream mask to her face. It all felt like a dream now, until he gazed at Moselle, lying still under the covers. *This is all kinda weird,* with the shake of his head, he thought.

Yawning, Jackson slid out of bed, hoping he could get to the door before Sabrina knocked.

"What's up?" Jackson asked as he opened the door.

"Hey, yeah, I need to talk to Moselle. It's really important," she explained, pushing past him.

"She's asleep."

With a long, soft groan, Moselle spoke up. "It's okay. I am awake."

"Moss, we need to talk."

"Can you fetch me a bottle of water from the kitchen downstairs?" Moselle asked Jackson.

Sabrina watched Jackson leave the room, peeking out the door to make sure he was out of earshot. When she was comfortable that he would not hear her, she turned, ran to Moselle's bed, and flopped down beside her.

"Something's wrong here, Moss. I swear I can sense an otherworldly nearby."

"You mean a malevolent one?" Moselle sat up, her wrappings tightening as she moved.

"Yes..." Sabrina shook as a chill ran down her spine. "Do you have werewolves in your service?"

"No! They would eat my cats!"

Sabrina turned her attention back to the partially open door and stared at it a moment. Years ago, before her father allowed her out on her own, she had trained in the use of her ability. She had honed it well and was able to identify the species of otherworldly beings that set off her senses. She swore there was a werewolf in the vicinity; it was almost as if she could smell the beast.

"Jackson! Fuck, Moselle, could your boyfriend be what I sense?"

"Heavens no, he is as human as they come."

No sooner did Moselle speak than the sound of a coyote's howl filled her room. Sabrina jumped off the bed and ran to the nearest open window. Sabrina could see nothing in the darkness except the outline of trees in the distance. Suddenly, from the front yard, a second howl echoed in the night.

"Attacked in the bathroom, nearly killed in my home, now this?" Sabrina shouted as she stomped out of room. "This has gone too fucking far!"

Moselle yelled to her to stop, but Sabrina was determined to put an end to the cat and mouse game she felt stuck in. She sprinted down the stairs, her fuzzy pink slippers off by the time she passed Jackson, who had just reached the bottom of the stairs, headed back up.

Sabrina passed two guards who stood watch like statues on either side of the front door and walked out into the cool night air.

Feet planted firmly on the patio, she stood strong, ready for a fight. Half expecting Alexander Kintner himself to step from the shadows of the weeping willow trees that lined Moselle's front yard, she called out brazenly.

"You want my wings, Kintner, you sick bastard? Come get them! That blast I gave you in the bathroom was nothing!"

Behind her, Moselle's guards did not flinch. Even when Jackson walked out the door past them to see what Sabrina was yelling about, the guards did not budge, their eyes fixed forward in a near comatose stare.

"Sabrina, you all right? You high or something?" Jackson asked as he stepped up beside her.

"What're you waiting for, Kintner? Come get me!" she screamed, taking two more steps away from the house.

Attached to one side of the crescent driveway was a small, five-car, parking area, where Sabrina's car was parked. Next to its trunk, a pair of eyes flared like burning matches. They were not at human height, nor were they at the distance from the ground a wolf would be; instead, they bobbed eerily in the middle.

"Gods!" she gasped as she watched the eyes move away from her car.

"Jesus, look at that. I haven't seen a coyote in years."

"Jackson, darling, please come inside now," Moselle called from the doorway.

"It's just a coyote. Turn on the lights and it'll probably run off."

"The lights are not on. Turn on the floods immediately," Moselle ordered the guards, cutting more linen strips off her legs with a silver-handled, curved dagger.

"Lady Moselle, the lights are switched on. There must be a fuse out or—"

"You don't need floodlights," Sabrina said.

"Sabrina, no, not here!" Moselle shouted. "Jackson, close your eyes!"

Enraged beyond reason, Sabrina unleashed her wings.

"You can't hide from the light," Sabrina yelled, emitting a pulse of bright multi-hued light from her wings.

The glow illuminated the front yard and startled Jackson who turned and came face to face with her shimmering wings.

"Unbelievable," he gasped.

"Thought you would hide in the dark, did you?" Sabrina screamed as the light from her wings revealed a beast that she could not clearly identify prowling near her car.

Howling louder than it had before, the creature's sudden movement caused her eyes to shift to the far side of her car, which had evidently been vandalized by the beast, its door torn off and lying in the grass.

Free of enough of her wrappings to move faster, Moselle grabbed Jackson and tried to pull him back into the house, ordering her guards to attack the invader. Unable to do more than budge him a few feet, Moselle covered Jackson's eyes with her hand, doing her best to shield him from the glow as it increased.

"You hurt Mira and I'm gonna kill you for that!"

"Guards!"

"What the fuck? I can't see!" Jackson shrieked.

"Sabrina, no! Stop!"

The beast shielded its eyes with its fur-covered forearm and released a whimpering yelp. Then, as Sabrina dimmed the glow of her wings, it climbed up the closest tree and launched itself recklessly over Moselle's fence.

"Run!" Sabrina screamed. "Run, you fucking coward!"

As soon as the beast disappeared, Sabrina's adrenaline started to ebb and she collapsed, shaking and sobbing on the lawn. As she began to pull herself together again, she finally noticed Jackson stumble and rub his eyes, as he repeated, "I can't see. I can't see."

"Fuck," she breathed.

"You'll be fine, my love. This, this affliction... it's only temporary. Right, Sabrina?"

"Shit! I knew he was beside me, but I wasn't thinking."

"Just put them away!"

With a deep inhale, Sabrina did as she was asked and returned her wings to their place just under her skin.

"Sorry, Moss."

"Lady Moselle?" one of her guards asked as they entered the house. "Your orders?"

"Search the entire property, check the walls for breaches, make sure that thing does not came back."

"Yes, Lady Moselle."

Moselle's guards filed out the front door two at a time, as Sabrina and Moselle led Jackson into one of the front rooms.

"I'm really sorry, Moselle," Sabrina repeated. "Was he facing my wings when I lit them up?"

"What the hell are you?" Jackson blurted out. "What was that outside?"

"Jackson, be calm, my dear."

"Calm? Fuck calm! Those weren't some cheap Halloween costume wings like you said they were in that photo you wanted me to fix, were they?" Jackson rubbed his watering eyes again.

"Jackson—"

"No. Okay? They're real. My wings are real."

Sabrina had just broken the first rule of all otherworldly beings: she had told a human the truth. She did so feeling little remorse; in fact, she didn't care at all. *Alexander Kintner knows my secret,* she thought. *Why not Jackson?*

It took a while before Jackson was able to see more than two white spots. When his vision returned, it came first in shades of gray. Shortly afterward, full colors started to appear, beginning with a bright shade of pink. He shook his head, as if it would help his eyes clear faster and focused his attention on Sabrina, who was sitting on the couch next to the one he and Moselle were on, examining her nail polish.

"Moselle, tell me the truth. You owe me that much, okay? What just happened?" he asked once he finally took his watering eyes off Sabrina.

Moselle looked pained by his question and when she didn't answer him, Sabrina spoke up.

"You were nearly blinded by my wings when I amped up their glow," Sabrina explained.

"Your wings? What do you mean? What the hell are you?"

Jackson looked from Moselle's disappointed face to her friend's impatient frown.

"I am a—"

"Sabrina!" Moselle tried to interrupt, to prevent her from deepening the mess they were already in.

"—fairy-kind."

Jackson began to question whether the girls were messing with him. Backing away from them, Jackson bumped a small table next to the couches and spilled its contents to the floor. A remote control landed on its buttons, turning on the TV. The picture snapped on to a newscast, the word "Homicide" prominently painted across the screen.

Jackson noticed Sabrina's eyes as they were instantly glued to the television. Like a nightmare that just would not end, the newscast unleashed another horror.

"...she had been missing for two weeks. If you have any knowledge about this crime, please call the number at the bottom of your screen. Brandy Canterbury's father, noted classical musician Karl Canterbury, has offered a reward for any information that leads to the arrest of his daughter's killer."

The TV's frame filled with a high school yearbook shot of a young, freckle-faced girl, full of life. By the way Sabrina's mouth fell open, Jackson knew something was wrong.

"This cannot be happening," Sabrina sighed.

"Is she...?" Moselle asked in a tone that suggested she already knew the answer.

"She is... *was* fairy-kind."

"Could this all be related?"

"There's no doubt in my mind that Alexander Kintner killed her. Fuck! I'm going to have to call my father." Sabrina dropped her head into her hands.

"I am not entirely sure that is wise, Sabrina," Moselle offered. "Perhaps we should talk it over."

"What the hell is all this?" Jackson snapped as he muted the TV. "Who is Alexander Kintner? Somebody tell me what's going on!"

After a few deep breaths, Sabrina explained everything that had happened in the last two days. Much of it sounded to Jackson like the stories he read in the newspapers. Acts of violence were not rare in New York City or Los Angeles, with the exception of one glaring element.

"So, you're some full-sized tooth fairy and he wants your wings?"

"I'm not a tooth fairy."

"Yes, Jackson, he wants her wings," Moselle answered.

"What the hell?" Jackson huffed. "How? Why?"

"Not sure, but I think this all has something to do with, DUST. I found some on one of the girls who attacked me at home. It's in my car actually," Sabrina explained.

"The drug? Then let's call the DEA or the freakin' ATF before anyone else gets hurt!"

"Otherworldlies don't meddle in the affairs of humans. Such a phone call would bring too much attention to our... my kind," Sabrina said, her eyes glued to Moselle.

"Otherworldly? You mean there are other things in this world? Other beings like that"—Jackson pointed to the front yard—"that thing? That was a werewolf, right?"

"Sabrina, you have said enough." Moselle shook her head.

"Fine, I guess I have to call my father."

When Sabrina excused herself, Jackson turned back to Moselle, his head swimming. He gazed deeply into her eyes; it was clear she was still pained by something.

"So, what are you?" Jackson asked.

"Excuse me?" Moselle gasped, startled.

"She's a fairy. That thing outside a—a God knows what, so what are you?"

A loud sigh was all Moselle gave in reply.

"Please, Moselle."

"There are punishments for breaking the highest codes of the otherworldlies, Jackson, but the knowledge you wish to gain makes me fear something much worse."

"Like what?"

"It makes me fear that you will dislike me."

"Not telling me the truth will—"

"So be it, Jackson." Moselle took a step into uncharted territory. "You want to know who I am?"

"Yes."

"I am Moselle Abdul Aziz Al Ghurair, daughter of Anmet Abdul Aziz Al Ghurair, child of Amen Rah Set, God of the Sun," she proclaimed, her head bowed and her arms up, palms to the sky.

Moselle's announcement was empty of one important fact. When seconds passed without another word, Sabrina stepped back into the room.

"And?" she prompted.

"And what?" Jackson replied.

"*And* I died nearly four thousand years ago, when my family was forced to flee our home in Thebes," Moselle finished.

"Stop joking around," Jackson said, but as impossible as it sounded, everything suddenly added up.

As his mind calculated the impossible equation, he took in the things he hadn't before: ancient pottery, idols, tapestry—and what was that glimmer he had seen through the door in the room opposite to this one when he first entered her house? *That large outline—the one that held the shape of a man. Could it be... could it really be?* With a mad dash out of the room and across the vestibule, Jackson reached the doors and before the guards could stop him he shoved them open.

Behind the heavy double doors, Jackson found exactly what he'd imagined he would: a large, golden sarcophagus. Propped against the wall, the sarcophagus was dimly lit by a beam of moonlight through a skylight and the flicker of a candelabrum in the center of the room.

"Oh my God."

"Jackson—"

"This..." He pointed. "This can't be."

Jackson shook his head as he stared at the sarcophagus. He had never seen one in person before, the nearest thing being a program on the Discovery Channel highlighting Tutankhamen. This sarcophagus was not as detailed as King Tut's was. As best he could tell, the vessel was made entirely of bronze or maybe even gold, but that was not what he found most amazing about it. The embossed shape, the outline of a woman, matched Moselle's height and body type perfectly. His heart was in his throat at the sight of an armband on the sarcophagus's figure —identical to the piece of jewelry that Moselle wore.

Jackson gazed down at Moselle as she joined him, still partially covered in strips of linen—the same kind he imagined a mummy would be wrapped in.

"What are you, some sort of freakin' zombie?" he guessed, covering his face with his hand, disgusted by his next thought. "Did I have sex with a zombie last night?"

Moselle tapped him hard on his chest with her index finger.

"Zombie? Do you think such an abomination could smell like lilac and sage?"

"I don't know. I clearly have no idea what the hell I'm doing. I mean look at me: I wrapped my girlfriend up like a mummy last night and now I find out she is one!"

"Relax."

"So, you're not a mindless, rotting corpse. I can see that but tell me I'm wrong; tell me you're not a mummy."

"Do I look like Lon Chaney, Jr., to you?" Moselle asked sarcastically, making Sabrina chuckled.

"Who?"

"Really, Jackson, mummy is such a detestable term. If you must know, my people are referred to as the cursed undead."

"This can't be happening."

Jackson paced, avoiding eye contact with Moselle. He thought of the intimacy he had shared with a person—*or thing*—that was four thousand years old. He could not free his mind, not until he heard Sabrina shout, repeating an announcement from the news, "Hey guys, Kintner will be lecturing at California State University of Los Angeles soon."

"I-I need to leave."

"No, Jackson, stay here with us, please." Moselle reached for his hand.

"What? Why?"

"Because I need you," Moselle beseeched him, her eyes widening as she spoke. "Please, just come with me, sit down and clear your head."

Regardless of what else she may have been, Moselle was beautiful, and her voice still had a calming influence on him. Taking her hand he said, "Fine, I guess, but we have more to talk about later."

"I know we do."

Chapter Eighteen

Revelations

The room held an eerie silence after Jackson left. Stillness had replaced the chaos. Sabrina had flopped back down on the couch beside Moselle, who stared off in the distance toward her sarcophagus. While Sabrina mumbled on about how her father might respond to her voicemail plea for help, Moselle thought of her own father... and the day he killed her.

It was an abnormally hot day, even for Thebes. Three slaves fanned her as she reclined on the cool, polished stone of Pharaoh Mentuhotep II's royal pool. The sensation of the sun baking her skin combined with the breeze from the palm leaves made her limbs tingle; it was a good day to be alive and a great day to be at rest.

Moselle gazed off at the palace. Her father never rested. Always busy, he seemed to conduct business at all hours, whether the sun was high in the heavens or hiding from the moon. On this day, her father was negotiating a deal between her family and that of a political opponent, Vizier Amenemhet I. Since her father was an elder advisor and beloved friend of the current pharaoh, her family was rewarded with many luxuries, but all that would soon change.

She would later find out that unbeknownst to her, within the hallowed halls of the palace, the Vizier was demanding her hand in marriage and more. In order to end her family's bloodline, he stipulated that he would have the right to destroy any child she bore. Amenemhet's request, an outright insult, enraged her father. As Moselle bathed in the lilac-freshened waters outside, words were spoken, actions taken, and any chance of alliance obliterated.

Later that night, Moselle slept, her belly full of exotic fruits from far off lands—things she knew not the name of but would say were utterly delicious without hesitation. It was a quiet night, but her peace came to an end when her father crashed through the doors of her bedchamber and shrieked, "The rule of Mentuhotep II has come to an end!"

Negotiations had failed with the succeeding ruler; her family was no longer safe in Egypt.

Her panicked mind, unable to fathom it all, filled with blending colors, a mix of sun and sand burning into one tint on the horizon. Sounds echoed where her thoughts should have gathered. Tears—her mother's had not stopped from the time they left Thebes to the day they reached a small, unnamed fishing village. Moselle heard only her mother's sobbing.

Seeking refuge in the village, they were quickly met with the sickening rumors that Amenemhet had sent twenty of his best warriors to hunt them across the burning deserts of Egypt. The new ruler had placed a sizeable bounty upon their heads, one that would set every thief, cutthroat, and scoundrel in the region upon them.

Moselle's father got right to work. Being a skilled negotiator, he promptly convinced the elder men of the village to grant him one wish before they turned him and his family in to the new Pharaoh of Egypt: allow him, Anmet Abdul Aziz Ghurair, to be the one who took the lives of his family.

Later that evening, the tangy taste of the sea bass filled Moselle's mouth as her throat collapsed. Violently gasping for air, she fell from her seat at the table to the soft ground. No matter how hard she tried to inhale, little air reached her empty lungs. Reaching for her father, she witnessed him do something she had never seen him do before: cry. Her muscles burned as they seized, and a violent convulsion arched her back. There was a swelling in her abdomen that made her think her insides were about to pop like a bubble. Her mind, ablaze with panic, repeated one question: "Why are you not helping me, Father?" As the pain reached levels she knew not possible, her heart stopped, and her human life ended.

"Hey, where did you just go?" Sabrina prodded.

"Oh, sorry. The past; it's all so dark now. It gets harder and harder to remember."

"I'm in my twenties and I barely have memories from my childhood. You're what, in your thousands? Do you really expect to remember everything from when you were alive?"

"I guess you are right."

"Yeah, that and you have no brain." Sabrina paused to let her snarky comment sink in.

"I told you before—"

"Wait!"

As if talking about memories had sparked hers, Sabrina unexpectedly remembered that her car held some proof of Alexander Kintner's involvement—the packet of DUST. On her feet in a flash, Sabrina yelled, "That bastard!" as she ran past Moselle and out the door.

The passenger door was still lying off to the side, but it was only when she reached her beloved sports car that she found the true degree of the heartbreaking damage. Deep scratches ran the width of her hood in two sets of five. When she placed her fingers over the apparent claw marks, the tiny hairs on the back of her neck stood on end.

"Asshole," Sabrina grumbled as she circled her car, tracking a trail of fresh footprints in the green grass.

"Sabrina, what are you doing?" Moselle called from the front door.

"I have proof! I just have to find it," she screamed as she climbed through the hole in her car that used to be a door.

"Come back in. Let us wait until the sun is high in the heavens to start any investigation. My guards will—"

"He could come back."

"My guards will defend your car, Sabrina. Now please, come back in."

Atop the hill, in the dense forest across the street from Moselle's home, Thrasher watched Sabrina through a pair of high-powered binoculars. An old friend of Thrasher's had called him from the East Coast the day before. The man piqued Thrasher's interest when he reported some sort of involvement between the one-time celebrity Sabrina London and Alexander Kintner.

Rex grumbled with frustration as he splashed water from an old, World War I, Army canteen onto his face. Not one of the foursome had known Sabrina was an otherworldly, let alone fairy-kind. In a roundabout way, it made sense to Thrasher. He had the most knowledge of otherworldly legend and, through his past encounters with the fairy-kind, had experienced that their scent was no different than that of a human's.

"Burned my eyes, that bitch did," Rex whined as he rubbed his face.

"You'll be fine."

"A bloody warning would've been nice." Rex's accent was always pronounced when he was angry.

"What are you talking about?"

"That the bitch is a fucking, nut-busting fairy! Could'a warned me, mate."

Thrasher shook his head before he returned to the binoculars. Bent over, Sabrina had given Thrasher a perfect view of her ass as it peeked out of tiny shorts. It had been years since he allowed himself thoughts such as the ones that rushed to his head now.

"Hold the fucking phone. She ain't wearing underwear, is she, Thrasher?" Barton chuckled in his deep voice.

"None, whatsoever."

"Damn, man, let me see that!"

Thrasher handed the binoculars to Barton and told him to enjoy the view.

"Hot damn!" Barton cheered. "You have to admit; that there is one smoking hot piece of fairy tail, Thrasher."

Thrasher agreed. The physical similarities between Sabrina and his dearly loved wife, Sue Anne, were so astounding that he could not help but think of her. Just like the fairy, Sue Anne had had long blonde hair and a petite frame. Although a proper lady of the nineteenth century, Sue Anne had married him, regularly saying he was the only man strong enough to handle her sickness.

Called madness by those who dared label her in front of Thrasher, Sue Anne suffered from seizures, during which she lost her mind, said crazy things, and often undressed. Whatever caused her illness passed with the birth of their first child, but Thrasher always worried a day would come when he would find his wife wandering the streets naked again.

Normally, Thrasher would not allow himself to even think his family's names; life was painful without them. As he stepped away from the other guys, he took a moment to wallow in grief.

"Oh, this girl is hot, muh man. Hot!" Clayton sung when it was his turn to take a look. "On her hands and knees like that... I'd give it to her doggie—"

"You mean Windigo style!" Rex joked.

"Amen to that, brother!" Barton laughed.

"What do you think, Thrasher?" Barton asked, stealing the binoculars to get another look.

"I'm more concerned with what one of the fairy-kind is doing in the house of an undead," Thrasher admitted with his back turned to the others.

"Undead?" Rex perked up.

"Yeah, the woman who owns this estate is cursed undead," Thrasher revealed.

"How do you know?" Rex asked, drying the last traces of canteen water from his beard.

"Sun Tzu, an ancient Chinese philosopher, once said 'know your enemy.' Rex. It's my job to know what otherworldlies call Southern California home."

Thrasher paced a moment, clearing his head of the past. Time was running out; he had to act now. With a whistle and point, he ordered his men to fall back deeper into the forest, away from Moselle's home.

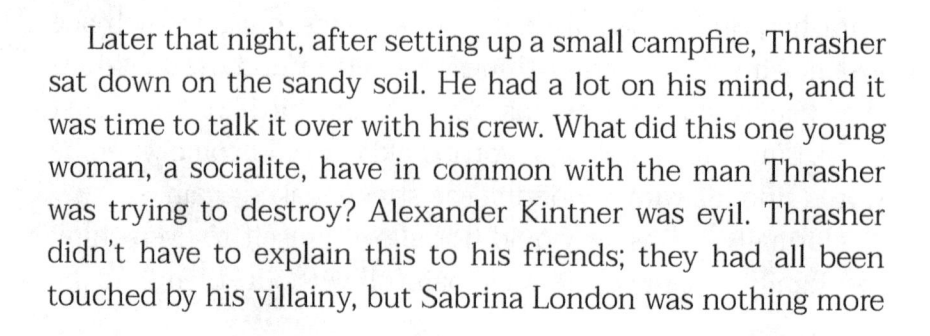

Later that night, after setting up a small campfire, Thrasher sat down on the sandy soil. He had a lot on his mind, and it was time to talk it over with his crew. What did this one young woman, a socialite, have in common with the man Thrasher was trying to destroy? Alexander Kintner was evil. Thrasher didn't have to explain this to his friends; they had all been touched by his villainy, but Sabrina London was nothing more than a dumb blonde who liked to party. Of course, the most plausible reason came to mind; perhaps she was one of Kintner's lovers.

If the two were lovers, then perhaps they had finally found what they needed to draw the man out.

"Maybe we should take her prisoner."

"Clayton, brother, that's a great idea," Thrasher declared as he gazed off into the distance toward Moselle's home.

"Hey, Rex, run down there and grab 'er," Barton joked, a bit of Rex's Aussie accent added to the sting of sarcasm.

"Wait. Before we do anything, we need to know what we're up against. This fairy is in league with the undead. It's a pairing you don't normally see."

"Why's that, boss?" Clayton asked scratching his coarsely bearded cheek.

"The fairy-kind represent life more than any other otherworldly. They've been around for ages, living in public and normally serving the greater good. Rumor is a large percentage of the London family's profits go to aiding fairy-kind still trapped in the United Kingdom."

"No shit," Clayton said, surprised.

"The undead represent foul corruption in every manner." Pointing in the direction of her home, Thrasher continued, "This undead woman has lived in the public eye for many years. She doesn't hide in the darkness like most of her kind do. You've all seen billboards with her; there's one on Interstate 101."

"I caught a glimpse of her a moment back there. Quite the looker, she is," Rex added.

"There was a time, ages ago, before I was even born, that the fairy-kind were much more in tune with nature. Their connection with Mother Earth has faded dramatically since the Industrial Revolution. Their proximity to humans has made them almost human. I've read how the fairy-kind once couldn't come in contact with the undead, or they'd become diseased and die."

"Must be in league with old Kintner; his dark magic must protect her from the undead sickness," Rex speculated.

"The one who owns this home, if she's who you say she is, she may be one of the ancients," Clayton suggested.

"Ancients?" Thrasher sarcastically huffed. "The Ancient Egyptians are nothing more than dressed up undead trash."

"They all need to be destroyed," Barton said with a rare seriousness.

"They all need to be destroyed," Thrasher concluded.

Chapter Nineteen

Wake Up!

Sabrina and Moselle knocked on the door to the guest bedroom where Jackson had exiled himself. For almost two hours, he had tried to sleep, but he could not get his mind to stop churning.; *Moselle was some sort of zombie. I had sex with a zombie.*

When the two women entered his room, they did so with smiles and gentle apologies. Moselle even brought him some tea to calm his nerves. The conversation started off simple, each person acting as if the events of the early morning had never happened, yet the pleasantries ended quickly when casual talk shifted to a laundry list of concerns the two girls had. As they rambled, Jackson stared hard at them.

He thought about Sabrina's beautifully detailed tattoo for a while. Her skin art had been the topic of many articles on fan sites and celebrity blogs. Jackson had often thought it was one of the hottest tattoos he had ever seen. Now he knew better. He didn't understand how it was possible, but somehow it wasn't art; she actually had wings. Curious, he ran his fingertips across her skin, causing her to shudder. To his surprise there was nothing, not even a bump that would suggest her wings were anything more than skin art. The longer Jackson looked, the more he wanted to examine her tattoo closer, but that would have meant removing her tank top first.

As he eyed her waist, where the end of the shirt sat, Moselle called his name under her breath. Jackson wondered what was going on. Moselle appeared to be annoyed, probably because she had to, *ad nauseam*, defend her side of the debate she and Sabrina were in the middle of. Jackson paid it all little mind. Oblivious to the finer details of the topic of their discussion he went back to his thoughts on seeing the rest of Sabrina's tattoo.

As he reached for her shirt again, Moselle suddenly snapped her fingers at him, and this time his attention shifted back to her fully.

"What?" he mouthed as he focused on how Moselle continuously sipped from a bottle of water.

Undead, he thought. It was hard for him to fathom what it meant to be undead. He had heard the term before, but its sources were an unsettling lot of horror movies and old Stephen King books. He started to wonder why she wasn't decomposing. *What keeps her from rotting?* Leaning toward her, he tried to smell her. Lilac filled his nose; she obviously did not smell of death.

"Jackson, are you listening to a single word we are saying?" Moselle raised her voice again.

"No. I'm sorry," he answered, and sat up straight.

"Look, I realize it's a lot to take in, but humans are not the only sentient beings on the planet," Sabrina mocked.

"I know."

"Do you? Obviously, you don't," Sabrina tossed her hair from one side to the other.

"The sooner you open your eyes to the possibilities, the easier the truth will be," Moselle added. "The legends of the past are, for the most part, true."

"Seriously, babe, think of the human Bible. It's one of the oldest books ever and trusted by billions. It's filled with the supernatural, but you humans put faith in it. Why not trust the words within the Vulgate Cycle equally?"

"Vulgate Cycle?" Jackson shook his head.

Moselle sighed. "The stories of the Holy Grail. Fairy-kind has always claimed authorship of the prose Lancelot."

"'Cause we wrote it and it's all true." Sabrina waved her arms around.

"Wait, are you telling me King Arthur existed?"

"That's common knowledge, darling, have you not seen the documentaries?" Moselle wrapped her lips around the water bottle in her hand to take the last sip of water.

Jackson sighed. Why hadn't he left? Why hadn't he just gone home to his quiet existence as a bachelor artist? Catching a glimpse of the side of Moselle's breast through the large opening of her sleeveless top reminded him in part. Undead or not, Moselle still exuded sex. *Shit, what is wrong with me? I still want to have sex with her—I want to have sex with a zombie...*

"What I'm trying to say is that for hundreds of years, scholars wrote of things that humans disregarded as nothing more than fictional legend, when in fact they were... fact," Sabrina continued passionately.

"Okay, so..." Jackson racked his brain for the name of an author who wrote about the fantastical. Not being well-read, he came up with one. "Bram Stoker?"

"Perfect example; all fact," Moselle quickly answered.

"Vampires? No way!"

"Oh, I'm afraid so, Jackson. Right, Sabrina?" Moselle nodded as she took his tea from him.

Sabrina's face twisted into a sneer like she smelled something foul; it was a moment before she answered. "Yes, Jackson, there are vampires."

"Do I know any?" he asked. "Wait, do I know any aliens?"

"Aliens? Are you for real?" Sabrina flopped backward on the bed.

"In all seriousness, Jackson, we are only telling you all this because we need your help," Moselle explained. "We need to confront Alexander Kintner. Sabrina thinks he may have kidnapped Mira."

Mira's abduction was news to him. "What?"

"She was hurt. I have to know if... I have to find her."

"Wait, what the hell am I supposed to do? I mean, I'm not a cop or anything. I'm a former athlete turned artist."

Silence claimed the room again. With all the discussion of their problems, it was clear to him that neither girl had given it much thought.

"He has a point, Sabrina. We need someone with a history of cunning and craftiness, someone who is no stranger to illicit activities. We need Cade."

"Cade Lawton?" Sabrina made the same face she had made when Moselle asked her about vampires—one of tremendous sourness.

"Do you have any knowledge as to where we can locate him?"

"Of course I do. He's underground where he belongs; right where I fucking buried him!"

Chapter Twenty

Huzzah!

Cade Robert Lawton was born on August 3, 1840, in the sovereign state of Virginia. Shortly after his twenty-first birthday, he enlisted in the Confederate Army and served as an infantryman under Major General George Pickett. Cade, like most men his age, had always done whatever was needed to survive, and as a soldier, that way of life did not change.

Cade didn't seek material items or wealth of any kind. He sent his entire pay—when he received it—home and lived off the land and what the Confederate Army supplied him. Known in his squad as "the Stalker," Cade had learned a variety of skills that helped him blend into his environment. Not only did this make him a great hunter, but it also gave him the opportunity to ambush Union troops better than anyone.

Although able to keep still and silent for days on end when on the battlefield, Cade was also branded a gossiper when in camp. Known to weave stories of his own adventures, Cade was a man full of pride and life until the day of the charge, July 3, 1863.

Cade and his fellow Virginians faced a brigade of Philadelphians guarding two Union guns. With a battle cry, he ran toward an old stone fence that would later become known as "the Angle." The Union soldiers fired their cannons directly at his line, a booming roll of thunder like the voice of God calling to his children to stop their bickering. A half-a-dozen explosions shook the ground beneath his feet, but that did not stop Cade; he kept on. Still running, he emerged from the cloud of dirt and debris that had enveloped him. Cade glanced down at the destruction and saw pieces of the men who had run beside him, men he knew by name, friends each and every one. Had he been able to hear, he would have been listening to the cries of dozens of mortally wounded Confederate soldiers; it was a blessing and a curse, as he could not hear his commander's orders either.

Doing as he was trained, Cade aimed his rifle and fired into the Union masses the moment he crossed over the stone fence. Braced against the wall, he loaded, aimed, and fired again, placing a bullet in the head of a Union infantryman who had set himself up in a sniper's position. Cade's fellow Confederates climbed the wall; first twenty, then fifty, soon three hundred of his brigade pushed forward. To his left, a group of men he knew from camp attempted to turn the Union cannons on their owners.

A sudden counter charge by the Union turned the gunfight into a vicious melee of bayonets and fists. Cade's ears popped, and he heard the thick Irish brogue of his opponents as they screamed "Huzzah" in rally. Cade fixed his bayonet to his rifle and waded deep into the sea of skirmishing men.

Muscles sore, face and uniform coated in blood, Cade fought on till he could barely stand. The battlefield had become so cluttered with the dead and wounded he could not return to charge even if his body had permitted it.

The desperate scream for help from an officer drew his attention, where his eyes settled on an injured Union artillery commander slumped over his horse.

Cade tossed his now-damaged rifle to the side and scooped a new one up from a dead man. It was loaded; maybe this *was* his lucky day. Cade aimed and squeezed the trigger, launching a bullet directly into the Union commander's mouth. Astonished by his shot and thrilled he had killed an officer, Cade turned back to his squad who had nearly dispatched the enemy around them. With the guns pivoted fully around, the Confederates prepared to fire upon the Union as reinforcements arrived.

But the ammunition had been depleted. He searched against the stone wall yet found nothing except wounded and dying men; their faces, smeared with a mixture of dirt, ash, and blood, had crooked lines where tears of pain raced down. As Cade's hands reached under the bodies, their hands reached up to him for help, pulling at his uniform in desperation.

Behind him, an alarm trumpeted and as he turned, a bullet struck his shoulder. The force of the impact made him stumble, but before he fell, another bullet pierced his belly.

Cade thought the wound would have been painful, but he felt nothing. Sprawled out atop three other men, Cade stared up into the blazing summer sky until a shadow fell across his face. He felt a man step on his chest, his body used to spring over the fence—then another and another. Suddenly, his view of the sky was blotted out entirely as something heavy fell on top of him. He wanted to stand, to join his battalion in apparent retreat, to tell them all how he had killed a Union officer that day, however he could not move. The bullet that had struck his stomach had also severed his spine. As darkness consumed the world around him, he heard screams, disembodied voices overlapping one another—then, he swore he heard someone call his name.

"Cade!" Sabrina shouted. "Cade Robert Lawton, can you hear me?"

A strong wind blew into Sabrina's back as she stood underneath the large, weather-beaten movie screen of an abandoned drive-in. Two years ago, this theater had a booming business; the throwback style included a small eatery with waitresses who served the customers' cars on roller skates. It had been one of Sabrina's favorite hangouts growing up.

She and Cade had come here many times during their whirlwind romance. He enjoyed the outdoors and the night air, and since the theater only operated from dusk till dawn, the drive-in was a perfect spot for a vampire to hang out.

Sadly, the drive-in had closed six months ago when the owner died of lung cancer. His children, not interested in maintaining such an endeavor, hadn't been able to sell it either. Sabrina had thought she would never return, but it was not the theater that drew her back; it was what was buried underneath it.

"Cade!" Sabrina screamed again.

Must sleep. Must sleep.

In the late 1990s, the elders of the Vampire Nation came to the decision that the new millennium did not favor their breed. The staggering advances in medical science had made it harder for them to hide in plain sight. Prophesying a great war to come that would shift man's attention from technology back to the basics of survival, the Vampire Nation withdrew from society to wait.

Must sleep. Must sleep.

With the exception of some of the more rebellious youth, vampires across the globe entered torpor, a deep sleep akin to a hibernation cycle, in the final days of 1999. Cade's clan followed suit, burying themselves deep in a cave near the Arizona–New Mexico border. Cade would have slept a hundred years if he had not been woken by an intensely sexual dream almost two years ago. From his bed of rock and soil, Cade rose, once more awake in the colorful world of the living. Restless and aroused, he was unable to reenter his slumber until his carnal thirst was quenched.

Must sleep. Must sleep.

Cade foggily lumbered down a highway until he found a gas station with a convenience store. Time befuddled, he knew not how long he had slept, or what year it was. All he knew—all his mind focused on was his desire. Not just any old flesh and blood would satisfy him this time; no, he needed something special.

The hum of florescent lights buzzed in his ears like gnats as he entered the convenience store. Unknowingly, Cade looked like a young homeless man—covered in a thin layer of dust—his mere presence put the store owner on edge.

Drawn down the magazine aisle, Cade took his first look at Sabrina London. The young woman graced the cover of *Maxim* magazine in a Union Jack bikini so tiny he barely recognized the flag.

Cade snickered when he read the title next to her: "Beverly Hills London-style". It was not only a play on her name; it was also a treasure map.

"Hot, isn't she?"

"Yes, sir. Who is this rare flower, may I ask?"

Cade spoke with a southern drawl—years of practice and still he could not overcome it. The store owner, an older man with a gruff exterior, was no exception to finding Cade's voice endearing.

"That there's Sabrina London, my friend. Don't you know? She's America's favorite new, spoiled-rotten, rich bitch. But damn, her tight, little body can sell a magazine like no other," he ended with a chuckle.

"Beverly Hills?" Cade pondered. "Do convoys, um, supply trucks pass through here on their way to the state of California?"

"You mean semis? Damn straight. Lots of drivers pass through here doing runs." The man took a long sip from the beer bottle gripped in his hand. "Why? You looking to hitch a ride, sonny?"

"Yes, sir."

"Huh, a boy like you shouldn't have too much trouble. I think you might want to clean up a little first," the man hinted, but Cade paid him no mind, he only cared about one thing: those beautiful pictures of Sabrina London.

"Thank you kindly."

"Cade! Can you hear me?" Sabrina yelled, handing a shovel to Moselle. "We should've brought your man. He should be doing this... this filthy work."

"Jackson would not be able to handle meeting Cade in this manner. He is disturbed enough by what he has seen today. If it were not for our intense sexual attraction to one another, I fear he would have run at his first chance."

"You're right," Sabrina shouted over the wind. "Hell, next time, do me a favor and pick a better human to fall in love with, okay?"

"I will try."

"And why do you look so refreshed? Shouldn't you be peeling or pasty or something?" Sabrina whined, annoyed that Moselle had not suffered as she had today. "Wait, did you? You didn't! Did you?"

"If what you refer to is draining my boyfriend of some of his life force in order to restore mine, the answer is none of your business."

"That's the real reason he's not here!" Sabrina tapped her index finger into Moselle's chest. "Did you kill him?"

"No. I would never," Moselle answered, but Sabrina continued to stare at her, waiting for an answer.

Moselle brushed the windblown hair out of her face before she continued. She knew how stubborn Sabrina was, and if she did not answer her, Moselle would be in for another long night.

"Look, if you must know, after you left the room, Jackson and I continued our conversation. We ended up lying down and he fell asleep. Once he was sleeping I-I could not resist the urge to sap him just a tiny bit to restore myself."

"You she-devil!"

Moselle grinned as she pushed the shovel deeper into the earth, striking something other than dirt and rock. Careful not to get dirt on her skirt, she knelt down and used a handkerchief to brush the loose earth off to the side just enough to reveal the face of a large, pink teddy bear. Not expecting to find a rotten stuffed animal, Moselle recoiled, stumbled in her heeled boots, and nearly fell.

"You buried him with a teddy bear?" Moselle's voice carried a hint of disgust.

Sabrina smiled as she recalled the moment she'd buried the teddy bear Cade had won for her at a carnival above him.

"Cade Robert Lawton, I know you're down there! Wake up! You have no idea how lucky you are. I was so tempted to buy this place and build a parking lot on top of you!"

"You would have done that? How wicked of you."

"Cade!" Sabrina yelled again. "Hand me that shovel, Moselle."

Shovel in hand, Sabrina dug slightly deeper, unearthing an old patch of burlap. When more was visible, she released the shovel's handle and pulled out a small bottle of perfume from her jeans' pocket.

"This should wake him."

With a flick of her wrist, she spilled a few drops of her perfume onto the burlap sack, stood back, and waited for Cade to rouse. After a moment, Sabrina stomped her foot like a spoiled child and screamed, "Why won't he wake up!"

A powerful gust of wind forced Moselle to take a step forward. The weather had taken a turn for the worse and added to Sabrina's bad mood.

"If I remember correctly, your perfume is not the only scent that Cade found desirable."

The look on Sabrina's face cleared. She reached out and asked her friend for the dagger she always carried. Moselle placed the tiny, silver-handled blade in Sabrina's palm with a nod. Sabrina could feel the scales on the embossed handle—a two-headed snake design. It was a beautifully crafted blade; too bad she had to soil it. With a quick, short swipe across her palm, Sabrina cut herself. Bright blood pooled slowly in her palm—she had him now.

"Oh, Cade... Ca-ade."

Cade heard a voice call to him from the darkness. He wanted to move, but his body felt stiff. Images of the war appeared in his mind's eye like camera flashes. Green grass, pale blue skies, golden sun, red blood—so much blood he could smell it wash away the darkness. However, there was something about the blood that smelled different. This was not the gunpowder and smoke-laced blood of his mates or the enemy he smelled; this was the sweet blood of a woman.

"Sabrina?" Cade called out with a desert-dry voice.

"Cade... Robert... Lawton." Sabrina made a sour face as she spoke.

"Has the hundred years passed?"

"Sure, Cade. I just look damn good for my age."

With his sharp fingernails he tore the burlap sack open and Cade was born again into the night air. His long unused muscles were taxed to their limit as he climbed from the grave. He was in pain, but never once took his eyes off Sabrina.

While he brushed the dirt from his clothes—dark jeans, old boots, and a partially buttoned black dress shirt—Cade sniffed at Sabrina, who held her ground fearlessly before him.

"Where is it?" Cade asked, his grey-eyed glare burned through Sabrina.

Hand up, she showed Cade the smear of blood from her open wound. In a burst of motion that made Moselle flinch, Cade snatched Sabrina's wrist and put his mouth over her wound.

Sabrina shuddered.

"Enough!" she snapped as she pulled her hand away from the thirsty vampire. "That's the last taste of me you'll get after what you did!"

"What did I do, sweet sunshine?" Cade asked, confused.

"What did you do?" she said, her hands curling two fists. "What did you fucking do?"

In spite of being hazy from sleep, Cade could hear the anger raging in her words. Luckily, he had learned early on how to handle her fits, and witnessing one now, he remembered just what to do: act stupid.

Oblivious to her exasperation, Cade ran his hand through his short, brown hair, returning it to its normal, perfectly messed look.

"You know, this is how I have worn my hair since the late 1800s. With the exception of an occasional crew cut, I've never changed it." Cade smiled at Sabrina. "You fashion folk like to think styles have changed a lot since my day, but they really haven't."

Cade knew that his statement, one he had made many times before, would irritate Sabrina. It was a great distraction from whatever it was that originally annoyed her and it normally worked... but not this time.

"You cocky fucking vampire, always fixing your hair when I'm trying to tell you about something serious."

"I'm sorry. What's wrong, Sabrina?"

Statue still, she drew in a deep breath and screamed, "The video camera, Cade! The damn camera video!"

"Video camera?"

"The one you had the night we broke into the laboratory."

"Ah yes." He grinned devilishly. "You were outright devious that night. I never would have guessed Sabrina London had it in her. You proved me wrong, my dear."

"Why did you have to record us?"

"I just wanted to have—"

"We—you lost the camera, Cade!" Sabrina screamed. "Don't you remember? You dropped it in the parking lot?"

"Lost it? What do you mean, it's here." He patted his pocket until he realized it was empty. "Oh..."

"'Oh,' Cade? 'Oh,'?" Sabrina turned red with anger. "You know what happened months later; months after you broke my fucking heart by asking me to bury you—the man I loved—under ten feet of dirt?"

"The camera was found?"

"Yes, Cade, it was found. Found by some kid who thought it would be cool to upload it to the web!" Sabrina's eyes watered as she shouted. "Several billion people saw what was on your stupid camera."

"All of it?" Cade fought off a smirk.

"Fuck! You weren't even awake when everything happened. I was arrested! You—you ruined my life!"

"Uploaded to the web?"

"That 'I was born in the 1800s' shit doesn't play with me, Cade! Wake up!"

After a giant yawn, Cade replied, "Sabrina, I took the video so that I would have something of you after you... when I rose in a hundred years."

"Don't try and confuse the point, Cade."

"Sabrina, this is not the time for such squabbling," Moselle interrupted.

Cade smiled warmly when his attention shifted to Moselle. He remembered her from his time dating Sabrina, and by the looks of her, she had not changed.

"Miss Moselle, look at you. You have not aged a day." Cade opened his arms for a hug. "How's death treating you?"

"Well. And you?" she said, accepting his greeting.

"Could be better. My dark slumber *was* just interrupted by an angry ex-girlfriend."

"Don't fall for his southern charm, Moss." Sabrina stood with her hands on her hips.

Above Moselle, Cade saw the silhouette of the massive drive-in movie theater screen. Upon spotting it, memories of the good times spent at the Starlight Drive-In returned. He walked around the screen, expecting to see lights, people, and cars, but all that was gone. All that remained was grey.

"What happened here, Sabrina?" He yawned again. "My senses... they are dull when I first rise. I thought the silence in my ears was... Wait, what year is it?"

"It's 2022."

"Hmm, the air smells different," he said, still gripped by disbelief at the abandoned theater.

"Are the gods about to grace us with rain?" Moselle tilted her head skyward.

"No, Moselle, and that's not what he smells."

"There's a renewed freshness surrounding you." Cade looked back at Sabrina. "When did you quit smoking?"

"I quit smoking when I quit you," Sabrina announced.

Sighing loudly, Cade knelt where weeds had broken through the cracks in the pavement. He tried to clear his head as he plucked some, pinching his sharp nails together, slicing the weeds in half.

As the veil of drowsiness lifted, another one of confusion draped over. The more awake he felt, the more befuddlement consumed him. Although he had slept for a little over a year, Cade did not feel rested at all. The slumber had been declared by the elders, and he was breaking that call for a second time.

Unfamiliar with his kind, with the exception of what they had read in old books, mostly propaganda placed by Cade's elders, Sabrina and Moselle had no clear idea of the complexities of being a vampire. A common misconception was a vampire's individuality. Often thought of as rogues, the truth was that the Vampire Nation had a hive-mentality. All vampires were related, all the children of one man, the original.

Sired by a vampire whose generation was not too distant from the first, Cade was sensitive to the nature of his kind. It was as if all other vampires set off a beacon in his mind. If there were a single vampire within a ten-mile radius, he would be able to seek that individual out.

Cade bowed on the cracked pavement, placed his cheek to the ground; he sensed nothing. It was that nothingness that left a void inside him, and like a black hole, it pulled at him. The slumber was calling. He needed to get back into the ground, to rejoin his clan in sleep.

"Sabrina, my love, I know you feel you had good reason to wake me. So please, do tell." His tone dropped and was serious now.

"Cade, we woke you because we need your help," Moselle answered.

"Help?" He peeked over his shoulder at the girls. "What kind of help?"

"Sabrina was attacked twice by a human who knows that she's a fairy. He seems to want her wings," Moselle explained.

"He... he has power over people; we think he may be controlling them through a new drug that will be released soon," Sabrina continued, her hands flailing nervously.

"A drug? You mean like cocaine?"

"No, a medicine to cure nicotine addiction," Moselle added.

"That bastard hurt Mira, and I don't know... she might... like, be dead."

"Mira?"

"My friend," Sabrina stated. "My—my bodyguard, okay?"

"Your father made you obtain the services of a bodyguard because of me, didn't he?" Cade laughed softly.

"No! Not everything is about you, Cade; it was to protect me from the fucking paparazzi." Sabrina turned her head to hide her emotions.

"My home was attacked by a shape-shifter today, possibly a werewolf, most likely in search of Sabrina."

Cade stood up; the girls' words had begun to solidify into an objective. Free of the weight of torpor, if only momentarily, Cade spoke a bit of vampire scripture.

"The more of our people in slumber, the more of us who will join them. The more awake, the more that will awake. The slumber has been decreed, and all shall feel the earth's pull and sink into the dirt with each step like quicksand under their feet."

"Why are you reciting this? What does that have to do with me, Cade?" Sabrina whined.

"If I do this for you, if I help you, I'll be consciously going against my whole nation. I'll be fighting my very nature."

"And?"

"I've seen my father conduct business enough to know what Cade is suggesting," Moselle stated firmly. "He expects payment, Sabrina."

"Precisely."

"Christ, Cade! Whatever you want, it's yours. Just help me, please."

Cade sneered as she spoke the Lord's name, but as that discomfort passed, a familiar sensation returned. This reunion with Sabrina had filled his head with images of their long nights of lovemaking. Cade had felt sad that he would never enjoy Sabrina London again as he had drifted off into the slumber a year ago. Now, it didn't have to be that way; now she needed him, and he wanted her.

With his vampire swiftness, Cade wrapped his arm around Sabrina's waist and pulled her into a tight embrace. Startled, she struggled a moment before becoming lost in his shiny grey eyes.

"I remember the night you buried me here. You cried for hours; I can still hear your tears like distant echoes of raindrops through the dirt. You cried my name over and over again. Do you remember the last thing you said to me?"

"Yes, I told you I loved you."

"Then you asked me if love was forever, and what was my response, Sabrina?"

"'Not forever; eternity.'"

Cade's sugary words had helped Sabrina forget why she was mad. The leanness of his hard muscles still apparent through his clothes, she remembered a time not so long ago when she thought she would never see him again. Looking into his eyes now made her want to melt. *Those lips*, she thought, *so perfect*. She wanted to kiss them.

"You know what I want, my sweet sunshine." Cade shifted his gaze to her perky breasts.

"Yes, I do," Sabrina agreed.

The sharpness of his index finger's nail cut open her shirt as he drew it down her cleavage.

"What the fuck?" she exclaimed. "This isn't even my shirt, Cade!"

She knew her words fell on deaf ears as Cade's hunger for blood had begun to surface. His tongue ran across his teeth to the tips of his fangs. Lips moistened, they shimmered like his eyes—and both were set to devour the feast of her flesh.

"I will have you one night now and one night after I save your friend," Cade announced.

"You want me to sleep with you as payment?"

"I can't think of anything I crave more than—"

"Asshole!" she spat in his face.

He tore open her shirt further, the fullness of her black lace bra now exposed. Sabrina held her ground. Hands to her hips, she took a defiant stance.

"You disgust me."

Sabrina hated Cade for what he was asking; she hated him for the power he had over her. *That bastard and his undead-asshole senses. He fucking knows I still want him.*

"Sabrina..." Moselle, who had kept quiet, watched the interaction between the former lovers. "You must face your demons, my friend. What are you willing to sacrifice in efforts to save your dearest friend?"

Thinking a moment longer, Sabrina whispered an answer that was wrought with defeat. It was exactly what Cade wanted to hear and she knew it.

"My body, my soul... and my blood."

"Looks like we have ourselves a deal, ladies. Huzzah!"

Chapter Twenty-One

Penetration

Moselle and Jackson lingered outside the guest bedroom Moselle had settled Sabrina in. Neither could concentrate on anything. It had been over an hour and Sabrina's long groans and deep grunts had yet to cease. Both frustrated and excited by the melody of pleasure coming from the room, the couple sat against the opposite wall, spellbound.

When Moselle began to feel uncomfortable, she told Jackson the story of how Cade and Sabrina met and how they fell in love. Ensnared by Moselle's storytelling ability, Jackson sat silently, his mind painting a dark picture of how a fairy and a vampire's forbidden romance put a strain on Sabrina's relationship with her family. *Vampire*, Jackson thought; suddenly Sabrina's comment that she had buried him made sense.

"Cade is a vampire?" he repeated for the tenth time since Moselle had said it. "Is this guy safe?"

As he spoke, a bright yellow-orange light seeped from the cracks around the door, and then pulsed like a strobe light.

"Safe? For whom?" Moselle frowned.

"Christ, all that screaming and moaning... are they having sex or killing each other in there?"

"A little of both, I fear."

Blood oozed from the many holes Cade had left on Sabrina's body, staining the white silk sheets. She felt no pain, with the exception of the very moment Cade's teeth penetrated her flesh. Her head felt light, as if she had taken ecstasy, but she was not high; it was the combination of blood loss and intense sexual desire that affected her.

As focused as she was on the pleasure, she couldn't help but hear her father's disappointed voice like a distant howl on the wind. Sabrina had never heard her father as furious as he was on the night she was arrested, and he'd made it obvious it was much more than just her illicit actions that upset him. Before that moment, the Londons had no idea their daughter had dated, let alone slept with a vampire.

"The fairy-kind stand against and combat such foul creatures, Sabrina! They do not spread their legs for them!" she bitterly recalled her father screaming when he confronted her about it that night.

Since then, she had been repulsed by the thought of ever sleeping with Cade again, yet how she felt changed the moment she saw him. A torrent of emotions returned to her, as if the days they'd spent together were just last week. *I have always loved you, Cade, and maybe*, she thought, *this time I can convince you to stay.*

"I want you to release."

Cade referred to her wings, something she had done a few times before while they had sex. On her hands and knees on the bed, she arched her back and spread her wings to the ceiling, their light so bright Cade had to look away. When his sensitive eyes adjusted, he moved his hands to the base of her wings.

Since the fairy-kind always had to keep their wings hidden, over generations they had developed an extreme sensitivity to touch. Sabrina had often considered her wings her biggest pleasure zone. Today the tips of Cade's fingers, as they pressed into the base of her wings, made her orgasm.

She held her breath until she nearly passed out, teeth gritting through the intense pleasure.

"Cade... I can't take much more," she moaned into the pillows.

"How do you feel?" Cade asked, as he tucked her wings under his arms so he could grab her waist again.

"Numb," she moaned. "You've fucked me numb."

"Admit it, my sweet sunshine, you're glad I'm back."

"Mmm, I am. Okay? Now finish up so I can just lay here and melt."

When Cade tightened his grip on the crests of her hip bone, Sabrina groaned. She loved it when he dug his fingertips into her hips. With only a spark of sexual power left, Sabrina bucked herself back into him. Although nearly spent, she knew her lover would enjoy it if she gave the last ounce of herself to him.

After another dozen long, rhythmic thrusts, Cade finished, growling like a wild animal as he erupted on her back.

Still outside, Jackson watched Moselle place her ear to the door when the guest bedroom grew silent. Jackson's fears that Sabrina was being harmed must have rubbed off on her. Although she said she knew better, she reacted nervously to the sudden quiet.

The sound of movement on the other side of the door caused Moselle to jump back to Jackson, and whisper, "I think he's coming."

"'Bout damn time," Jackson mumbled to himself.

When the door opened, Jackson wanted to look away and pretend he was doing something other than eavesdropping, but he could not help but stare; he had never seen a vampire before. Jackson was immediately surprised by how young he looked, even younger than himself. Cade had model good looks; someone Jackson would refer to as a "pretty boy." Cade's angular face had high cheekbones and a small nose and since he was shirtless, Jackson got a good look at his skin, which shined like polished ivory. A circular scar sat above his belly button. If the blemish did not exist, Jackson would have thought he stared at Michelangelo's David.

Cade smirked when he took his first look at the two of them.

"Miss Moselle, if you wanted to watch, you should've simply asked. Like that one time, remember?" Without taking his eyes off of her he asked, "Who is the blood bag? Is he mine?"

"No, Cade, he's mine."

Facing Jackson, he extended his hand.

"Then good luck to you, my new friend," he chuckled.

Jackson took his hand and squeezed it. He wanted the vampire to think he was not afraid of him.

"Where are you going?"

"There are many hours before dawn; I need to hunt."

"Be careful. The shape-shifter could still be out there," Moselle offered.

"Nope." Cade pointed to his nose. "Would've smelled him. Ain't nothing but deer and rabbit in those woods."

With a spring in his step, he walked to the stairs. As he buttoned up his shirt, Cade called to Moselle.

"Miss Moselle, do you think anyone would notice if one of your neighbors went missing?"

"What?" Jackson nearly choked.

"Cade, not on my street!" she replied sternly then turned to Jackson to do damage control. "Never mind his words; he crafts them so people will fear him more."

"To be honest, he doesn't look all that scary. I think I could take him in a fight."

"Keep thinking that, darling." Moselle's gazed into the guest bedroom. "Would you excuse me a moment? I would like to check on my friend."

"No problem," he answered, not sure what to do with himself.

Jackson caught a glimpse of Sabrina through the door when Moselle walked into the room. Although no lights were on, he could see Sabrina lay on her stomach naked with her wings a flutter above her. The glow from her wings was brighter than any bulb and the colorful glimmer sparkled with an amazing rainbow-like effect that held his attention until he spotted the red splatters on the sheets. Every thought, every feeling he had moments ago, changed the moment he realized what he stared at was blood.

"I... I guess I'll just go downstairs... maybe catch the scores."

"Thank you, darling."

Moselle listened to Jackson call out to one of her cats as he descended the stairs and finally shut the door, one arm up to shield her eyes. Moselle announced herself softly, so as not to startle her friend.

"Hey." Sabrina mumbled into her pillow, sighed, and yawned.

Moselle could feel her skin bake under the light of her friend's wings, not unlike the day she sunbathed next to the Pharaoh's pool so many years ago.

"Could you withdraw your wings?"

"Don't kill my buzz, Moss," Sabrina stated bluntly. "Okay?"

"I'm sorry, my friend, you may leave them unfurled, just dim them a bit so I can see you."

Sabrina dimmed her wings and able to see again, Moselle gasped in horror as she looked down at the gore. Dozens of small pools of blood covered the sheets and Sabrina's skin.

"By the gods, are you well?" she inquired, afraid to even touch her.

"Little weak... but fine."

"He bit you!"

"Yeah, I know."

"No, what I am trying to say is that you have bite wounds all over your buttocks and shoulders, Sabrina."

"I'm okay. It's fine. It's only scary the first couple times." Sabrina sighed. "I mean, Cade has a way of teasing me with his tongue before he bites me on my inner thigh. I scream because I'm afraid he's going to bite my—"

Sabrina rolled over to her back, the full length of her body exposed. Moselle covered her mouth in shock. The dozens of red marks she had seen on her friend's backside were nothing compared to the ones on her breasts, stomach, and pelvis. There must have been twenty more wounds spread across her body, sparkling red, like tiny rubies, blood oozed from them all.

"I can't believe you let him bite you like this, Sabrina," Moselle interrupted.

"It only hurts a second, like getting a shot."

"You mean like shooting up."

"Moselle, please, your hoity-toity attitude is really spoiling my high."

"You're high?" Moselle raised her voice. "You came to me in a panic, devastated that your friend was hurt and possibly abducted yesterday. Now you're high from some sort of kinky vampire sex? What about Mira?"

"Mira," Sabrina sighed. "I'll never forget the day she showed up at my front door. She came with a note. Did I ever tell you that? She had a note from the ranking officials of the Otherworldly Assembly. It explained who and what she was. Yeah, my father wasn't eager to speak to me anymore, but he still sent me this one last gift and you know what I did?"

"What?"

"I left her sitting outside my door for almost a week. I told her I didn't want her. I told her to go home."

"Yet she stayed."

"Like you said earlier, Moss, she was just doing her job."

"She is your friend now."

"Yes, she is." Sabrina closed her eyes. "My bodyguard, my friend, and more. Mira understands me better than any of you do."

"Does she now?" Moselle crossed her arms and shook her head with frustration.

"Yes, and she would understand that tonight... tonight, I just need to rest."

Chapter Twenty-Two

Confrontation

Jackson waved a few times at the security camera, waiting for Moselle's guards to let him in. He wondered if they were surprised he was back? In part, he found it a bit unbelievable himself.

Last night, his exit had been abrupt. He was not proud of the way he had left things with Moselle and found it somewhat unsettling how she did not argue with his decision to go. She had simply waved her hand at him and ordered one of her guards to bring one of her cars up from the underground garage for him to use. He hoped she wasn't mad.

Jackson yawned widely while he waited for the gate to open enough to fit Moselle's car, a 1960 Jaguar XK 150, through. Last night, he had thought he would sleep soundly—safe in his own apartment—but he thought wrong. A week ago, he might have, but that was before he knew that there were things out there in the night that hunted people. *Monsters*, he called them in his mind, *creatures that have existed for years undaunted by mankind and its technology*. He had lain awake most of the night, focused on how it was possible that man could be so blind. *How could they not know about vampires, werewolves, and fairies?* According to Moselle, most otherworldlies hid in plain sight while others had adapted to the invasion of man's technical toys.

The gurgle in his stomach reminded Jackson that in the entire day he and Moselle had spent together after returning from New York City, they hadn't eaten. Had he found anything edible at home, with the exception of expired cans of soup and stale potato chips, he would have devoured it all. As he parked Moselle's car next to Sabrina's damaged vehicle, Jackson thought about the previous night.

"Yes, one quart of sesame chicken and one pint of pork fried rice. Oh, and two egg rolls. Delivery please," Jackson told the woman who answered at the Chinese restaurant.

"Address?" she asked.

Eyes on the newspaper from the day before, the headline caught his attention: "Suspected Serial Killer is Food Deliveryman." It made sense to him; vampires could take jobs as nighttime deliverymen, and easily gain access to people's homes.

"Address? I need your address!" the lady yelled again.

"Ah—"

"The address?"

Jackson slammed the phone down; he refused to make himself such easy prey. If this was what the world really was, he needed to adapt to it and fast.

Hand still on the gearshift, Jackson looked into the classic Jaguar's rearview mirror. A diehard fan of old gangster movies, he quoted *The Untouchables* when Ness confronted Capone, "'Never stop, never stop fighting till the fight is done.'"

When he finally got out of the car, Moselle was at the front door. She leaned against one of the stone pillars adorned in black leather pants and a tight black top that made her look more appealing than ever. *If that's even possible,* he thought.

With his duffle bag slung over his shoulder, he walked to her confident and strong.

"I thought you might never return to me, Jackson."

"I'm sorry I left like that."

"All that matters is that you are back."

Jackson stared at her hips and the way her high-heeled boots accentuated the curves of her leg muscles while she spoke. Living dead or not, he still wanted her. Jackson wrapped his arm around Moselle's waist and pressed into her for a kiss. In the little time they had been together, he had never handled her so aggressively, and by the way Moselle's body wilted in his arms, she liked it.

"Look, I called work and told them I'd be gone for a few days. I'm here for you."

"My heart is warmed to hear you say so."

"I want to know all about you, Moselle, the real you."

"You know, I could be burned for telling you the truth." She inhaled his scent as she spoke.

"I—"

"It is a risk I willingly take for you, Jackson."

Suddenly uneasy, Jackson looked back at her car, and when he did, Moselle smiled. "Did you enjoy my automobile?"

"Yeah, it's a great car."

"You are wondering if it was I who purchased the vehicle." Moselle ran her hand through Jackson's hair. "The answer is yes, my love, I did."

"Really? It has your style."

"It was a rainy day, as I recall. My father had joined me but wanted me to make the transaction. You should have seen him, Jackson; the dress of the late nineteen fifties did not flatter my father at all. His strong Egyptian features did not mix well with the James Dean style of that time. He looked ridiculous."

Jackson chuckled. He wondered if she still had her clothing from those days; the imagine of Moselle driving off the dealership lot, dressed to the nines in the fifties most expensive garb, filled his mind's eye.

"I've seen lots of artifacts in your house—amazing things—but I have to ask: did you keep any of your clothes from back then?"

"I would be shamed in the eyes of Hathor if I did not," Moselle ran her hand across Jackson's muscular chest. "Would you like to see my wardrobe?"

On the third floor of Moselle's home was a room she had spent much time and money converting into a large walk-in closet. The space, originally designed as two bedroom suites, had been combined into one room almost twice the size of her bedroom. As they approached it, Jackson heard a sound he had not heard in any other location inside her spacious home: the humming of an air conditioner.

Moselle turned the key in the lock, and when she opened the door, Jackson was hit with a gust of cool air that held the scent of plastic and old clothes. The room, unlike the others on the third floor of her house, was not lit with a skylight or candles; this room had a light switch that turned on several overheads, 60-watt lights.

He walked into a vast storage space filled to the inch with racks of clothes. At first, Jackson felt like he was staring at costumes for a Broadway musical. He was no stranger to on-set wardrobes, but the amount of clothes before him was astounding.

Moselle dashed off with a silly laugh that was unlike her. When she disappeared into the depths of the climate-controlled room, Jackson had to track her voice to find her.

"This is incredible, Moselle."

Every article of clothing was preserved perfectly, stored in acid-free plastic bags and appeared to be organized on the racks according to date.

"Here we are," Moselle exclaimed when she found what she was looking for.

Jackson joined up with her near the back of the room where a full-scale fitting area was set up.

Moselle pointed to an old high-backed chair and said, "Wait here while I change into an outfit I've owned since the Second World War."

"You have clothes preserved from World War Two?" Jackson looked over his shoulder at a rack of clothes that held long gowns. "I keep thinking we should use these for photos. Just imagine all the cool ads we could create with these outfits."

"I would really enjoy that."

"Hey, do you have anything from the Renaissance? Oh, were you living in America during the Civil War? Do you have anything from then?"

"It is endearing that you find my collection so exciting, Jackson, but I am afraid I was neither living nor in America during your Civil War."

"Too bad, you know I visited a bunch of the battlefields with my parents when I was in elementary school. There's a lot of interesting history here in America."

"Darling, I am Egyptian born. I know very little about your country's history. If it is American history you desire, speak to Cade; he loves to tell tales."

"Really? Was he alive during the Civil War?"

"For the most part."

Moselle emerged from the dressing room with an extra swing to her walk. Dressed in a yellow and black crepe cocktail dress, she appeared to have stepped out of the war-torn days of the 1940s. The cut of the dress may not have flattered her body type like her current ones did, but she was the picture of sexiness nonetheless, with her black full-armed gloves and matching fur coat. All she was missing was one of those tiny bonnets, and she would have been set.

Moselle pulled her long, wavy black hair up over her head and spun slowly around to give Jackson the entire view.

"My hair would have been doubled up those days mind you."

"I don't think I've ever seen you so covered up."

"Your observation is keen, my love. Even as I stand here these sleeves are making my arms itch."

"World War Two. I still can't believe it; that's almost a hundred years ago, and yet here you stand, dressed like you did then."

"Well, I wore this dress when I went out at night. My father owned a small, officer's dance club."

"Those must have been exciting times."

"More like terrifying," Moselle corrected as she slowly lowered herself down onto Jackson's lap.

"The war—"

"No, I was used to war," Moselle interrupted Jackson. "It was the world that frightened me. I was still very much a newborn to the modern day."

"Wait... I don't follow. I thought you've been alive for several thousand years," he said while Moselle nuzzled his neck.

"No, I said I died four thousand years ago," she whispered. "You see, it took my parents many, many years to find my burial place, so I was not resurrected until 1935. In life, I lived twenty-three years. In death I have only existed for eighty-seven years."

"Did you say, resurrected?"

"I did. In time, I will share with you the disturbing details of my death. Tonight, let me begin with what happened afterward. As chronicled by my father."

As Moselle explained the circumstances of her resurrection and how she came to exist as one of the undead, Jackson hung on her every word.

Gripped by an uncontrollable fear that treachery had tainted his ranks, Amenemhet I took his most precious treasures to Libya and hid them deep under the sand. Throughout the final years of his rule, Amenemhet ordered his most loyal men to build a tomb in the Sahara, just outside of Kufra, an oasis in southeastern Libya, a shrine worthy to be his final resting spot. In it, he placed the woman he wished to take as a bride in his afterlife: Moselle Abdul Aziz Al Ghurair.

Assassinated, Amenemhet did not get a chance to retire to his secret tomb as he had hoped, and in time, its whereabouts were forgotten—lost to the desert. In 1935, almost 3900 years later, Moselle's father finally unearthed her tomb.

The region was packed with foreigners; a war was on the horizon. In the midst of the fascist dictator Benito Mussolini ordering his men to build a fortified city, Moselle's father, Anmet used the great wealth he had accumulated through the years to excavate the buried tomb, all under the guise of another Italian military project.

After three long weeks of excavation, an entrance was discovered. The air tasted stale, even to Anmet, who did not require breathing to survive. With torches lit, he and ten of the Libyans he had hired to help entered the tomb. From the journals Amenemhet kept, Anmet knew he had yet to finish his tomb. Some of the catacombs would no doubt lead to dead ends, which would increase his search, but at least he did not have to contend with booby traps, since the fallen pharaoh's body was never put to rest there and his most loyal men were killed. If it were not for its secluded location and the unyielding hunger of the desert, it would have undoubtedly been pillaged hundreds of years before. Nevertheless, plunder was still a fear Moselle's father carried with him. He always worried he would be too late.

The torches painted the dusty walls reddish-yellow, revealing the lack of hieroglyphics on the walls. They were bare, yet another sign the tomb was unfinished, as Amenemhet would have no doubt glorified his rise too. Anmet braced himself as he descended the steep tunnel. He could sense he was close to his lifelong goal. He would find his daughter; he would reunite his family.

At the bottom of the passage were two chambers. One was empty, untouched, unfinished. Torches lit the second chamber. As the men crept deeper into the room, they realized that Amenemhet had completed part of his tomb—this one chamber, the location of his most valued treasure. A series of hieroglyphics on the wall adjacent to the door read: The pharaoh's greatest prize, a woman with raven hair and onyx eyes. Here lies the eternal bride of Amenemhet I.

One of the Libyan men shrieked in terror as the flames of his torch lit a pedestal in the corner. Atop the stone platform sat a bronze sarcophagus.

"Gods be praised," Anmet said in polished Libyan Arabic, as his eyes feasted on the resting spot of his beloved daughter.

His orders were delivered with a newfound haste; it was time, so he prepared to return his daughter to this world. Each of the ten men he had brought down into the tomb carried a tiny jug of liquid that contained water from the Nile, blessed by Egyptian holy men, priests who believed in the old ways, the ancient gods. When all ten canisters were lined up alongside the sarcophagus, Moselle's father instructed two of the men to open the casket.

The two men, struggled to lift the lid of the sarcophagus and when the smell of death wafted into the air, they dropped it. The heavy lid crashed to the floor echoing loudly in everyone's ears.

"Avert your eyes!" Anmet shouted; he did not want his daughter looked upon by common laborers.

Steeling his nerves, Anmet gazed down into the sarcophagus and laid eyes on his daughter for the first time in nearly four thousand years. Although wrapped from head to toe in long strips of rotten linen, her body had shriveled. The wrappings which had once held her supple skin tightly were now draped loosely over most of it. He ran his hand over the exposed skin of her shoulder; it felt like stone. Anmet had much work to do.

With the first two canisters of holy water uncorked, he doused his daughter's mummified corpse. One after another, he emptied the jugs until the last drop of water was gone, every ounce absorbed by her skin.

Anmet stared at his daughter a moment; now came the part he dreaded most. Head bowed, he whispered a plea for forgiveness.

"Line up, men; it is time I divvy up your reward."

From his large backpack, he removed a long tube carefully wrapped in dark cloth. With his back to his men, he unwrapped the package: a Soviet Union sub-machine gun. When he turned around, he pulled the trigger, spraying the men with bullets. The muzzle of the machine gun lit up the room with vermilion flashes, while Anmet yelled, "I am sorry" over and over in Arabic.

The men fell to the ground.

"A sacrifice for you, Anubis, ten men in trade for my one daughter," Anmet said in the ancient Egyptian tongue.

Anmet knew exactly how his daughter would feel when she awoke. Moselle would experience resurrection the same way he and her mother had all those years ago.

Unable to move, she would want to open her eyes, to seek answers, to call for help, but there would only be blackness and silence. With no voice in her throat, she would begin to panic, but fear would vanish when sensations returned.

Anmet recalled the first thing he had felt upon his return: the touch of cold air as it blew over his bare skin. To this day he had never felt anything so powerful as that touch.

"Do not be afraid, my daughter, I have you now."

Cradled in his arms, Moselle's father placed her on the floor next to one of the dying Libyans. The man screamed as he pawed at the bullet holes in his stomach. Unable to endure the noise a second longer, Anmet kicked the man in the head until he was quiet. He withdrew a thick-bladed knife and proceeded to shear the linen wraps from his daughter's right arm. As delicately as a father holding the hand of his newborn baby, he carefully placed her palm on the dying man's chest.

"Feed, daughter. Take what is left of this poor man's life energy so that yours may be replenished."

Moselle's hand, which looked like old, dried, hardened leather, slowly began to glow pale purple.

He knew her mind would be fractured, unable to comprehend what had occurred or what to do now, but her body would follow its natural course; it was her way now, the way of the cursed undead.

Nearly invisible to the eye, the man's energy drained from his body and pooled above him like an aura. As quickly as it formed, it was siphoned into Moselle's open hand.

Soon the young Egyptian woman's withered form changed. At first only small details were noticeable, like the tone and texture of her skin; no longer dark brown and wrinkled like a spoiled fruit, its youthful radiance began to return. When the first man expired, Moselle moved her arm of her own accord, in search of another source of energy.

Anmet pulled the next closest man by the leg to Moselle. The man, who had just slipped out of consciousness, laid still, a bullet lodged in his hip, another apparently inches from his heart. *A good thing for him, not to see his end*, Anmet thought as Moselle's hand, covered in the last man's blood, left a snail trail of sticky gore as it traveled up the hired man's pant leg, past his hips, to his chest.

"Hurry, my child. Their grip on this world fades fast. I can sense it."

After she drained two more men, Moselle took in her first breath since death, but it was not to fill her lungs with air; it was a gasp of terror. Her decayed form had finally healed enough for her to peel open her eyes, and the sight she was welcomed by was as confusing as it was horrifying.

"I know this all looks strange to you, but I will explain everything to you later," Anmet said.

"Thirsty," she called.

"Yes, my daughter, I remember the sensation well. I have brought you gallons of water; it awaits you on the surface, along with many more men to consume."

———∽———

When Moselle began her story, Jackson had been rubbing her leg, slyly moving his hand ever further up her thigh. At some point, he had stopped and his hand rested motionless.

"My father kept journals that explained everything from his and my mother's resurrection to his long search and discovery of the tomb I was hidden in. He is very detailed; that is how I can tell you that he tricked those poor Libyan men before shooting them, all in his efforts to return me to this world."

"I don't know what to say," Jackson told her as he pulled his hand out from under her skirt, a puddle of sweat between his skin and hers.

"Have I made myself unattractive in your eyes?"

"No, you might have freaked me out a little, but I still see you as the most beautiful woman alive."

"Alive?" Moselle turned her face toward him, brushing her nose against his.

"You know what I mean."

"Kiss me then."

No sooner did their lips touch than a voice interrupted. Sabrina stood in the doorway, calling out to Moselle. With no answer, she forged into the room.

"If you guys are screwing, you might want to tell me before I see something I don't want to."

Moselle withdrew her mouth from Jackson's.

"We're in the back, Sabrina, near the dressing room."

"Are you guys naked?" she asked snottily.

"No," Jackson answered.

"Good. Unlike you, I don't want to interrupt your... moment," Sabrina stated as she came face to face with them.

"How may I aid you, my friend?"

"Cade will rise soon," she stated, looking at them both. "Play time is over. Dress up and kissy face will have to wait until after we find Mira."

"A change of attitude from last night?" Moselle asked with a slight trace of sarcasm.

"You know what, Moselle? All I have is one word for you."

"And what word is that, Sabrina?" Moselle said rising from Jackson's lap.

"Redemption."

Chapter Twenty-Three

Back to School

Moselle, Sabrina, Cade, and Jackson arrived in the primary visitor's parking lot of California State University of Los Angeles an hour and a half into the lecture Alexander Kintner was giving in the auditorium. Their plan was to corner him and force him to release Mira by any means necessary—that is, if she was still alive.

"I can hardly believe it. Overkill put out another album?" Cade exclaimed from the back seat as Moselle's 2010 H2 Hummer settled into park.

"They sure did," Sabrina answered smugly.

"And you have the *From the Underground and Below* gold record?"

"Well, it's in my penthouse; hopefully no one stole it," she answered as she nervously crossed and uncrossed her legs.

"I certainly hope not. I want to see that prize myself."

"Overkill? The thrash band? From the 1990s?" Jackson turned his head around from the driver's seat. He wanted to get a full look at what the vampire in the backseat was doing.

"Some of their best albums were released in the 2000s," Sabrina corrected Jackson.

"You listen to that music, Sabrina?"

"Hell yeah," she answered with a smile and a slight head-banging motion for emphasis.

"She doesn't share that secret with everyone, buddy." Cade smirked. "Only the ones of us she likes."

"You like them too?" Jackson asked Cade curiously.

"Bobby 'Blitz' Ellsworth's voice, Overkill's ripping melody—they make me feel. Sensation is important when you're dead. Right, Miss Moselle?"

Moselle nodded.

"Vampires listen to heavy metal music." Jackson chuckled, his new reality more and more amusing by the minute. "I thought you were all goths."

"Cade actually knows the vampire who turned Bobby 'Blitz' back in 1993 before the *I Hear Black* album."

"Wait, the singer is a vampire?" Jackson exclaimed.

"I guess his bandmates dug him up again to sing for the new albums..." Cade supposed. "You would be surprised how many bands had vampires... before we all went underground."

"No shit?" Jackson asked. "Hey, remind me to download *Dracula* when we get back. All of a sudden I want to watch it again."

"The 1931, 1992, 2014, or 2018 one?" Cade asked as they got out of the car.

"What?" Jackson replied only partially hearing Cade's question as he shut his door.

"Which *Dracula* are you gonna watch? The 1931, 1992, 2014, or the 2018 one?"

"*Bram Stoker's Dracula*? The Coppola one?" Jackson guessed.

"Good choice. I challenge you to not want to have sex with Lucy."

"Cade! Jackson!" Sabrina interrupted. "You two can pal around later, okay? We've got to get moving."

"Fine. You all head to the top of the walkway up there and wait one hundred or so yards from the auditorium, just in case he has guards posted. I'm going to scout around a bit; I'll meet you there in fifteen minutes," Cade explained, and then looked at Sabrina. "We good?"

"Good."

Moselle, Jackson, and Sabrina followed Cade's instructions and held back a safe distance from the auditorium, which had its doors open to help cool it off. Even from their distance, they could hear the cheers of the people inside.

"It's been a few years, you know, but it feels kinda good to be back on a college campus. What about you guys?"

"Never been." Sabrina answered first.

"You went to college, right, Moselle?"

"I did. Victoria University of Manchester," she said with a smile. "*Arduus ad solem.* Striving towards the sun."

"Where is that?"

"England." Sabrina and Moselle answered together.

"Ah..." he replied, trailing off.

Familiar sights filled Jackson's eyes: students rushed to classes weighed down by bags crammed with textbooks they had spent ridiculous amounts of money on and probably only opened once or twice. Between him and the auditorium passed a sea of letterman's jackets; they must have belonged to the offensive line of the college football team, he guessed. Jackson remembered that feeling, the enjoyment of being part of a team. On the ice, he knew the men to his left and right would gladly go down protecting him. With a ponderous glance to his left and right now, he wasn't so sure.

A wave of loud applause poured out from the auditorium into the courtyard. When Jackson looked at Sabrina, she appeared to be in discomfort, fidgeting with her bracelet and wincing from time to time.

"You okay, Sabrina?" he was compelled to ask.

"Yeah..." she grunted and nod.

Although the socialite was dressed down—wearing sweats and a pair of oversized sunglasses—she looked good, *perhaps too good*, Jackson thought as he noticed some of the male students begin to swarm as they recognized her. As the minutes ticked by, a large group of guys formed not far from the entrance of the auditorium just to stare at her.

"Sabrina London?" one boy asked as he approached them.

"Yeah?" Sabrina answered without thinking.

"Wow, it is you! I knew it! I used to love you so much! Oh my God. Can I take a quick photo with you?"

"Wait no, not me. I just look like me, I mean her," she said, adjusting her glasses to better cover her face.

"So, you're *not* Sabrina London?"

Cade walked up from behind the boy and tapped him gently on the shoulder. When the young student's eyes met Cade's, they stopped.

"That's not Sabrina. Just another pretty girl, that's all." Cade enunciated every word and when he was done, he waved a hand in front of his face.

His back turned, the boy said, "Sorry, you're not her."

"No problem."

The boy was a few steps away from the group before Sabrina called out to him.

"Hey, if I was Sabrina, what else were you going to say to me, or her?"

"I was just going to tell Sabrina I hope she gets her life back together, and that she was super hot."

Sabrina smiled.

"What did he just do?" Jackson whispered to Moselle.

"Vampires can mesmerize people with a combination of their voice and a thing they do with flicks of their eyes and third eyelid. Once they have their subject under control, they can give a simple command."

"Third eyelid? Wait, has he done that to me?" Jackson whispered again.

"No." Moselle took Jackson's hand and smiled when she answered. "And he can hear you, my love. There is no need to whisper."

"Oh, yeah. I knew that. So has he ever done that to you?"

"It only works on humans and a scarce few species of animals: dogs, dolphins, and primates for example."

"Good to know that you're safe, but now I feel bad for all those poor dolphins."

Chuckling, the vampire spoke up. "Anything happen here while I was gone?"

"Nothing at all," Moselle answered. "What took you so long?"

"Hard to sneak around. This place is covered in lights, it's like Dodger Stadium. Speaking of which, I really hope I can catch a game before I return to the slumber—"

"Cade, what really took you so long?" Sabrina interrupted, her hands on her hips.

After a smirk crawled across his face, he answered, "Strawberry blonde."

"I knew it. You fucking smell like cheap perfume," Sabrina sighed. "How disgusting."

Cade displayed his toothy grin. "She may have had bad taste, but she tasted good."

"What?" Jackson imagined some defenseless student dying in a dark corner of campus; the thought ignited his anger. "Why the hell would you—"

"Have to build my strength, buddy. Don't fret; I didn't kill the lass. She'll be just fine."

"Oh. Good."

"Look, I found a rear exit to this circus. The man you want will most likely take that door, to avoid the crowd out here. We can set up a perfect ambush for him in the passage between this and another building. That being said, just in case he avoids us, I think we should dispatch Moselle's beau to the target's car to sabotage it."

"Okay, so you want me to do that now?"

"No, tomorrow morning!" Sabrina snapped sarcastically.

"Moselle, will you be safe here without me?"

"You have nothing to worry about with me, Jackson." She smiled as she ran her hand down his cheek. "Go find our enemy's vehicle."

After Jackson ran off, Cade led the girls around the auditorium to the passage he had mentioned. The path from the back exit passed between the edge of the auditorium and a tall maintenance shed and created a bottleneck. As the trio approached it, Sabrina began to twitch with anxiety.

"Shit!" Sabrina blurted. "I think I sense his guards."

Cade inhaled deeply, "I smell four. You didn't tell me there were four of them."

"I only saw one, Cade. How was I supposed to know?"

"Well, I reckon I would have brought a rifle, sweetie. You know I hate to fight more than two of those beasts at once. Remember that one time—"

"Shh! Look!" Moselle motioned to the back doors as they opened.

The tiny blue light of the security lamp they stood under flickered as Alexander Kintner and two other men dressed in designer suits exited the building. Kintner seemed preoccupied with a tablet computer as they walked down the path. With a point of his finger and nod of his head, Cade instructed the two girls to move back into the shadows. Once they were safe, he honed his senses and counted: there were three people, but he smelled four otherworldlies. *Where is the other one?* he wondered.

"Now!" a deep voice screamed from above the maintenance shed.

Like bombs dropped from the heavens above, four black bear-faced beasts hit the ground in front of Alexander Kintner with such force the ground shook. Cade instantly recognized the things: windigos, not werewolves as Sabrina and Moselle suggested, but equally as dangerous.

Unseen by either group, Cade faded further into the shadows with the girls.

"Kintner! After so many years." The biggest windigo frothed at the mouth as he growled. "You die tonight, you sick aberration!"

"Not by your hands!" the man replied.

Gunfire rang out as Alexander Kintner's two guards engaged the windigos. Although hidden safely around the corner of the maintenance building, Cade told the girls to run. As they bolted, back around the auditorium to the front, he heard Sabrina scream, "My wings are gonna pop!"

Cade climbed to the top of the maintenance shed, the very place the four shape-shifters had been hidden before they sprung their ambush. Littered with cigarette butts and other debris, the flat roof gave Cade a bird's-eye view of the battle below.

The smell of fresh human blood filled the air; the windigos had already gutted Kintner's guards and surrounded the man himself in the small space below. Kintner Co.'s CEO had no escape, but Cade saw little concern on the man's face.

"I knew a public outing would bring my enemies into the light. Now that I face the bothersome insects trying to spoil my day, I can personally squash them."

Chapter Twenty-Four

Crash and Bash

"Take his arms first!" Thrasher ordered, but his words were useless; he may as well have whispered for all the good it did.

"Kintner, you killed my brother!" Rex growled through his snout. "You die!"

Rex lunged in, with Clayton right behind him. As Rex's claws were about to strike Kintner's chest, they fell through open air. Clayton's attempt to tackle the man also missed. Witness to the failed strikes, Thrasher watched as Alexander Kintner stepped from the shadows where the shed and the auditorium met. Thrasher didn't know how he did it, but he must have moved with lightning speed to avoid both Rex's and Clayton's attack.

The man raised his left hand and it glowed white, until a spark of electricity leapt from the spotlight above the exit to his palm. Instantly, his other hand fired out a bolt of electrical energy. The bolt branched out like a hundred miniature strikes of lightning all hitting Clayton and Rex as they turned to engage him.

"No!" Barton grumbled, frozen in his approach. "Stop! Stop!"

The sight of his friends'—their thick fur on end as they sizzled with high voltage—made Thrasher sick. He held his breath, unable to speak as he listened to the sound that emanated through Rex and Clayton's clenched teeth—not screams, but deep, spine-chilling groans.

Thrasher knew his enemy was powerful, but he had no idea the madman held command over the elements. Thrasher stomped his talon-nailed feet as he moved; shoved Barton to the side and bravely approached his foe. The glimmer of arrogance in Kintner's eyes flashed as Thrasher growled, his full set of jagged teeth bared.

The bolts of lightning Kintner cast abruptly stopped when the power to the auditorium failed. As darkness swallowed the tiny alleyway, Clayton and Rex fell to the ground like rag dolls, all the while vapors rose from their bodies like mist from morning dew. The blue emergency light intensified, but Thrasher didn't need man-made lights to see. Ears back and flat to his head, Thrasher lowered from his tall grizzly bear stance.

"Get them to safety."

"I think Clayton's dead, man," Barton replied.

"Get them to safety!" Thrasher roared.

His eyes keen, Thrasher saw the air around Kintner's hands change; denser and nearly opaque. Suddenly, the energy that engulfed the man's right took the shape of a large mace, while the left formed a medieval shield.

"Your kind prides itself on its hand-to-hand combat, so let's do it."

When Kintner swung out at Thrasher with the elemental-mace, the beast-man felt the breeze as it approached. Ducking under the swipe, Thrasher planted his hands on the ground before he slammed himself shoulder first into his enemy's nearly invisible magical shield. Kintner fell backward into the metal door, his back jarred. Thrasher cocked back his arm but before he could strike, he saw movement from both his left and right sides.

"You fool, that's not me." Alexander Kintner's mirror image stepped from the shadows.

Thrasher was distracted long enough for the man on the ground to land a blow to his thick left leg. Hurt, Thrasher howled as he stumbled backward, and suddenly there were three of Alexander Kintner in his view, but Thrasher wouldn't be fooled by such trickery; he only smelled fear from one: the one in the middle.

He braced himself against the swing of his enemy's translucent mace by stepping into the attack. Locked under Thrasher's arm, Kintner raised his shield to protect his face and chest, as Thrasher pounded his fist into the barrier that now looked like thick, smoke-filled air but felt like cool stone. As many times as he struck it, he felt no give in its structural stability. Muscles weakened and lungs burning, Thrasher pushed on.

"I will kill you!" he growled.

Hands tight on the man, Thrasher spun his body around and he threw his opponent into the shadow-painted wall to his left. Lost from Thrasher's view for a second, Kintner returned with his mace and shield reformed into two new weapons.

The magical fields that encompassed his arms fired out of the shadows, expanding until they struck Thrasher's barreled-chest like two battering rams and drove him into the wall. Nearly unconscious from the blow, Thrasher's bleary eyes watched his mortal enemy step closer, the force of his magic weapon instantly withdrawn to his fists.

"Campus security will arrive at any moment, but they won't find me. All they'll discover is the corpse of some worthless ecoterrorist."

"You haven't won yet." Thrasher looked up at him as he pressed the speed dial on his cell phone.

"Oh really?"

Kintner formed the magical force over his left hand into a thick blade and aimed at Thrasher's heart. When he plunged it, Thrasher moved, and the blade meet only with the concrete below.

Out of the way of Kintner's weapon, Thrasher popped up strong on the man's left. Claws out, he drew them across his side and tore not only the magic wielder's jacket and shirt, but also his soft skin underneath. The cell phone in Kintner's hand dropped; the voice on the other end screeching out the entire way down.

"Bastard!" he cried out.

Kintner lashed out with his magically bladed arm almost instantly but missed as Thrasher moved in for a second strike. After all these years, Thrasher was within inches of taking the life of his mortal enemy, but where was the fear in his foe's eyes, he wondered.

With the thought of his wife and children in the forefront of his mind, Thrasher moved to end Alexander Kintner. A punch landed, and another. Thrasher threw an uppercut that collided so hard it dazed the man. Arm cocked back, Thrasher spread his claws and ripped six deep lacerations down his foe's arm.

"Time to die!" Thrasher roared.

His next strike should have hit its target—but it didn't. At the last second, a powerful gust of wind struck Thrasher and threw him all the way out of the tight alleyway. Although Thrasher was unharmed by the wind, it gave his opponent enough time to stumble toward the auditorium and pick up one of his guard's dropped guns. Kintner pulled the trigger four times.

The first two bullets struck Thrasher's chest, the third his leg. Hobbled, he dropped to his knees. The fourth bullet flew by his face, nothing more than a whoosh in the night air. While Thrasher drew upon reserves of strength he had never used before, he witnessed his rival do the one thing he had prayed he would not do: escape. Doubled over, the man responsible for so much of the sorrow and rage that filled Thrasher's tragic life opened the auditorium's back door and stepped back inside.

His head tilted to the sky, Thrasher released a guttural howl so loud it even drowned out the distant police sirens.

Cade watched the whole ordeal motionlessly, both stunned and amused. This man, Alexander Kintner, was more than just human; he was something else. His powers were not the only thing that suggested a taint of ancient evil; Cade could sense something different in his blood.

Not wanting to be found at the scene of the crime, Cade jumped down to where the battle had just raged and ran his fingers quickly across a drop of blood that had fallen from Kintner's arm.

"Over here! Call for back up!" a voice echoed close by.

Cade sprung to the top of the maintenance building with ease. He glanced one last time to where the largest windigo had fallen. The man-beast was gone, but his trail, a cloud of dust, and fine splatter of blood, was clear as day; simple to track even for a novice, and Cade was no amateur.

Chapter Twenty-Five

Information Exchange

An emergency alert rang and sent text messages to every student's cell phone on campus. There had been gunfire reported at the Eagle's Nest Gymnasium/Auditorium. Panicked students ran from all areas of campus toward the parking lots and security stations. Amongst the fleeing crowds, Sabrina held her breath. She had to concentrate on her wings to keep them hidden, but the mass hysteria that surrounded her made it nearly impossible.

Moselle led Sabrina back toward the car. Sabrina wanted to leave, regardless of Moselle's suggestions to duck into a bathroom or empty classroom where she could release her wings in private.

"Moss, I can't hold them much longer."

"You're going to have to, or you risk revealing yourself to everyone around."

Sabrina spotted Jackson from afar; he had retrieved the Hummer and was speeding across the parking lot toward them. He dodged students as they raced to their own vehicles, honked the horn, and flashed the headlights clearing his way toward them.

The car came to a screeching halt, whipping a cool breeze over Sabrina.

"Jackson, cover your eyes!" Moselle shoved Sabrina inside and slammed the door behind her.

The entire car lit up with an intense flash of light that scared a group of students as they passed. One girl screamed and pointed, cried out that there was another shooting, and fell to the dirt when she ducked for cover. Sabrina might have laughed if the moment had not been so dreadfully serious. Instead, she crumpled herself up into a ball over the back seat, her wispy wings bent against the ceiling of the car.

"Are you okay?" Jackson asked, looking at her in the rear-view mirror.

"Just peachy."

"Good call getting the car, darling," Moselle said after she sat down into the passenger side seat.

"I heard gunfire. Where's Cade? Is he okay?"

"Bullets will not harm him," Moselle answered.

"This turned out to be a real cluster fuck!"

"Sabrina!"

"I'm sorry, Moss, but we didn't even get to talk to Kintner, and…" Sabrina sat up, holding together the scraps of her top. "And I think I ruined your Juicy fleece hoodie."

"No worries. I have another at home. Juicy Couture sent me two dozen of those when I did that shoot with them," Moselle replied.

"They did?"

"Indeed, a myriad of colors and sizes. Why do you think I had a pink one in your size?"

"I don't know. I didn't think about it really."

"You modeled a bikini for them in some television advertisement maybe two years ago, or am I mistaken?"

"Music video, yeah," Sabrina corrected her, her voice fell off into a sigh.

"Did they not send you some complimentary samples?"

"I got to keep the suits I wore during the shoot is all."

"How odd."

"Hey," Jackson finally interrupted, "shouldn't we be doing something?"

"We are," Moselle replied. "We are waiting for Cade."

Jackson sighed and rubbed the bridge of his nose.

"Seriously, why didn't they give me some extra swag?" Sabrina whined.

"I'm sure I do not know—"

"Did you complain a lot? Argue with the director?" Jackson asked, clearly frustrated, and that only agitated Sabrina further.

"Well, Jackson, the asshole kept having his assistant oil me up. I told him any more oil and I was gonna break out, but he didn't listen to me, and I hate breaking out on my chest. It's gross."

"Have you shot with them since?"

"No."

"That's your answer," Jackson surmised.

"What's my answer?"

"I think Jackson is trying to tell you that you would catch more flies with honey than vinegar." Moselle winked at Jackson before taking a sip from her water bottle.

Sabrina wanted to yell at them both, but she caught the meaning of what they were saying and telling them both to fuck off would have only proven them right. Instead, she closed her eyes, held her breath, and counted to ten. At ten, she drew her wings into her body. *Why is this happening to me? Why are my wings causing me so much trouble?*

"Feel better?" Moselle reached back for Sabrina's hand.

"A little bit... thanks."

Cade stood downwind of Thrasher on the roof of the gymnasium, until the shape-shifter transformed back into his human form. Cade could smell the severity of its wounds. They were clearly fatal, which meant he wouldn't be strong enough to change shape again. In his human guise, the windigo was no match for an aged and powerful vampire.

Careful not to make a sound, Cade snuck up on the windigo, who had taken refuge under a large satellite dish.

"Come to finish the job, vampire?"

No longer in need of the darkness, he walked out into plain view only a few feet from Thrasher.

"Not at all."

"I thought I sensed you back there. You make a lousy bodyguard, vamp," Thrasher coughed. "I nearly had the bastard; you failed your master."

"Alexander Kintner is not my master."

"Then why are you here? Why are you even awake?" Thrasher tried to stand but collapsed again. "Your kind should be asleep."

"You're dying," Cade stated bluntly.

"Fuck you!" Thrasher spit.

"I know what you need to survive your wounds," Cade said, as he knelt over Thrasher's damaged leg. "You have something I need; care to barter?"

"Barter?" Thrasher grumbled and groaned. "What do you want, bloodsucker?"

"Information."

Chapter Twenty-Six

School's Out

Ten minutes had passed, and Cade hadn't returned. Police from two different townships had arrived in the meantime. Jackson stared at two female police officers as they moved a barricade into place. The southern exit to the parking lot they were sitting in was now blocked. It would only be a matter of time before they wouldn't be able to slip out anonymously.

"Where's Cade?" Jackson asked again.

"Maybe he caught Kintner?"

Sabrina leaned forward between the driver and passenger seats to get a better view. She clutched the fabric of the torn hoodie in one hand and pointed with the other. Instead of looking where she pointed, Jackson was staring at her tattoo. Still amazed by its detail, he reached down and traced its outer line with the tip of his index finger.

"Stop that, it tickles." Sabrina wiggled.

"I don't see him, Sabrina."

"He was right over there like a second ago, Moss," she pointed again.

Jackson continued to trace her wings, slowly moving down to the small of her back. When he reached her hips he redirected his finger to her spine, and moved it toward her butt crack, which was creeping out from her pants.

"Quit it," Sabrina said containing a laugh. "These things are super-sensitive, especially today."

A knock on the glass next to Jackson scared him so badly he jumped, pulling his hand away from Sabrina so hard he slammed it into the roof of the car.

"Cade!" Sabrina shouted.

Impatient, Sabrina crawled across Jackson's lap to the door so she could press the unlock button. He gazed at her svelte body as she slithered across his lap, and briefly fantasized about her, the touch of her skin, the smell of her hair, the taste of her... *What the fuck am I doing?* he suddenly thought. *What's wrong with me? I can't stop myself from thinking about her.*

As Sabrina backed off him in reverse to return to the backseat, her hand accidentally brushed his groin. Practically nose to nose, she let loose with a tiny, whispered sorry.

"Miss me, children?" Cade quipped as he stepped up into the car.

"Cade!" Sabrina wrapped her arms around him.

Moselle's eyes locked on Jackson, head titled, she leaned over slowly to speak softly into his ear.

"Relax, my love." She reached her hand down to where Sabrina's had just been. "You are fine."

Jackson closed his eyes a moment and collected himself.

"Where the hell did you get that jacket?" Sabrina asked as she pulled out of Cade's embrace.

Jackson and Moselle twisted around to see Cade wearing a letterman's jacket that was easily two sizes too big.

"Best way to blend in with the enemy."

"Did you kill the owner of that jacket, Cade?" Jackson asked.

"Who me?" He shrugged.

"Might I suggest we retreat from this university before we discuss the details of Cade's escape?" Moselle interjected.

"Huzzah, Miss Moselle," Cade cheered, fastening his seatbelt.

Before he put the car in gear, Jackson asked the question most on his mind. "This is a school shooting. The police have the exits blocked. How the hell are we just going to leave?"

"Simmer down. That's easy, my friend," Cade said, unfastening the seatbelt he'd just done. "Let's all switch seats for a moment."

Cade pulled the car up to the barricade at a snail's pace and rolled down his window. The policeman, a man in his late fifties, walked over to the car cautiously, flashlight up and pointed directly at Cade.

"Good evening, Officer."

"How may I help you, son?"

"My girlfriend is in the midst of a serious panic attack; she's terrified. I was hoping to take her home."

"Sorry, no one leaves campus for the time being. Pull over and wait," the policeman commanded.

Sabrina sobbed louder, a performance she would, no doubt, expect accolades for later.

"As you can plainly see, she is very upset," Cade explained, as he positioned himself to best make eye contact with the policeman past the bright beam of his flashlight.

"Wait, aren't you that girl... Sabrina London?" the cop asked when the beam of his flashlight illuminated her.

"Officer, look at me. You don't see Sabrina London; you see a very upset young lady. You feel deep remorse for her and want us to leave. We are harmless."

"Get her home and get some rest," the policeman ordered.

"Thank you kindly, Officer."

Cade drove the H2 carefully around the barricade and then sped away from the college. Once the university had faded from the rearview mirror, Cade slowed to just below the speed limit. Sabrina's faux tears turned to laughter as she yanked the jacket off and tossed it out the window.

"How do you do that?" Jackson asked from the passenger seat, where he stared totally enthralled.

"Fuck all that!" Sabrina spoke before Cade could answer. "What happened back on campus with Kintner?"

"I wouldn't believe it myself had I not seen it with my own two eyes."

"What transpired, Cade?" Moselle prompted.

"The windigos came to kill Kintner."

"What?" Sabrina smacked Cade's arm in disbelief.

"Praise *Menhit* they were successful in their ploy." Moselle bowed her head as she spoke.

"Did they kill him?" Sabrina asked more clearly than Moselle had.

"Not even close. Kintner was way too powerful for them. I think he killed two, almost three, of the four beasts."

"Moselle, what the hell is a windigo?" Jackson sounded more confused than ever.

Moselle held her finger to her lips, so she could listen to the rest of Cade's story.

"Kintner may have escaped tonight, but he did so under the false pretense that the battle's won." Cade's grin grew. "No, he's tired—wounded and I don't even have to track his blood to find him."

"What are you talking about?"

"Thanks to the windigo, I know exactly where that Yankee will go to tend to his wounds... his home."

Chapter Twenty-Seven

Knowledge is Power

After Cade put a good mile between them and the university, he pulled over so Jackson could drive and he could further detail his encounter with the shape-shifter.

The monster that attacked Kintner had shared an abundance of information, much of which sounded like the plot of a science fiction movie to Jackson. He listened as carefully as he could, but his attention kept flagging. All of it sounded crazy, and while there were bigger things to be concerned with, there was something the vampire said when he parked the car, which seemed to punctuate all the madness, and repeated in Jackson's head. Cade had nonchalantly stated how much he hated driving cars, that they scared him ever since the time when he crashed a Model T by rolling it down a steep hill. It did not make any sense to Jackson. Cade, was a seemingly ageless monster: intelligent, and immensely powerful, yet he was scared of cars...

It all left Jackson with a surreal sensation. He felt like he was swirling down a drain and the only way to stop the sinking momentum was to gain some measure of clarity: starting with the difference between werewolves and windigos.

"Werewolves have existed since the dark ages of Europe," Cade briefly explained, Sabrina nodding in agreement. "Their kind began when a powerful witch cursed a man to transform into a wolf once a month at the full moon."

"Humans do not know this, but the Reverend Sabine Baring-Gould was fairy-kind."

"Who?"

"He wrote *The Book of Were-Wolves*, another bit of prose Sabrina likes to point out as being created by her people," Moselle cut in.

"It was!"

"So, what is a windigo then?" Jackson asked again.

"Windigos are men who are cursed forever with a cannibalistic spirit," Cade explained. "This normally occurs when a man consumes human flesh through an act of desperation or depravity. From that day forward, he no longer ages, but has to turn into a bear-shaped creature to eat and survive. You know, to be totally honest, I have never heard of them traveling in groups. To see four of them together like that was terrifying."

"Eat people?" Jackson's face was horror-struck.

"My people's account say the first windigo came into existence when the Aztec gods cursed a priest who was slaughtering children and—"

Jackson did not want to hear the rest. "So, both werewolves and windigo are evil?" he interrupted.

"Good, evil, really, Jackson, there is no black and white anymore, only shades of grey." Moselle sighed, and then returned to filing her nails.

Jackson suddenly had a powerful realization. "It's like 10:00. Is anyone other than me really hungry?"

"I ate back at the college," Cade joked.

"Can we stop for a burger or something? Are you hungry, Moselle?"

"Ha! She doesn't eat. Duh!" Sabrina replied sarcastically.

Before Jackson answered, he ran through his interactions with Moselle over the past few months.

"Wait a minute, you brought me fruit and bagels at work the other week. I saw you eat some grapes."

Moselle reached over and patted his leg. "Most people think my lack of eating is due to a strict diet for modeling, but the truth is, I do not eat because my body does not require such nutrition and would not process the food anyway."

"At the club, you had food on your plate," he said with certainty.

"I have become very good at sleight of hand. You would be surprised how much food a napkin can hold."

Jackson shook his head in disbelief. "What, you don't eat because you're... dead?"

"Undead."

"But I see you drinking water all the time."

"Our bodies can absorb fluids, just like yours. In fact, I require lots of fluids to stay hydrated," Moselle explained.

"And you?" Jackson turned his head to look at Cade when he could not find him in the rearview mirror.

"I only consume blood... and gin on occasion."

"Okay." Putting all this new information together, Jackson nodded. "Let me guess, all fairy-kind are vegetarians?"

"Hell no! I eat meat. Lots of it."

"That's the best news I've heard all day. So, wanna get a burger and fries with me, Sabrina? My treat."

"I would love to."

"Cade," Moselle interrupted. "Could you tell us more about the windigo?"

"Yes. As it turns out, this guy, Thrasher, he's the leader of a gang of windigos that have been sabotaging Kintner's company for some time. They want to kill him but have never been able to get close to the man—well, not until tonight, and as I said, Kintner was too strong an opponent for them. Thrasher, the poor bastard, he was gravely wounded in the fight, not allowed a proper death on the battlefield," Cade shook his head. "He failed, and with no other option fled to the roof."

"Kintner had powers? What did Thrasher say about this?" Moselle's voice cracked as she asked.

"He believes Alexander Kintner is some sort of powerful, ageless shaman."

"Did he know whether Mira was still alive?" Sabrina asked.

"He didn't know anything about Mira, but he did say that the drug Kintner created has an otherworldly main ingredient: crushed fairy wings."

"Gods no!" The reality flattened Sabrina.

"I'm afraid so." Cade nodded. "You're the seasoning in his stew, sweetheart."

"Jesus man, ease up!" Jackson interjected, knowing Sabrina must have been terrified by the thought.

"Worst of all, that drug won't even cure nicotine addiction. It's just being used to control the minds of its users. Once consumed, the user's mind bends to Kintner's commands like a beaten slave… and we all know slavery is illegal."

"At the very least this explains your assailants, Sabrina," Moselle surmised.

"How can all this be happening?" Sabrina asked. "Doesn't the Otherworldly Assembly have agents whose sole purpose is to prevent things like this from happening?"

No one had an answer. Or one they wanted to hastily share.

Chapter Twenty-Eight

Lines Crossed Cannot be Uncrossed

Sabrina's question brought up an interesting point. The legends of the otherworldly warriors who policed human affairs any time a human stepped out of bounds were well-known to Cade. Although Cade's un-life had been a little longer than Moselle's, he was sure she at least knew the story of the most famous human who'd crossed the barrier into the otherworldly realm; his name was Adolf Hitler.

With the aid of Nazi occultists, Hitler had discovered many of the otherworldlies' secrets; however, it was not until April 1945 that the man the world had learned to hate above all others captured one. Although the stories never disclosed what species of otherworldly was in the Nazi leader's clutches, it had long been rumored to be an air spirit because of the term Hitler used during one of his speeches to the homeland: *Gefallenen Engel,* fallen angel.

Cade recalled these days better than Moselle, because he had assumed the identity of an American paratrooper during later stages of WWII and fought in the Battle of the Bulge. Drawn to conflict like moths to flame, thousands of vampires roamed the European Theater of Operation, yet he was one of the few that took up arms for the allied forces.

In the final days of April 1945, Cade encountered two of his brethren as they fled the German countryside. The vampires, both older than himself, gave him a warning: the wraiths were coming to Germany. He had heard scant tales of such creatures. Never once had he paid the legends mind. Until that day, at that moment, when he feared the wraiths were coming to Germany for him.

Now Cade knew much more. The wraiths were once elementals, or so say the elders who dare tell their story. Sacrificed by the Mayans to ensure prosperity, it was the otherworldly gods who answered their slaughter. The elemental's souls who were sacrificed were deemed desecrated and not permitted passage to the next world. Enraged, the souls twisted into what they were now, ghost-like, malevolent to their core, their thirst for vengeance forever unquenched.

It took many generations, but a way to direct the wraiths fury was finally found, and now, anyone, human or otherworldly, who breaks the rules or wrongs the Otherworldly Assembly faces their weapons-three unstoppable bloodthirsty souls.

Cade would never forget the day he read the headline of *The Illustrated London News* while sitting in a café the night of May 3, 1945: "**HITLER DEAD.**" The news had reached him the day before: Hitler didn't commit suicide; the wraiths had found and destroyed him.

Chapter Twenty-Nine

Father

Across the small parking lot, not far from the entrance to the restaurant they had stopped at, Moselle stood with her arms crossed. She took no pleasure in the way Jackson joked around with Sabrina so casually—not when he should have been at her side. *Look at him, so human. Sitting at a picnic table, enjoying a meal—it must be so nice to be normal. Not a care in the world. He has no idea.*

"Would you pass me that ketchup packet, Lady Sabrina?" Jackson asked in a faux English accent.

"Gladly, Lord Jackson," Sabrina replied in kind.

Cade had asked Moselle to join him for a moment out of Sabrina's and Jackson's earshot, who were busy anyway, putting on an act as if they were the king and queen of England outside the tiny, roadside burger joint. Although distracted by her boyfriend's behavior, Moselle knew what was on Cade's mind before he even spoke it.

"Your concern is painted clearly across your face. You're worried about the wraiths."

"Aren't you?"

"I am now."

"She's too young to realize the danger we're all in." Cade nodded in Sabrina's direction.

"Then the rumors are true…" After a cleansing exhale, Moselle continued. "When the wraiths are dispatched by the Assembly to deal with an issue, they not only destroy their target, but any otherworldlies who have come in contact with it."

"Not just otherworldlies, Moselle. It would be a clean sweep. No witnesses." Cade pointed to Jackson. "So, him too."

Moselle did not need Cade to tell her; she knew Jackson was in jeopardy as well.

"What of my parents?"

"Well, there was a guy I knew in Canada, he and his clan lived in a tiny town way up north. So, one night his sire was caught feeding on a live television broadcast. It was a weather report, and my friend's sire was way off in the background. Most people would not have even known what was going on. It looked like a romantic moment being shared between two consenting adults. But to the trained eye, the eye of any other vampire, the truth was obvious. My friend's sire had enemies, and those enemies tipped off the Assembly. Moselle, the wraiths destroyed them all." His story was as chilling to tell as it was to hear.

"What do you mean 'them all'?"

"Being connected as we vampires are, the wraiths killed the sire and his whole lineage, including my friend. Thirty-five vampires in total. Hell, I heard the wraiths even killed the clueless weatherman."

Moselle's mind was wiped clear by Cade's story and filled with pure dread.

"We have to do something, Cade. What do we do?"

"I reckon we rush to Kintner's, rescue Mira, and set us an old-fashioned, Confederate-style ambush." Cade motioned as if he was holding a rifle to his shoulder, firing off a shot.

"Kill him before the Assembly gets wind of this disaster?"

"Indeed."

Moselle's memory was poor and dependent upon visuals to spark the largest part of her recollection; a result of having most of her brain matter removed through her nose during the mummification process, she hated to admit. At home, Moselle kept a series of detailed diaries in which she recorded all her most important daily events. When a memory eluded her, she referred to them—that was not a luxury she had at the moment.

There was something important, she needed to remember now, but couldn't seem to dredge up. Watching Jackson, as Sabrina dangled a French fry over his mouth, kept Moselle's thoughts solely on him and the idea that he might be killed if the Assembly sent in the wraiths. Moselle couldn't allow that —Jackson was innocent.

The ring of another customer's cell phone suddenly ignited her memory. *Phone... phone... phone...* "Sabrina!" Moselle ran to her side. "Sabrina, did you call your father?"

"Huh?"

"Did you call your father? Did you? I must know!" she demanded as she shook Sabrina by the shoulders.

"Fuck, Moselle! Stop shaking me!" Sabrina yelled, trying to swat her friend's hands away.

"Did you call your father, yes or no?"

"I did, okay, chill."

"Wait, you called your father, Sabrina?" Cade asked as he walked up to the group.

"Yes, after the attack at Moselle's."

"Am I right to assume your father is still a ranking member of the Assembly?" Cade put his hand on her shoulder so she would turn to look at him.

"By the gods, Sabrina, what did you tell him?"

Sabrina stood up suddenly, waved her arms with anger, and snapped, "What the hell, can't I just eat in peace? Mira's gone and some madman wants my wings. I'm doing my best to hold my shit together, okay? I need a break!"

Jackson forcefully swallowed his mouthful of cheeseburger. "Moselle, what's going on?"

"Sabrina, my sweet sunshine, just inform us, please, what did you tell your father?"

"Nothing, okay? I left him a message to call me back and the bastard hasn't even bothered to return my call," Sabrina yelled, drawing even more attention. "He doesn't give a fuck about me anymore, okay? Happy?"

Her face covered; Sabrina ran to the car in tears.

"What just happened?" Jackson whispered.

"Sabrina has paternal issues. I will go speak with her."

"I'll go too."

Cade walked with Moselle to the passenger side of the car. Sabrina had crawled in the back and pushed herself into the corner behind the driver's seat. Head low, Sabrina sobbed, harder than she had in months.

Moselle and Cade stood a moment in silence. Moselle had felt great sadness in her un-life but seldom found a way to release or express it physically. For the Cursed Undead it bottled up inside, but that was not the way of the Vampire Nation. Moselle had known Cade long enough to recognize he responded to woe and depression the same way he did anger, with expending the energy, often resulting in violence. It was that Sabrina expressed her emotions so differently from Cade and Moselle that made bearing witness to her crying so captivating. For the undead, the memories of their own tears were like long lost dreams.

"Sabrina, my dear, please. We did not mean to offend you with our persistence."

"Darling, we are just worried that the Assembly may become negatively involved in this affair."

"Well, don't worry about it! All I asked him to do was call me, and he couldn't even do that!" Sabrina cried.

"Why does he refuse to speak to you?"

"You, Cade!" Sabrina spit, her eyes pink.

"Me?"

"Your fucking camera. Damn it! You have no idea the damage it did. That video had things on it my father never should have seen! Never should have heard!"

"I highly doubt that your father is so naïve, Sabrina, to believe that you were still a virgin."

"*No, Cade*, he knew I wasn't, but I guess he'd thought I'd be having sex with someone, something, a little less dead, you know?" Sabrina sighed loudly, eyes on the clear night sky through the sunroof. "The gods make it so damn easy for vampires; they can fuck whatever moves and there are no repercussions, none at all!"

With a step back, Cade spoke under his breath. "The damn Quakers where less uptight about sex than you fairy."

"Fairy-kind and vampires *are* mortal enemies." Moselle stated.

"How do you think he felt when he watched his little girl fuck a vampire? A vampire, Cade, the very thing he raised his daughter to fear and loathe?" Sabrina grumbled. "Not to mention—"

"Fine, but he's also a member of the Otherworldly Assembly, so he deals with vamps all the time."

Sabrina stomped her feet, slammed her hands on the seats and screamed. "My father is one of the fucking elemental kings!"

This information was something she had no doubt sworn never to reveal to anyone outside the fairy race. A taste like vinegar filled Moselle's mouth; she wanted to speak but all she could do was stand there in disbelief until Sabrina finished.

"His own daughter disgraced him in front of the whole world when she committed a crime side by side with her vampire lover—embarrassed him in front of the entire Otherworldly Assembly. He told me my life was over a year ago, so I tried to kill myself."

Jackson, who had respectfully kept his distance until then, finally joined the others at the car.

"I had no clue your father was a king," Cade admitted.

"Nor did I." Moselle wondered why her friend never told her.

"Wait, did she say her father was a king? Doesn't that make her a princess—" Jackson began.

"Don't say that!" Sabrina kicked the seat in front of her. "I hate that stupid word!"

"My deepest apologies, Sabrina. I truly had no idea." Cade took her hand in his.

Moselle watched Cade's cold hands gently squeeze Sabrina's thin fingers and listened to him apologize again and again. He repeated what he told her the night they dug him up, how he wanted the video for a memento, but now understood it was wrong, and agreed he should have erased the digital video the moment they reached her car that night. In this dire moment, he had put aside his selfishness, and was saying-doing whatever was needed to calm Sabrina down.

Cade got into the car with Sabrina, wiped the smeared mascara from under her eyes, and brushed her hair to the side so he could kiss her forehead. Moselle suddenly felt like a third wheel, so she led Jackson away from the car.

"So many years passed as friends, and I knew not that her family was royalty," she whispered to Jackson as they walked.

"So, her father is what? The king of all fairies?" Jackson asked as he sat down on a bench.

"Not the only king, one of the four. The fairy-kind rule over the elemental world—a vast kingdom."

"Earth, air, water, and fire?" Jackson guessed.

"Precisely, my love." Moselle sat on his lap.

"Which one does her father rule?"

"A week ago, I would not have been able to wager such a guess, but having met Mira, I would safely bet the kingdom of water."

"It must be hard for her to live with such guilt. This explains why she nearly jumped off her roof a year ago." Jackson realized something as he spoke. "Wait, if she can fly... was that really an attempt to kill herself?"

"Yes, Jackson." Moselle's voice dropped. "For a fairy to jump to their death; it is quite a statement."

"Wow."

"Yes. I now know, sans any doubt, that Sabrina is mentally and emotionally much stronger than I." Moselle stared across the parking lot, wondering what was being said inside the car. "I would have collapsed under such pressure by now."

Inside Moselle's car, Cade wrapped his arms around Sabrina and held her tight. Neither spoke. Sabrina's tears had dried, and she'd calmed down a bit. She knew Cade cared about her, and she felt his love, but it was not his amorous aura that made her shiver; it was the chill of Cade's flesh against hers. Cade's body held no heat. *Why would it?* she thought. *He's dead.*

Since all this chaos had started, Sabrina had craved the warm touch of another living being, but it seemed that, in her life, she was destined to be surrounded by individuals whose bodies felt like ice against hers. Thinking back to the last time she felt this way, she recalled a bender and an Irish pretty-boy actor who, to this day, still e-mailed her.

She had not thought of returning to those days in some time—not since Mira had helped her overcome so many of her vices. Her best friend had become a crutch, and without that support, she wanted to fall back on old habits.

"I could totally use some whiskey and a cigarette." She chuckled. "Maybe some blow."

"Would that help you feel better, my sweet sunshine?" Cade asked, gazing into her pained eyes.

"Everything is all fucked up, Cade. I need to get away... Yeah, I think it might help."

"Anything else?"

Face in her palms, she whispered, "Mira. I need Mira."

Chapter Thirty

Breaking and Entering

An hour had passed since they had left the college campus—it was thirty minutes longer than Cade would have liked to spend when time was of the essence. After he explained to the group that they may still have time to reach Kintner's home before him, since his car was disabled and the college was sealed, the group agreed to start on toward San Bernardino. While they sped down the highway, Cade went on to explain that after Mira was safe, he would stay behind at Kintner's to catch him unaware and kill him. In the end, he decided not to mention what he had discussed with Moselle about the wraiths. There was no reason to upset Sabrina more, and Jackson wouldn't understand anyway. *The human*, Cade thought, *to be extra safe, it's for the best that he does not learn any more about the Otherworldly Assembly until after this disaster is averted.*

On the outskirts of town, in a neighborhood Jackson would have considered bad—if he felt it was a strong enough word—Cade tapped his shoulder. Startled, Jackson turned to look, and was greeted by a sly, toothy smirk that raised Cade's already high cheekbones.

"What?"

"Pull over." Cade pointed to the side of the road.

"Here?"

"You'll be fine. I only smell humans around." Cade nodded to the side of the road.

"Only humans, yeah, that's settling."

"I saw a gun shop one block back. Let me off here and then meet me out front of the shop in five minutes."

"Gun shop?" Jackson repeated, slowing the vehicle down.

"I need a weapon, and I suggest you all get a change of clothes there."

The moment they came to a stop, Cade jumped out and disappeared into a dark alley. Jackson would have sworn the vampire didn't make a sound when his feet hit the pavement, but he could not be sure over the hum of the engine. Nevertheless, he found it creepy.

Moselle's nose twitched, a precursor to a sour look spreading across her face. She had told Jackson before how much she hated the big cities: their litter, smog, and other unidentifiable filth. It all left a scent in her nose that made her want to gag. Jackson understood; it did stink out.

"I'll shut the windows."

"Yes, do that, while I prepare a solution."

Moselle rummaged through her handbag until she found a small hand-knit pouch.

"Incense," she announced as she poured the tiny flakes into the car's cup holder.

Fascinated by what she was doing, Jackson watched Moselle, as she pressed the car lighter and held it to the dried leaves and herbs after it popped out, heated. In a matter of seconds, the lighter burnt the incense, which created a tiny plume of orange smoke that filled the front seat of the car with a pleasant aroma.

"If you two are done," Sabrina grumbled, "we really should go meet Cade."

When Jackson pulled into the empty, four-car parking lot of the gun shop, Cade slunk out from the shadows of the back alley alongside the building.

"You know this place is closed, right?" Jackson pointed at the sign in the barred window.

"What do you think?" Sabrina bounced from the car to Cade. "Get some?"

"Of course."

"Wait, we're breaking in?" Jackson looked around to see if anyone was close enough to hear him.

"Not at all. The back door was open when I checked it." Cade laughed. "Let's make haste."

At the back entry, a reinforced-steel fire door hung from its hinges as if it had been blown open with dynamite. The damage to the door was all the proof Jackson needed to finally accept that Cade was a lot stronger than he looked. It also helped ease his concern; Jackson felt much more confident that they would defeat Kintner now... whatever *he* was.

Once everyone was inside, Cade pulled the damaged door shut and latched it. An emergency light gave the store a dull amber wash; it was almost impossible to see more than a few feet. Jackson followed Cade, who marched through the store like he owned the place, and when the vampire approached the gun cases, he looked like a kid in a candy store.

"I need to find a pistol and a rifle. While I look for those, can you get find me a bowie knife, Jackson?"

"You know, something bothers me about the way you say my name, Cade."

"Oh, really? You got a nickname?" Cade asked, his eyes still glued to the pistols in the case.

"Stonewall, but you can just call me Jacks."

"Hold your horses." Cade lifted his gaze slowly from the gun case and planted it on Jackson where he stood not three feet away. "Did you say 'Stonewall'? As in Stonewall Jackson?"

"Yeah. My teammates gave me the nickname in college."

"I *knew* Stonewall Jackson. For a time, I served under the man. He was a brilliant strategist. I have honored his birthday each year like he was my father," Cade revealed.

"You knew him?"

"Yes, and *you* are not him."

The vampire shook his head with distaste as he returned his gaze to the pistols in the case. Even though he was silent, Jackson could tell that Cade was still mulling over his remark, and quickly found he agreed; his days of being called Stonewall were long since passed.

"Yuck, this place stinks of cigars." Sabrina crinkled her nose. "I need to pee. Is there a bathroom here?"

"Far wall." Cade pointed to the end of the shop, where a corner was swallowed by shadows.

"Way over there?" Sabrina timidly replied. "Hey, big guy, can you come with me and stand outside the bathroom? I don't want to go alone."

"Yeah, big guy, go pee with the girls," Cade teased.

"Real funny."

"Jackson, be a dear and go with her, will you? I will procure Cade's blade."

"Fine, you guys rob the gun store; I'll just stand guard while Sabrina London pees," Jackson grounded out.

"Look, men, there is Jackson, standing guard outside the girl's potty like a stone wall." Cade chuckled loudly.

"Fuck this," Jackson said, walking off, wondering how hard he would have to punch Cade in the face to break his undead nose.

The aisles were packed with merchandise, some covered in dust. Jackson spotted a rack of green and brown camouflage clothing as he traveled down one long aisle toward the side of the store the bathroom was on, so he pointed at them and asked Sabrina what size she was. He snatched up a pair of boys' small pants and a men's small shirt and waited outside the bathroom. With no desire to listen to the socialite piss, he tried to focus on Moselle's voice as it floated to him in the darkness. She was asking Cade a lot of questions, but the gloom of the store swallowed the details, just like the ambient glow of the emergency light.

"Hey, Stonewall?" Sabrina called through the bathroom door.

Jackson hung his head and sighed; he wished he'd never mentioned his nickname. "Yeah?"

"Can I ask you a question?"

"Sure thing."

"What's having sex with Moselle like?"

"Yeah, okay, was not expecting that. We've only had sex a few times, but it's great... I rock, of course."

"Naturally," she giggled. "I mean what's she *feel* like?"

"Feel like..." He paused to think how to answer.

"Her skin?"

"Oh, it's soft and—"

"Cold?"

"Yeah, I have noticed she *is* kinda cold," he answered over the flushing of the toilet.

"She's cold because there's no blood circulating in her veins. She's not like us."

"Because she's undead," Jackson calculated. "Is Cade cold too?"

"Cade's skin feels like ice against mine. It's something that's hard not to notice, like when you dip your toe in a pool and the water is so cold it sends a chill all the way up your spine," Sabrina continued through the bathroom door.

"I guess I'm used to the cold. I used to play hockey."

"Lucky you." Sabrina's voice wavered. "I hate it. Everyone I choose to love has a chill to their touch. Mira, for example. I mean, she looks human and all, but she's made entirely of water, cold... cold water."

"Really? When we save her, I can't wait to see what she really looks like."

"She can take on many forms, human or otherworldly, thanks to ancient fairy magic, but no matter who or what she looks like, she's still cold when you lie next to her. You're not cold too, are you, Jackson?"

"Not at all. I've been told I seem to run at a temperature higher than most. Some girls even call me hot." He smirked at his own pun.

"Do you have that change of clothes for me?"

"Sure do."

When he answered her, a sudden flash of light emerged from the cracks of the bathroom door.

"Come in, but do it quick; my wings are out and I don't want to light up the whole damn store, okay?"

Jackson opened the door and stepped in as fast as he could. Hand up, he recoiled with discomfort, his vision washed away to white. Like a prolonged glance at the sun, a pulsating glow was all that filled his view until slowly the outline of Sabrina sitting on the closed toilet seat appeared.

"Can you see me?"

"Kinda. Man, your wings are bright."

As Jackson's eyes further adjusted to the glare of Sabrina's wispy wings, he noticed she sat in a state of near undress on her folded jogging suit.

"Can you see now?" Sabrina unwrapped the arm that covered her breasts and bared them fully for him.

"Totally."

Resting there in her tiny panties, topless, with her wings aflutter behind her, Sabrina was a sight too attractive to look away from.

"This is what I am, Jackson."

"You are much more beautiful than I ever imagined. Just... incredible."

"I am fairy-kind, a child of the sun, born into the soft caress of the daylight, yet seemingly cursed to live in the chill of night."

"Sabrina, are you all right?" Jackson unglued his eyes from her breasts a moment. "What's that white stuff on your face?"

She slowly brushed the fine white powder off her upper lip and nose, then rubbed what remained on her fingertips across her gums. Jackson may not have done drugs before, but that did not mean he had not seen them used—he was certain of it, Sabrina was sniffing cocaine.

"Do you like my boobs? You can touch them if you want." Sabrina ran her finger back and forth between her breasts.

Although much smaller than Moselle's, Sabrina's breasts were flawless, a perfect handful, as Jackson would have described them. He cupped her breast and squeezed it tenderly. It was soft, yet firm, like the rest of her body appeared. Lost in the moment, Jackson pinched her nipple until she released a soft moan.

"Your hand is so warm," Sabrina sighed. "Oh, the things I could do for you, big guy, things you could never imagine."

"Are you sure you're all right?" Jackson inquired as he slowly removed his hand from her body.

"I would be much better if you held me. Would you do that? Would you share your warmth with me?"

When Jackson stepped a bit closer, Sabrina grabbed his groin with an authoritative hand and then looked up into his squinted eyes.

"Is this what I felt in the car earlier?" She gave him a little squeeze.

"Yes."

"Are you thinking about fucking me right now? Is that what made you all—?"

"Yes."

Without another word spoken, Sabrina turned around, pushed her thong to the side, and bent over. Her hands gripped the cistern of the cold porcelain toilet as she lifted her wings to the ceiling and spread her legs.

The scent of wildflowers—buttercups, daisies, and tulips—filled his nose while sparkles of light shed off Sabrina's wings and floated through the air in the tiny bathroom like flurries of snow. He watched in awe as the little embers dissolved into his skin—it all felt like a dream.

"How often do you get a chance to fuck a horny fairy, Jackson?"

Jackson unbuckled his belt, but before he could free himself from the confines of his pants, a knock on the bathroom door startled him.

"Jackson, Sabrina?" Moselle called out.

Panic stole the voice from his chest.

"Just give me a few minutes, Moselle. I just need a few minutes," Sabrina replied in haste, clearly frustrated.

"Where is Jackson?"

"I don't know, somewhere I guess."

When Moselle opened the door, Jackson felt like his heart would explode. He stood to the side, looked away from Sabrina, and carefully positioned his hands over his crotch. Although Sabrina had stood up fully, her back was still to him and the door. There was no doubt in his mind that Moselle had a perfect view of Sabrina's misaligned panties.

"Shit!" Sabrina growled as she fixed herself. "Shut the door, for fuck sake."

Moselle joined Jackson and Sabrina in the tiny room, not a second wasted before she snatched her friend by the wrist and spun her around so they were face to face. Ashamed, Jackson stole a glimpse at Moselle before he returned his gaze to the floor. To his surprise, her face didn't show even a hint of anger, only disappointment.

"Sabrina, I know you are going through a molting stage and I know what happens when this occurs, but I have not given you permission to use my lover in such a manner."

"You know what? You have no idea what I feel." Sabrina thumbed her own chest aggressively as she spoke. "I'm in agony."

"And you thought I would be okay with this?"

"I. Don't. Care!" Sabrina yelled.

Jackson had no idea what was happening; all he knew was that he had messed up and all he could do now was apologize.

"Moselle, I'm sorry, I—"

"Jackson, darling, you have no fault in this matter. Please just leave us."

"I'll be outside if you need me," he said, and hastily made his exit.

―――― ∽ ――――

Once Jackson left the jam-packed bathroom, Moselle's keen nose caught a new scent: one masked by the abundant pheromones Sabrina exuded.

"What have you insufflated?"

"What?"

"I can smell the coca leaves on your skin. Do you have any idea the effects of such a drug on your molting?"

"For fuck sake, Moss, I just don't care anymore. My life is a wreck, and now my wings need to shed. I mean what the hell's next, my period?"

"Drugs are not the answer, Sabrina."

"Oh, stop. You sound like my mother."

"Will you be able to complete even one half of the Negative Confessions?" Moselle asked. "'Not have I polluted myself,'" she recited.

"Moselle, really, I'm sick of your Doctrine of Ma'at. It doesn't apply to my people."

After a moment to regain her composure, Moselle tucked a loose strand of hair behind her ear. Sabrina held her ground, standing strong with hands on hips, bare chest before her friend. Although Sabrina had pointed out Moselle was not her mother, Sabrina acted like an aggressive, rebellious teenager.

"Can't Cade help?"

"I need sun! Warmth! Body heat at least, Moss. You and Cade have none, remember?"

Moselle raised her hand to her face. "Well, what have you done in the past?"

"A number of things and people. You know this. You've seen me molt before. Remember the Maroon 5 concert that one winter?"

Sabrina grabbed the clothes Jackson had brought her and dressed in a hurry. With just the pants on, Sabrina amped up the glow of her wings. Moselle understood what she was doing, this was a *fuck off* statement from her friend.

The door to the medicine cabinet above the sink thrown open, Sabrina discovered an open pack of cigarettes with a single stick spilled out. She snatched one and placed it in her mouth then pulsed up her wings, igniting the tip.

Sabrina puffed away on her cigarette like a spoiled brat. Moselle covered her eyes a moment; she wanted to reprimand her friend but had grown tired of it all.

"I want to help you, Sabrina, but you're making it hard."

"You know what, Moselle? I don't need your help."

Chapter Thirty-One

Newborn

Cade crossed the store toward Jackson as he exited the bathroom. Slung over his arm was a small backpack containing everything he needed to rescue Mira and take down Kintner. Cade could tell something was wrong by the look on Jackson's face and since he felt slightly bad for the joke he'd made earlier, he asked, "What troubles you, Jacks?"

"This... this is all crazy."

"Oh, I see. Reality has finally started to overwhelm you? Don't worry, friend. Better humans than you have buckled under the pressure of knowledge of the otherworldly realm," Cade said as he patted Jackson's shoulder. "President Regan for example, they called it Alzheimer's, but I believe he could not cope with finding out Gorbachev was a—"

Jackson interrupted, "What the hell am I doing here? We're robbing a store and—"

"What else?" Cade's nose tickled when he caught the scent of Sabrina's pheromones. "Hey, if that smell is what I think it is, Sabrina just dosed you with a ton of fairy dust. Whatever just happened in there is not your fault."

"The girls are fighting..." Jackson began. "Did you say fairy dust?"

"Jacks, you should know, the fairy-kind have many natural defenses, one of which is the release of a pheromone that can sway a human's mind."

"All the weird thoughts, the ones I've been having about Sabrina?"

"Not your fault. Hey, by the smell you're giving off, Sabrina must be ready to shed her wings."

"Shed her... yeah, I'm not sure I want to know."

Cade laughed out loud and squeezed Jackson's shoulder. Cade understood how he felt; there had been a time not so long ago when this world was new to him too.

The breeze had significantly cooled. Cade was pinned underneath something heavy, most likely other dead or dying soldiers. He thought death would have been swifter. He had seen many men die, many of them he had killed himself, and always it seemed that death was abrupt. One moment a mind full of ambitions, the next a chest full of hot lead. *Perhaps,* he considered, *I am being punished by God for all the killing I have done.*

The weight on his body seemed to shift to his lap and chest. He tried to open his eyes, but all that welcomed him was blackness. He prayed that this was the end, that he would finally fade away, but as time passed, he did not. What little sensation he had left was suddenly jolted by a taste of something strong. A substance as thick as the sweet, Virginia maple syrup his mother used to pour on his pancakes as a young boy filled his mouth. Try as he might to cough or turn his head, he could not. As the thick fluid poured down his throat, he gagged from its saltiness; it was blood—lukewarm, gooey blood.

His mind burned as he ingested it. Cade had seen corpse piles before. Blood had a way of trickling from the top bodies all the way down; its thickness painted those on the bottom pure red. The men in the Confederate Army called those unlucky individuals "Blood Devils," often remarking on their inhuman, ghastly features. Now, as best he could figure, he was one of them, a body at the bottom of a pile.

Again, he questioned why he was not dead yet and came to one simple conclusion. Perhaps, Cade thought, he was not dying after all; maybe he had recovered to some extent. The fear of death no longer filled his heart and was replaced by the terror of staying alive.

Self-preservation told him all he had to do was free himself from the tomb of bodies; afterward, he would be alive and well again. He tested his inert limbs. When he tried to move his leg, his foot wiggled. A sudden burst of strength, unlike any he had ever felt, fueled his muscles, reminding him of their purpose.

As the weight on his chest lessened, Cade tried to move his right arm. Hand clenched to the ground, he felt the dirt push under his fingernails. There was room to wiggle his fingers, roll his wrist, bend his elbow, but the realization that his arm was free only came the moment he lifted it several inches from the ground. *Good God*, he thought, *I can move!*

Cade shoved himself to his feet with a scream and a swing of his arms—this potency that filled his body was a godsend. There were no obstacles in his path. *What happened? Where did the bodies go?*

When Cade's eyes finally peeled open, he was greeted with a sight he never expected; a woman so beautiful she could have been an angel stood before him. Braced against the blistery winds, the woman's pale blue dress outlined her thin frame when a strong gust sealed it to her body.

"Am I dead?" Cade spit blood from his mouth.

"'Bout bloody time!" a man's deep voice emerged from the shadows, coated with a British accent.

The woman raised her finger to her lips, but Cade only saw her three-inch-long manicured fingernails. Bewildered, he stared at the woman; in time, he realized that her lovely blue dress was covered with trails of blood. *Is she hurt? No, but how do I know this?*

His concentration broke when the angelic woman spoke, her language one he had never heard before. Although aggressive in nature, the words seemed to be a request for help.

"Ye don't speak Russian, do ye? Well, it be good thing for all that I do!" the hidden man said.

"What happened to me?" Cade called out to the dark, where the male voice came from.

"Shot and left to die, like so many others."

"I was in a corpse pile."

"Aye, ye were, but not for long. Shortly after dusk, Dunyasha pulled your sorry hide out from the bottom."

"She pulled me out from under a corpse pile? Impossible."

"Do yerself a favor bloke: never underestimate that lady there."

Cade's eyes searched around, finding only unfamiliar surroundings. When suspicion took the place of confusion, he reached for his gun.

"Where is my sidearm?"

"Same place yer boots went I'd wager," the odd man laughed.

Cade had not realized until then, but his feet were bare. If it were true that he was left for dead, then he must have been looted.

"Damn filthy Yankees!"

The Russian woman stepped closer to Cade, her movements like those of a large spider: pronounced, yet with total certainty. When she spoke, Cade noticed she repeated what she had said the first time.

"She's saying that she saved yer life for one reason and one reason alone. The lady needs yer aid, friend."

"What could you possibly need me for? Who are you two? Are you working for the North? Have you taken me prisoner?"

"Prisoner?" The man chuckled. "Never thought of it like that," he said almost to himself.

"What?" Cade slyly looked around for something he could use as a weapon if need be.

"Dunyasha is simply calling for aid against a common foe."

"Then you are Confederates?"

"No, no, no, my new brother..."

The man finally stepped out of the blue, night shadows. He wore a thick, hooded rider's cloak covered in dust and dirt. When he reached Cade, he pulled back the hood to reveal his features. His face was hideously scarred on one side, the clear sign of a man who had been nearly burnt to death. Witness to such wounds before, Cade did not recoil at the sight, but what the man did next sent a chill down his spine.

With what sounded like a hiss, the odd man opened his mouth and revealed a set of long, sharp fangs.

"Not Union. Not Confederates. Not human. No, we be vampires."

"Get away from me, demon!"

Cade shoved the man hard to the ground. Stunned by his own strength, he paused a moment to measure the distance in his mind; it must have been at least twelve feet from where the man had just stood to where he just landed. Cade turned. There was no better time to escape, but before he could flee, the Russian woman blocked his way.

"How the hell?" Startled by her speed he raised his hands in defense.

"Cade Robert Lawton," she announced with a seemingly bottomless accent.

"Yes?" he was compelled to answer.

Her eyes were like crystal clear pools; they were calming enough to lose oneself in.

"Cade Robert Lawton."

Cade noticed that her mouth did not move and her words did not sound normal either; they reminded him of echoes from a great distance.

"What do you want?"

"She's talking in your head, ain't she?" the scarred man asked with a touch of jealousy in his voice. "She must really like ye, bloke."

Cade watched the woman's lips; he waited for them to separate next time she spoke, but they did not. He did not know how it was possible, but he heard her voice in his head, speaking his language. Soon all other sensations faded away, and only the blurred vision of her motionless lips and the resonance of her voice as she explained to him why she needed his help remained.

As Cade listened, he began to understand why she had chosen to give him life after his apparent death—because he was an excellent soldier.

"Beasts who strive to end my bloodline have infiltrated your enemy's ranks. Have you not heard of this General Wolfrum?"

"Yankee bastard runs nighttime raids on our encampments once a month. That man is a butcher. He's slaughtered scores of my fellow confederates, good men with families, and that Wolfrum never leaves any survivors."

"Wolfrum is not the man he appears to be; he is both a wolf and a man."

Cade had heard her words before. He had spent a lot of time in the company of Indians. Werewolves were commonly known Indian lore; he had thought it was only savage talk until this moment.

"His very existence threatens the lives of my whole family." She paused. "That includes you now, Cade."

"I don't understand."

"You will understand all things in time, my child."

As hard as it may have been to believe, he knew deep down she spoke the truth.

"What are you?"

"We, Cade." She smiled. "You are born of my blood now."

"Then what are we?" He shook his head in frustration.

"We are vampire."

Chapter Thirty-Two

An Attempt

Alexander Roosevelt Kintner's home was massive.

Off of CA-18, deep in the California forests, sat a city called Arrowhead Highlands. Arrowhead Highlands was an odd conglomeration of the many geographic features of California: a sprawling forest, rolling hills, and beachfront property, albeit on a lake. Alexander Kintner's property, a gated lot so large even Cade's enhanced vision couldn't see the end of it, consisted of half the town.

They parked on the road several hundred feet from the main entrance, a tall gate which sat atop a hill that dipped into a dark valley where the house sat. Not a single person in the group knew what to say as they stared at Alexander's home, until Jackson blurted, "Holy shit, that place is bigger than the HP Pavilion. Here I thought *your* house was huge, Moselle."

"My home is but a pebble at the base of this mountain," she agreed, stunned by its size.

With no security cameras evident, Cade waved the others to the gate.

"No cameras. No guards. I wonder if he is using magic to lock the gates," Cade thought out loud.

"Mira could be anywhere in there. How the hell are we gonna find her?" Sabrina pointed through the bars.

"I can track her scent." Cade pulled the lever on the gate.

"I can search for her as well," Moselle added.

"No, Moselle, it's too dangerous."

"Jackson is right; there's no place for women on the battlefield," Cade firmly stated, as he pushed the gate open with ease.

From the top of the hill, the group looked down the driveway to where it dipped into darkness. Cade stopped when a hint of movement in the shadow caught his eye. He took a knee, raised the hunter's rifle he had stolen from the gun shop, and gazed through the scope.

"Looks like a bloody Yankee encampment down there."

"Seriously, Cade." Sabrina tied the bottom of her shirt up through the neck hole to make it look more feminine. "A what?"

"There must be over three hundred people down in the valley there."

"Really?"

Hushed by both Moselle and Cade, Sabrina sneered at both in response.

"Take a look."

"Why would there be people camping out on his front lawn? Are they newscasters?" Jackson asked.

Cade looked at Jackson with a raised eyebrow; he wondered how naive the human could be. Cade hadn't lived as long as he had without using his brain as much as his brawn; he knew exactly who the people were the moment he saw them.

"Best guess. These must be his lab rats, which, if his medicine works as Sabrina and Moselle tell me, also makes them loyal soldiers too."

Moselle turned at the same moment Cade did—*she smells it too*, he thought, *the stink of unwashed clothes*. Behind them were at least another thirty of Alexander Kintner's apparently mind-altered slaves advancing on them steadily.

"Bastet protect us," Moselle whispered as she placed her hand in Jackson's.

Cade knew there was more to be discovered about this situation. Looking around, he spotted a helicopter pad in the distance; the aircraft was still glowing with a heat signature Cade could detect.

"You said you found Kintner's vehicle at the university, right, Jacks?"

"I found a limousine and flattened the tires just before all hell broke loose. Why?"

"You must've hit someone else's ride because I fear we are the ones being ambushed here," Cade admitted.

The path back to the car was blocked by a large group of people; they would soon be surrounded. With his keen eyesight, Cade could see the flicker of the lights off the large knives in the hands of the men and women approaching them. This was worse than he originally thought.

Last to realize they were trapped, Sabrina shrieked when one of the men in the mass pointed at her and shouted, "Wings!"

"Jacks, get the women to safety now! Go, man! Retreat!" Cade yelled.

"Where?"

"Just run for the gate! I'll clear the way!"

Rifle up, Cade aimed and squeezed off two quick shots, the heads of the two closest attackers popped.

"Holy fuck! Did you see that?" Sabrina yelled as she ran hand in hand with Moselle.

"Disgusting but unavoidable I fear."

The explosion of a bullet from Cade's rifle echoed in the night as another man dropped. Although in imminent danger and anxious for the others to escape, Cade hadn't had this much fun since his days fighting in the Battle of the Bulge. Targets acquired; he fired off another three shots.

"Not so fast!" Alexander Kintner's voice emerged from left of the gate, where Cade had spotted the helicopter.

Seemingly out of nowhere, the man arrived with a pleasant look about him. "It's rude to drop by uninvited, but at least you brought me a noteworthy gift."

Kintner pointed as he spoke, and a gust of wind swirled in front of him.

"Lucky for me it's such a windy night!"

The wind spun in front of Kintner until it formed a tornado only three feet in size. Cade paid his magic trick little mind, placed his crosshairs on the man's right temple, and steadied his aim. As he was about to squeeze the trigger, he heard distant gunfire. Three bullets struck Cade's back: two in his shoulder and one in his right leg. The unexpected blast knocked him off balance, his shot spoiled.

"Go! Keep running!" Cade yelled to the others.

Undaunted by the gunfire, Jackson pulled Moselle and Sabrina behind him. He tried to focus on the cracked open gate in front of him and nothing else. Just like his days on the ice, Jackson could feel himself on a breakaway. Cade's shooting had cleared the line to the gate; all Jackson had to do was get through the last man.

"Stay close!" he ordered as he released both girls' hands.

"Be careful!"

As Jackson ran ahead of the girls, Kintner released his mini vortex directly at the trio. It ripped the grass from its roots as it sped across the yard into Sabrina and Moselle. The girls were toppled, like bowling pins, falling backward into the crowd of attackers.

Jackson dropped his left shoulder toward the last man before the gate then, with footwork he had never used off the ice, he rammed into the man. The collision jarred the man's knife out of his hand and threw him hard into the bars of the half-open gate. As the man fell, his head split like an overly ripe melon against one of the metal posts.

"Jackson!"

Sabrina screamed at the top of her lungs when two of Kintner's mind-slaves grabbed her. Both women, one in her late thirties, the other near Sabrina's age, looked sickly, their too-big clothing hanging off their bodies. It appeared to Jackson that Sabrina had finally decided she should fight them off and yanked free of their icy grips, shoving the younger woman into the older one.

"Help Moselle!" Jackson shouted.

"No! Flee, Sabrina! Run while you can!" Moselle finally pushed herself up to her knees.

The enemy was ignoring Moselle, their eyes all on Sabrina and when Jackson looked at Kintner, he heard him give a command, "Get the fairy, bring her to my home. Kill the rest!"

Cade's wounds closed quickly. The bullets spilled to the ground, one by one, after they were rejected by his undead flesh. It had been years since he had been shot. It hurt worse than he remembered, but underneath the severe pain was the suggestion of failure; Cade hated failure.

In the time it took for him to raise his rifle, the fight had shifted. *Everything has gone to hell*, he thought. When he heard the second volley of gunfire behind him, he dove to the ground.

A dozen or so bullets whistled as they flew over him and struck the men and women who had surrounded Sabrina.

"Cade!" she screamed in fear.

"Get down!" Cade suspected Sabrina was unaware that those shots had not originated from his rifle. "Get down now!"

Jackson looked around; sweat poured down his brow and moistened his forearms. Another round of gunfire echoed in the distance; he was just as surprised to be alive as he was shocked that Sabrina and Moselle were—but for how long?

Moselle dashed to Sabrina, waved her arms, and shouted, "Sabrina, listen to me. You must fly out of here now. Now, Sabrina!"

Jackson watched Sabrina tilt her head back, and he mimicked her, the night sky filling his senses. *It must be so easy for her*, he thought, *a flap of her wings and she is up off the ground; she could float away—so why isn't she?*

"I-I can't!" Sabrina shouted back.

"You must!" Moselle replied.

Jackson was unsure how it happened so fast, but the girls were surrounded again. Feet dug into the ground, he launched into a sprint.

"You don't understand, Moss—" Sabrina began.

"Moselle! Look out!" Jackson yelled as he raced back to the girls.

Although only ten or so yards away, no matter how hard Jackson taxed his body, he couldn't run back to Moselle and Sabrina fast enough. With each step, he watched the horde close in on them; with each breath, their brandished blades were closer to the girls.

"Moselle!"

One of Alexander Kintner's minions, a thin man wearing a red, hooded sweatshirt, drew back a knife-wielding hand then released it in an upward swing that struck Moselle so hard it lifted her to the tips of her toes. The Bowie knife was so long that its point instantly emerged from her chest just beneath her sternum. Moselle's eyes widen; her jaw fell open.

Jackson stared in sick disbelief. Moselle, the woman he loved, was being killed, gutted before his very eyes. In the blink of an eye, he was nearly on top of the red-hooded man. Jackson's shoulder crashed into him, like a battering ram, he slammed his enemy to the ground. As Moselle fell to her knees behind him, Jackson raised his foot above the man's throat and dropped it on his neck like a blunt guillotine.

Hell-bent rage howled from Jackson's mouth. With a strength he had never before discovered, he picked up the dead man's body and threw it at three of the men who moved to attack him. Then, with another loud grunt, Jackson stomped his feet on the ground like a bull about to charge.

"I'm going to fucking tear you all apart!"

"Jackson..."

To his surprise, he heard Moselle's voice, weak yet steady.

"My God, Moselle!"

"Please, take—"

He did not wait to hear her next words. He didn't waste another breath of his or hers. He simply scooped her up into his arms and dashed off toward the open gate.

A minute passed with Kintner's full attention glued to Jackson as he ran off with Moselle in his arms. Cade saw his opportunity to strike. Out of bullets, he planted his hands in the grass before him then lunged forward like a predatory cat, Alexander Kintner his prey.

"Vampire, you stand no chance of striking me," Kintner laughed.

Kintner magically created a barrier in front of himself, one that repelled Cade as if he had run directly into a brick wall.

Dazed and hurt, Cade turned to Sabrina; she was in the clutches of two men and one woman—he had failed her. Cade's desire to fight was still strong, but when he tried to stand, his worn-out legs gave out from under him.

"Do you idiots have her this time?" Kintner yelled to his servants.

"Let go of me!" Sabrina whined, no longer with even the strength to struggle. "Get your hands off me."

"Knock her out," he ordered.

One of the women rotated her knife and with the blade firmly gripped in her hand, she struck Sabrina in the back of the head with the handle.

"Very good."

"Let her go!" Cade demanded as he rose up, his strength, like his love for Sabrina, endured.

"Next time I see you, vampire, I will light my cigar from your burning remains. Consider yourself lucky that this has been such a long night and that I find your kind so insignificant. I have what I need. Now be gone to your sewers or wherever it is you sleep."

Kintner turned his back on Cade and walked away, down the path to his home. In all his years, Cade could not recall a time when he had ever felt so insulted. He was a proud Confederate, a WWII veteran, and above all else, a bloodthirsty vampire; he was meant to be respected, to be feared, not disregarded.

His rifle reloaded, Cade took aim and fired at Kintner's head, but the bullet, like his body moments before, struck an invisible wall.

Kintner gazed over his shoulder at Cade, a deep sense of disappointment in his eyes. "Very well then."

With a wave of his arm, the hundreds of people who had held still in the encampment at the bottom of the hill began to charge. They were men and women of all ages, some clearly children as best Cade could tell from this distance. He knew he would be able to fight off the first twenty or so, perhaps even all of them, but this was not the time for such combat. Cade had lost today's battle, but the war was far from over.

Chapter Thirty-Three

Blood

Jackson ran with Moselle cradled in his arms, never once looking back. All he cared about was Moselle. When he reached her car, he flung the back door open and attempted to lay Moselle on the backseat, but the Bowie knife that speared her chest was still inside her.

Jackson had seen plenty of movies and recalled from most that if he removed the weapon, he risked more damage, so he left it in. In fact, he assumed, it was the knife's existence inside her that kept her alive but would eventually kill her.

"Please, Jackson, listen to me—"

"I have to get you to the hospital as fast as possible," he interrupted.

"Jackson, no, listen to me."

It was too late for words; Jackson had slammed the door shut and already run to the driver's side. As soon as he was in the car, he started the engine and dropped his foot heavily onto the gas pedal.

———∽∾∽———

"Jackson."

Moselle called his name repeatedly, but he didn't answer. The blade in her back burned, but she did not feel the pain as her lover would have if it had been his flesh the weapon pierced. To her, it felt like a massive splinter. She could feel her skin tighten; it had been quite some time since she drank anything. It had grown late, and her body required its nightly attention, the ritual she performed to keep herself fresh and young—even more, now, to repair the damage done to it. If Moselle was to avoid a permanent wound, she needed to get the knife out of her body now and get home as quickly as possible.

"Jackson, please, listen to me."

She saw him look down at his hands as he drove; he turned them over and over.

"Where's your blood? Jesus, Moss, where the fuck is your blood?"

"I don't bleed; there is no blood left in this body."

"What?"

"Jackson, you must listen to me. You cannot take me to a hospital. Such an error in judgment will be the end for both of us."

"You're hurt bad, Moss."

"I... will... be fine. Please, just take me home."

Moselle gripped the end of the knife with the tips of her fingers and wiggled the weapon until it loosened. She prepared herself for the pain, reached around her body again, and finally found the handle of the knife. Once it filled her hand, she pulled it out with a sigh of relief. Moselle laid silently in the backseat exhausted, her gaze locked on the ceiling, watching the lights from passing cars and streetlamps as they flashed. *The lights are moving so very quickly*, she thought, *Jackson must be speeding*.

Moselle closed her dry eyes for just a moment. It felt so good to rest; sleep summoned her. As she began to drift, she wondered: *What would the doctors think? What would they do if they found out what I am? The wraiths would be sent to destroy any proof of my existence; I know this for fact. Could that be what happened to the other Ancient Egyptian Cursed Undead? Where are they? The old archaeology journals—they are filled with tales of priests who used evil curses to ensure those mummified would never die, just rot for eternity. The others must be hiding, hoping to never be found out.*

As Moselle wrestled with consciousness, she heard the voice of Amenemhet, the words, that forever altered her family's path.

"Great Anubis, damn him, this mortal man who has deemed himself fit to decide when his family should go on to the afterlife. Damn him, he who seeks to leave this world without your guidance, my Lord."

Moselle jerked awake, sitting up suddenly.

"Jesus Christ!" Jackson screamed when she popped up in the seat behind him.

Eyes off the road, Jackson swerved across the double yellow lines before he tried to right his course and force his heart back down from its location lodged in his throat.

"Moselle, what the fuck?"

Gripped in her hand was the knife that had only moments before been buried deep in her torso.

"What's wrong? Wait, how are you sitting up?"

"I am better. I just—"

"Can you drop the knife?"

Moselle hadn't even realized the blade was still in her possession. When she opened her hand, the weapon fell to the passenger seat with a thud, where Jackson stared at it a moment.

"Where's the blood?"

"Jackson, would you calm down, stop the car a moment, and listen to me, please?"

It must have taken him a mile to pull over, but once the car was in park, Jackson took a ponderous glance down at the tear in her blouse, the evidence that the blade had run her through.

"How are you alive?"

"Jackson!" Moselle yelled. "Listen to yourself!"

"What?" He shook his head as he answered.

"'Where is your blood?' 'How are you alive?'" Moselle repeated his questions. "Jackson, I'm not alive. I'm undead, remember?"

"Oh my God."

Suddenly, the logic sunk in. Even though he had seen things that were extraordinary, he was still thinking within the realm of the normal world. Moselle crawled up to the front from the back with an obvious stiffness about her. She plopped down haggardly beside him and brushed her hair back with her fingers.

"You're fine?"

"Weak." She smiled. "I require remedial aid, but not in the human sense."

"I thought you were going to die."

Jackson wrapped his arms her.

"I love you, Moselle."

The words came out ahead of his thoughts, but before he could really register that he'd made the statement, his fingers brushed across her skin and went knuckle deep into the jagged gorge that was her wound.

Once more he looked at his fingers. When Moselle caught his glance, she took his hand in hers and spoke softly. "You see, my love? No blood."

"How do you heal?" Jackson asked, still concerned and confused. "What can I do?"

"Take me home."

Chapter Thirty-Four

Cold Slither

Moselle's guards rushed the door the moment Jackson and Moselle arrived. They had known something was wrong when their mistress had missed her curfew; she told Jackson she had never done that before. Their panicked voices overlapped with one another; their foreign tongue echoed through the house. It was not until the guard Jackson had conflicts with before stepped in front of him, hand on his shiny gun, that Jackson realized what was being said.

"Give my mistress to me and leave now, boy! Do yourself a favor and never return to this house. Go now, or I will kill you where you stand."

"Step aside," Moselle whispered, her head nuzzled into Jackson's chest as he carried her.

"You heard her: step aside."

"Listen to me, boy. If the mistress perishes, so shall you."

"Take me to my room," Moselle whimpered.

Jackson ascended the stairs, determined to show all who watched him his strength. Even as he reached the halfway mark, when his calf muscles burned and his arms felt like they held up the weight of a car, he did not show strain.

"We should've sent your guards after Kintner. Maybe they would have had better luck."

"My guards must obey the rules set by my father. They cannot leave this property without his orders."

"Are you kidding me?"

"No. They are not human... they are like Mira—different."

"Of course."

"Each guard wears an ancient, scarab brooch bestowed to them by my father. It is through this jewelry that my father controls them. If they refuse his orders or remove that brooch, they will turn to sand."

"That... I have so many questions," Jackson stated.

"Later my love, first tell me, you say you think Sabrina was captured. What of Cade?"

"No idea."

"If he survived, he will no doubt seek fast retribution. Vampires cannot deny themselves revenge." She sighed. "Place me on my bed."

Unable to push the bedroom door open with his hand, he tapped it open with the toe of his sneaker.

"Almost there, Moselle. In just a second, I'll lay you down on your bed and then you can explain to me how I can help you heal, okay?"

Jackson entered with only the light of the moon to guide him.

"Okay."

Only five steps into the dimly lit room, he stopped.

"What the hell is all over your floor?" Jackson asked.

She lifted her head from where she had buried her face in his warm neck and cast her eyes to the floor.

"Jackson, do not move."

"Snakes?" he blurted out, when his eyes adjusted. "Holy shit, Moselle, there must be fifty snakes in here! Where the hell did they all come from?"

"I will explain later. Right now, you need to reach my bureau without getting bit."

Coached by Moselle, Jackson tiptoed to her bureau. With each step he took, she identified another snake by its markings, letting him know if it was venomous or not. Of the nearly three dozen she had spotted, three were clearly a danger to his life and those emitted a rattle loud enough to wake the dead.

"In that pearl-handled box is an herb. I need you to gather a handful for me."

Shaken by the night's events, Jackson knocked the lid off the box and scooped up an overflowing handful of its contents. Instructed by Moselle to move back to the doorway, Jackson did so as fast as he could, the last four feet cleared by a jump, with her still tightly wrapped in his arms.

"Now take the herb and draw a line from the hallway into the room."

"What will this do?" Jackson asked as he sprinkled the herb on the floor.

"It will attract my cats."

No sooner did she speak than her cats appeared. Some raced from the opposite ends of the hallway while others ascended the stairs, all of their tails pointing straight to the heavens as if they were antennas to the gods. Silently, they poured into the room; some even bounced through Jackson's spread legs.

"Do your job, my children," she coaxed as they attacked the snakes.

Jackson stood in awe as he witnessed the calculated battle. Moselle's cats killed the snakes with such proficiency he could have sworn they were trained. In pairs, the cats pressed their assault—one in front would draw a snake's toxic fire, while the other lunged from the side—a classic flanking attack.

The hisses from the snakes and the cats began to overlap, a sickening symphony that thankfully only lasted a few minutes. In little time, the snakes were dead and being removed from the room, limp in the mouths of the cats.

"When my cats have left, it will once again be safe to enter the room." Moselle pushed her face back into his warm skin.

"Did you teach them to do that?"

"Yes."

Jackson laid Moselle out gently on her bed then took a step back to survey the room. One cat had returned and paced the floor anxiously. He may not have understood how it was possible, but Jackson had a hunch the cat was there to double-check the room to make sure his master was safe. Curious what powers she had over the cats, Jackson raised his hand to his face to examine the flakes that remained stuck to his moist palm.

"What is this stuff?" he inquired with a sniff.

"Nepeta Cataria."

"Is it magical?"

"It's catnip," she explained with a weak chuckle.

"And here I expected an ancient mixture of rare ingredients put together by a crazy alchemist."

"I grow it in my garden."

Much more relaxed now, he sat beside her on the corner of the bed.

"You don't look well," Jackson declared, when he noticed some dead skin on her pale face. "You need me to wrap you?"

"That would be lovely."

"What should I do for your wounds?"

"You know so much already, I guess there is no reason to hold anything else back," Moselle said after a brief pause. "Jackson, like vampires, we cursed undead need to sap the life-force of humans to heal."

"Then do it. I'm willing to take the risk."

Moselle did not speak. He could see in her eyes that she was touched by his sentiment, but it was her lack of words that made him think she hid something. Moselle pulled his hand to her breast and held it there a moment before she admitted, "I cannot take from you... again."

"You already took from me?"

"I siphoned just a bit from you the other day, it pains me to say. I am very sorry."

"Well..." Too tired to argue or question her further, he simply accepted her comment and moved on. "Okay."

"I took very little."

"But this time you would require a lot, right?"

"Yes."

"Then I will—"

"Worry not, my love. My guards have no doubt already prepared a solution for me. What you need to do now is help Sabrina before it becomes too late for her. Find Cade; he will know what to do."

When Jackson stood up, he felt sick to his stomach. The thought that Sabrina and Cade both might be dead because of his cowardice made him ill, but his brain and heart played a deadlocked game of tug-of-war. He thought back to what he had just seen. Kintner controlled all those people with little more than thought. How would they be able to defeat such insurmountable odds? As he contemplated the answer, he was interrupted by a ringing cell phone.

The ringtone's origin was somewhere down the long hallway. Upon its third chorus, Jackson figured out whose phone it must have been. His sudden dash out of the room startled Moselle, who had almost fell asleep.

In less than a breath, Jackson reached the guest bedroom Sabrina had stayed in. Inside he could hear her phone again. Door open, he spotted the phone's pink glow across the room where it sat on the floor amongst some discarded clothes. Jackson snatched it and looked at the screen. Sabrina had four new messages—all from her father.

"Hey, Moselle, Sabrina left her phone behind. It just rang. Looks like her father called her a few times tonight," Jackson shouted as he walked back to the room.

When he reentered the room, he found Moselle bent over at the waist, fast at work with a pen and a tiny piece of parchment. The moment her hand finished the last stroke, she gave the paper to Jackson in trade for the cell phone.

"You must go to this address right away. Find Cade, save Sabrina; put an end to this all as fast as possible."

"But what about you?"

"By the time the sun is at its apex tomorrow, I will be fine. I promise."

"Tomorrow?"

"You must go now, my love. Please, go now."

Chapter Thirty-Five

Voyagers

Cade heard motorcycles in the distance, the roar of their engines like the howls of predatory animals, a warning to their prey that the end was near.

The woods across the street from Alexander Kintner's home were thick enough for Cade to disappear in, but not thick enough that their canopy could hold out all of the daylight.

Cade hoped he could backtrack to the main road in time to intercept one of the bikers. With a motorcycle, he might be able to win his race against the sunrise. Fleet of feet, Cade traversed the forest floor as if it was an Olympic track, clean and flat. When he reached the street, he was happy to see the headlights of two bikes speeding toward him.

He would have to kill both riders and take the best bike, he decided. As the wind shifted, a scent wafted from the bikers' direction. His senses soon told him not *who* but *what* the riders were: windigos.

Thrasher slowed his motorcycle when he spotted Cade in the middle of the road and waved to Barton to do the same but motioned for him to hold back a bit too.

"What'll it be, vamp?" Thrasher kicked his stand down.

Cade told them how he had planned to kill them up until a scant moment ago. "That is, I *was* going to kill you both, until I smelled you... windigo. You look well, friend."

"I ain't your friend, sucker, I owe you one is all, understood?"

"Understood."

Thrasher squinted and frowned as he looked in the direction of Kintner's property.

"Spill it. Why are you here? What do you hope to get from Kintner?" Thrasher sounded exhausted.

"You know I was here to kill him." Cade calculated his time left until sunrise.

"And you failed, huh?"

"He ambushed me," Cade grumbled. "The bastard took my girlfriend prisoner."

"You mean the other undead, right?" Thrasher asked.

"No, sir. Sabrina is no undead; she's fairy-kind, warm and soft as the clouds in the sun-drenched heavens."

"You idiot! You just handed him the one thing he needed most!" Barton tilted his handlebars in Cade's direction and revved his engine.

"If Kintner took the fairy, then she's already dead, man." Thrasher shook his head.

"Not if he wants her wings she isn't."

Cade's comment ensnared both men's full attention.

"What do you mean?"

"I'd be glad to explain, but I would prefer not to do it here."

"What's the matter, vamp, time almost up?" Barton mocked. "Don't ya wanna see the sunrise with us?"

Thrasher hushed his friend.

"There's an old roadside bar ten minutes down the interstate. I'll take you there if you explain to me what you've discovered. Then and only then will we be even. We may enter this bar as allies, but I assure you when we leave, it will be as rightful enemies."

"Huzzah! That saves me the trouble of having to kill you both where you stand. Let's ride!"

Cade jumped onto the back of Thrasher's bike before he could respond. His swiftness caught Thrasher off guard and startled him so much that he almost tipped his bike over. Clearly embarrassed, he did not speak, just revved the engine and then gunned his bike down the road.

Chapter Thirty-Six

Infatuation

With a violent sweep of his arm, Alexander Kintner wiped the top of his desk clean in the main study of his mansion. His laptop slammed against the floor, and tumbled end over end until it came to a sudden stop against one of his many bookcases. Several dozen sheets of paper floated to the ground like a handful of feathers, as pens from an old, hand-carved cup spun in circles on the hardwood floor.

Still feeling the aches and pain from his fight with Thrasher, he impatiently ordered his guard to lay the fairy out on his desk. His guard, a man in his late fifties, but built like a man twenty years his younger, was not from the group who had captured Sabrina outside. Those were test subjects; this man had been in his command for years. Loyal to the finish, he knew who and what Kintner was and, more important, what he was capable of.

Still unconscious, Sabrina lay motionless on her back across his desk, her platinum blonde hair tinted red at the crown, where the handle of the bowie knife had struck her head.

"You're bleeding, sir, you may need stitches."

"Strip her down." Alexander ordered.

"Sir?"

"There was a day when the fairy-kind did not wear clothing. The light of their wings kept them warm all year round. It was not until they joined humanity, the day they stepped down from their elemental mantle and mixed with the huddling filthy masses..." Alexander's back to Sabrina, he retraced his steps to the door of his study. "They were once pure, like their elemental kin."

After Alexander's man speedily cut off the new pair of camouflage pants and Go Army t-shirt Sabrina had taken from the gun store, he lowered his palm-sized pocketknife to her and asked again, "All her clothes?"

"Yes! I detest seeing them wrapped in such rags, especially this one. Her fashion sense escapes me."

"And what of her bracelet?"

"Is this your first hunt, Christoph?" Alexander asked sarcastically—he knew it was not.

"No, sir."

"Then don't act like a rookie. You know, I collect their bracelets after they're dead."

The moment Alexander Kintner heard the scraps of cotton that had once been her bra and panties hit the floor, he sharply ordered his guard to leave.

"Should I prep the helicopter, sir?"

"Just leave."

"Yes, sir."

"Shut the lights off, and make sure no one disturbs me till morning."

"Yes, sir."

With the lights out, Alexander's office was lit only by the eerie glow from the moon through the large bay window.

"Well, my dearest prize, here we are," Alexander whispered as he slid a chair from a smaller table to the front of his desk.

A foot from the table, elbows rested on his knees, he stared at the naked woman on his desk in deep contemplation.

When Alexander had the presence of mind to consider it again, he realized he didn't know how much time had passed since he'd been studying Sabrina so intently. It must have been hours, he guessed, as the sun had risen on a new day.

Mesmerized by the intricate pattern of the tip of her embedded right wing, where it crept up onto her shoulder blade, he had given himself pins and needles in both legs. Lost in thought, Alexander repeated over and over in his head, *Success*.

To find and catch her now was no coincidence; this was pure fate. As he sat in his study, he recalled just how much he had begun to question his faith in the past years. There always seemed to be something or someone who prevented him from obtaining his goals. He had worked hard, tirelessly at times, but now, at long last, he saw something he had never seen before: the end of his journey; victory was within reach.

A sinister smile, formed on his face when he said her name out loud. "Sabrina London."

Alexander had made it his habit to learn about his prey. When his men identified a target, he tried his best to study it for days, even weeks, before he made his move. On his company's servers, he had a database with a profile of each of the fairy-kind he had captured and killed. Included within the database were hundreds of surveillance photos.

This one fairy was special for many reasons. Sabrina London represented the last stage, the first of the final ingredients he would need to finish his project. With her wings, Alexander would be able to conclude production of DUST. Soon a full release would be made across America and every last person who suffered from nicotine addiction would be his slave.

Yet that was not all she represented to him. After their fight in the women's bathroom in New York, Alexander had delved much deeper into the past of this particular target.

All it took was a simple Internet search to discover countless photographs of Sabrina London, brazenly in the limelight. Her courage intoxicated him as much as her beauty, yet not all media was kind to Sabrina. Mistakes were made and the paparazzi had chased her down a fateful spiral until she vanished into the darkness. It was a story Alexander very much enjoyed, especially given that, unlike the other fairy-kind he had hunted, Sabrina's past was mapped out before him in glorious full-color photographs.

Of all the photos, one set particularly held his attention. Labeled by the paparazzi as Sabrina's worst drug-hazed night, a bouncer captured nineteen images of her as she stripped down to her bra and panties. The bouncer must have known he could have made thousands on the photos, but instead of trying to sell them, he tweeted every last one for the world to see instantly.

Unexpectedly, the bouncer's smartphone camera framed Sabrina's flawless body artistically... perfectly. Each drop of sweat glistened like a priceless diamond. Her dance atop the bar, every twist of her waist, every bounce of her breast, were like a sonata to Alexander.

Short of his master plan, Alexander had never wanted anything more than he wanted her, and now that he had her, he questioned himself as to why. Was it simply because, with her wings in his grasp, he would be closer to the end of his quest, or was it something else? As he gazed at her naked body, he began to wonder if he desired her flesh more than her wings.

A flicker of dim light from his laptop drew his eyes from Sabrina for a moment. A slideshow of the photos he had collected of her from the Internet had been on loop since the moment he came back from the college campus. He could barely see it from where the laptop had landed on its side, but he could still make out the motion.

Aroused, he took another look at his prize. With the exception of her chest's rise and fall as she breathed, Sabrina had not moved an inch since her body had been laid out on the cold cherry wood of his desk. Her legs were spread, draped over the end of the table in a fashion that highlighted their length.

"Let us see how toned those legs truly are, Miss Sabrina London."

On his feet for the first time in hours, he shook the numbness from each limb and positioned himself between her legs, running the tip of his finger from her knee up to her inner thigh. Just as he expected, her skin was amazingly warm.

"My slave must have hit you hard. Not too hard, I hope. I need you awake to prune your wings."

Suddenly, a new thought came to mind. Alexander engaged his power and increased the density of the oxygen molecules to the point that they became almost solid. Focused on the space beneath Sabrina's feet, he formed the air into a pillar shape with his mind and manipulated it up from the ground until it settled under the heel of her right foot. Once in place, he raised his hand and lifted the air pillar, and Sabrina's leg with it, up to shoulder height.

As his eyes feasted on her body, he felt his arousal grow. She had what he wanted, and he could barely wait to take it.

With Sabrina's ankle grasped tightly, he rolled her over onto her stomach; now he would have a clear look at her wings. Although embedded under her skin, he could sense the energy from them like the hum of static electricity.

"Outstanding."

Alexander thought the design her wings made upon her flesh was magnificent when he first saw it, but to examine it more closely, he was stunned by its seemingly endless detail. However, its presence baffled him. Of all the fairy he had hunted, none displayed their wings like this; they hid them, and only a reddish blotch of skin remained on their backs——a mark that resembled a bad case of psoriasis in his opinion.

"Can you all do this trick? Can you all paint your back with your wings so beautifully?"

To wear their wings in public would make them too easily recognizable to the human masses; they must know this. She must know this. Or is Sabrina so bold she does not fear the risk of being found out? His laptop's screen once again caught his eye, a picture of Sabrina in an elegant dress at some unnamed gala. Alexander came to another possible conclusion when he saw it. *Perhaps you are too vain to walk around with an ugly, red spot covering your back; or is it that you are just too naïve to care? I'd love to know. It's a shame you'll soon be dead.*

The vibration of his cell phone stopped his train of thought. Freed from the depths of his pocket, he read a text from one of his top scientists.

"Maybe if we had met at another time, Ms. London," Alexander sighed.

A pen that had been given to him years ago by a man he idolized crunched under his right foot as he walked around his desk. He gazed down at it as ink spilled from its broken body. For years, the pen had held a sentimental value to him, but tonight it was no more than a broken twig, trash beneath his feet. Nothing else mattered now but his goal.

Deep inside the bottom drawer of his desk, Alexander retrieved an old pair of metal shackles. The short chains attached to them rattled loudly.

"You might not believe this, but these very shackles once restrained my hands. I've kept them all these years as a reminder that such a thing will never happen again. I was brought to America a captive; ironic that it will soon be America that is my slave."

Still unconscious, Sabrina did not reply. The cold iron around her wrists, Alexander half expected her to wake up from the harsh, bitter temperature. Once locked, he dropped her bound hands to the small of her back and walked around his desk to her head.

"Such a pretty halo," he remarked as he touched the red ring the blood had made at the crown of her head.

With his power over the elements, Alexander stretched a thin pillar of air out from his finger to the intercom button and pressed it down.

"Sir?"

"Prepare the helicopter. It's time to go to work."

Chapter Thirty-Seven

Trophies

Sabrina awoke with a deep inhale. Her eyes could not adjust to the abundance of light that crashed into her corneas, so she squeezed her eyelids shut. *What is that smell?* she thought. It burned her nose, made her want to sneeze. She shook her head and scrunched up her nose. A dull pain throbbed from the crown of her head, growing stronger every moment. Confused, she raised her hand to shade herself from the bright lights but quickly found she was restrained; the heavy chains rattled loudly behind her.

"What the hell!" She reopened her eyes.

A blast of cold air from the overhead vent helped rouse her, but it barely registered when she saw the last person she ever wanted to see: Alexander Kintner.

"Ammonium carbonate," he announced clearly. "You can always depend on it to do its job. I would applaud its creator, but you see, the man who produced smelling salts was never given proper credit. Rest assured, all will know DUST is my brainchild."

"Let me go, you sick fuck!" Sabrina shrieked, realizing she was sitting there nude. "What've you done to me?"

"Do you smoke, Sabrina?"

"What?" She shook her head with confusion. "Is this a hospital? Why am I here? Where are my fucking clothes?"

"Answer me."

Overwhelmed with her situation, Sabrina didn't answer, and when she didn't, Alexander screamed, "Do you smoke?"

While looking past Kintner, down a long hallway behind him she finally said, "No. Yes... no. I mean, I did."

"Which is it?"

"Mira helped me quit... Mira! Where's my friend? What have you done with Mira, you bastard?" Sabrina shook her seat so much, she and the chair mutually appeared to bounce.

"You mean the water spirit?"

"Where is she?" Sabrina snapped forward with a bite.

"There was a time in my youth when my powers were at their apex, that my full control over the element of air also gave me the ability to manipulate water. I could reach out to the clouds with my mind and make it rain, then cover myself with the wind so I did not get wet. Feels like a lifetime ago."

"Where's Mira?" Sabrina yelled again. "Where's my friend?"

Kintner shushed her and continued, "While I've only had sparing moments to spend with the water spirit, I must admit, I have taken a great deal of pleasure in your elemental friend's capture; in fact, I—"

"What did you do to her?"

As he formed a fist, Kintner siphoned the oxygen from Sabrina's lungs, putting a stop to her questions and her ability to breathe.

"I personally collected her shapeless form off the floor of your apartment and brought it back here to my labs to... to help her," he finished with a small bow of his head.

After a gasp, Sabrina cried, "She's hurt. I need to help her."

Closer and closer to her as she spoke, Alexander Kintner placed his hands on the arms of her chair, leaned in, and face inches away from hers, he enunciated each word carefully, "Your friend can wait."

"No."

"Yes, my beauty; you, on the other hand, need my direct attention," he whispered as he brushed his finger down from the nape of her neck to a spot between her breasts where a large freckle decorated her skin.

"Don't touch me! My father—"

"Your father?" Kintner smirked. "Your father will what?"

"My father is part of the Assembly. He will—"

Alexander snatched Sabrina by her chin, between his thumb and index finger.

"What will he do, Sabrina?" He squeezed her face.

"You're hurting me," she whispered.

"Do you think your father will send more fairy-kind here to rescue you and destroy me? He would only be doing me a favor."

"I don't know." Sabrina began to panic, more afraid of the look in Kintner's eyes than she was his hand on her face.

He took a step back, shaking his head.

"I have studied you very closely in the short time since we met, Sabrina London. I know you; your perceived stupidity is only part of a character you play for your public. Yet here you sit before me, unaware of the power your own family possesses."

"I'm confused," she huffed, her breath more and more erratic.

"Perhaps this is not an act." He paced away from her. "I had a theory, one that came to me just last night. I thought perhaps your infamous fall in the public eye was all a hoax, one perpetuated by the Otherworldly Assembly to take the spotlight off one of its fairy princesses."

"Don't call me that." Sabrina hung her head low.

"But then I dug deeper," Kintner said. "Do you know what I discovered, Sabrina? Sordid details of a life no father would want for his daughter."

"Stop it." Her voice shook with a mixture of fear and embarrassment.

"Apparently, I gave you more credit than you deserve." He paused. "But, this is not about your past. This is about my future. This is about one thing and one thing alone, Sabrina: fairy wings."

"Let me go."

"Go? You just got here, and I have something very special to show you."

He grabbed by her underarms and lifted from her seat. Placed suddenly on the ground, her bare feet slipped on the highly polished linoleum, and she dropped hard to her knees.

"Careful, my dear."

"Why the hell am I naked?" she questioned, her voice weak with exhaustion.

"Do you know anything about your ancestors, Sabrina?" Kintner snidely asked. A hand on the back of her neck, he returned her to her feet. "Do you even know the story of the first fairy, and how it came that you all wear bracelets?"

Scared to look at him and fearful of where he might take her, Sabrina glued her eyes to her own feet.

"Yes," she whispered, and then peeked to her wrist where her bangle remained, lodged under the shackle—a welcome surprise that he had not taken that from her too. "Our bracelets are worn to honor the past. They symbolize—"

"Your enslavement to the human race. Forced for so long to wear shackles and chains, now the fairy-kind all wear decorative bracelets."

"How do you know this?" Sabrina asked, her scared voice echoed in her own ears.

They walked in silence. Sabrina could not tell where she was, but she was sure this was not Kintner's home, as the checkered linoleum floors made her think the place was a hospital; it even had the familiar sickening scent.

The noise Sabrina's flat feet made as they landed one after another on the cold, hard floor filled her ears. With each step, she noticed a stickiness building.

"Least you could've done was given me a pair of slippers," she whispered under her breath.

"Excuse me?"

"Never mind."

"Sabrina, Sabrina, Sabrina... Humanity has truly spoiled your people. If I could only open a window in time just to show you how the fairy-kind were not so garish in the Middle Ages," he sneered, "I gladly would."

"How would you know?"

"I know because I survived those distant days."

She turned her head sharply, trying to take a quick peek at her keeper, but her long hair stuck to the sweat on her brow. With pursed lips she blew it to the side and took a long look at the man's face. *His skin is flawless for a man of his age*, she thought. *How can he be so old, unless he's like Moselle and Cade?*

"You're undead," she guessed, eyes narrowed. She investigated him another second.

"You insult me," he laughed. "I'm not undead. I'm something else."

"What?"

"What matters is you, Sabrina," Kintner dodged her question. "As I was saying, your people were once majestic, but in joining with the humans, your bloodline was forever tainted. I mean, look at you. Your kind was once three feet tall at best."

"So what? We were short. What does that matter to you?"

"It matters to me because it was your people who attempted to alter the path of my life. A sad mistake for your entire species, Sabrina, as it was the day that the fairy-kind revealed itself to me and tried to steal away my memories that I came up with the idea for DUST."

"So that's it? Revenge? You want to hurt me for something my ancestors did to you?"

"Here we are—my special room." Kintner pointed to a black door at the end of the hallway. "You see, I like things of beauty and perfection, Sabrina, and the fairy-kind were once the most alluring of all beings alive. There are many days I wish I could steal away one of your ancestors for my collection."

"What collection?"

Kintner unlocked the black door and showed her the way inside, his hand on the small of her back, just above where her wrists were bound with chains. Sabrina watched him flip a set of light switches with the mere point of his finger. *What the hell is he?* she thought.

The overhead lights turned on; one row after another they snapped into existence with the crackle and buzz of energy. When all four rows were on, Alexander Kintner's proud accomplishment was revealed.

"What is this, an art gallery?"

In six rows of twelve, hung large glass plates. Each glass plate was two feet wide by four feet long and fixed to the high ceiling with two long, metal chains. The rows were large enough for Alexander Kintner to stroll down each without the risk of his shoulders striking either side.

"This is more than just a gallery, Sabrina."

The room's walls and ceiling were painted stark white, and its white linoleum floor had a polish so bright that it sparkled. The only color besides the curious items pressed between the glass plates was a chrome air vent in the back of the room.

"This room was designed with state-of-the-art environment controls. Highly sensitive air-conditioning and dehumidifiers manage the temperature. It never dips below seventy degrees or rises higher than 30 percent humidity. Three HEPA-filters keep all harmful airborne substances clear from my prizes. Even the lights themselves are a temperature and color that will not harm what I have preserved between the archival glass you see before you."

As he spoke, she couldn't help but think of Moselle's closet.

"Don't you know what you are looking at yet, Sabrina?"

"I can't tell from here," Sabrina squinted.

"Then please, take a closer look," he stated, shoving her forward.

"Asshole." Sabrina sneered over her shoulder after she regained her balance. "Fine, I'll look at your nice, little craft projects, then you'll give me my clothes back and let me go home."

Sabrina's heart sank when she reached the closest glass panel. The item pressed between the sheets of glass made her recoil with disgust. Her weak legs suddenly buckled, her head felt light—before she knew it, Sabrina had collapsed.

"You sick fuck! Wings! These are all wings?"

"A five-by-five-inch section of inert wing off each fairy I have slaughtered to further production of DUST," he explained as he approached her from behind. "A token, you might say, to remember each by."

"How many are there?"

"Seventy-one and yes, Sabrina, there is one spot open right there in the back left corner for you, my most renowned prize."

Sabrina trembled; she had never been so scared in her life, yet emotions never ran singular within her. For as afraid as she was, she was equally angered.

"You prick!" she spat. "You'll never take my wings."

Kintner grabbed her by the neck and rammed her face-first into the panel in front of her. The impact busted her lip and splattered blood all over the floor. Dazed, Sabrina did not see the glass panel as it swung away from her, only to swing back and strike her again across the bridge of her nose.

"I have killed far worthier opponents than you, Sabrina London!" he screamed into her ear. "Now, show me those beautiful wings!"

"I can't," she mumbled through the pain of her swollen lip.

Kintner spun Sabrina to the ground where she landed on her shoulder, slid several inches due to the layer of nervous sweat that coated her skin, and finally was brought to a stop when her head bounced off the floor.

"You all deny me!"

"I—"

"You're not the first of your kind to resist me. I know your weakness to the aura of powerful magic. Behold."

The man took flight, but it was not flying as Sabrina knew it—he floated. *What next? she thought.* Elevated three feet from the floor, Kintner leaned his body forward, his upward direction changing pitch as he moved toward her.

Sabrina blinked her eyes half a dozen times, yet it did nothing to clear her vision as she began to see double.

"Stop!"

Woozy, she held her breath in the hopes she wouldn't faint, but instead of better, she felt worse. Her eyes closed; she felt weightless, and when she opened them again, she realized Kintner was not the only one aloft.

"Please let me down, stop, I don't feel well."

"Don't feel well? Maybe if I took off your shackles."

Sabrina could feel the air pressure around her wrists change. The touch of something solid at her back and a loud clicking sound made her look, somehow Kintner was using his powers to turn the tumbler and open the locks that held the handcuffs.

Able to move her hands again, she rubbed her eyes. "Put me down, please."

"Drop or fly; your choice!" Kintner shouted with frustration.

Sabrina dropped to the ground on her hands and knees. Her stomach spun and emptied on the floor beneath her, a green-yellow viscous fluid that smelled as gross as it looked.

"I feel—"

"You feel what, Ms. London?"

Kintner lowered himself beside her, a handkerchief in his hand. When Sabrina spotted the pearl white fabric, she thought maybe he had felt some compassion for her, that maybe he was going to offer her some aid in this moment of need, but he didn't. He reached past her with the handkerchief and wiped the speckles of her blood off the glass.

It was this that made her the angriest.

"You think you know so much about my people simply because you hunt and kill us?" She paused to sit up on her knees. "Then tell me what you know about this."

With a strained grunt, Sabrina unfurled her wings. This time, they did not glow or crackle with energy; they hung limp at her back, colorless, lifeless, like old rice paper.

"What is the meaning of this?" Alexander stepped back, eyes wide.

"Don't you know?" Sabrina yelled as she stood up cautiously. "Don't you fucking know, asshole?"

Hand out, he brushed his fingertips across her right wing and when he did, it fell off. Slowly, the wing floated to the ground and crumbled to dust on impact.

Kintner dropped to his knees and scooped up the powder in both hands. As he stared at the remains of the wing, which had further disintegrated in his palms, Sabrina backed away. When she got close enough to one of his glass panels, she rubbed her back against it, scrapping what was left of her other wing to the floor.

"No don't!" Alexander scrambled on his hands and knees to where the other wing fell, only to watch it disappear into oblivion.

"Happy?" she mumbled through her increasingly swollen lip. "You got my wings, now go to hell."

Chapter Thirty-Eight

Broken Down

Sabrina sat alone in the dark.

She wished she was stronger, she wished she could have fought him off with everything at her disposal, but no matter how hard she struggled, she was no match for his strength. *I'm simply too weak. I need help.*

Kintner had shoved her inside a small office, directly into and over an executive's desk. Eyes locked on an overturned, tall-backed captain's chair; Sabrina could not recall her collision with it. She only remembered the table, and how she'd slid over it briefly before crashing against the floor, elbow first, her back jarring so hard that her spine hurt.

Everything was fuzzy. Alexander's magic, the shock of all the severed fairy wings—she was muddled. Blood still oozed from the wound on her lip. As he wiped it clean the thought about what he'd said before he left returned: he had called her a failure. The anger inside the words stabbed at her pride, but the way he slammed the door terrified her.

Sabrina had slammed doors many times in her life, and had many doors slammed because of her too, but something about the force with which Alexander closed the office door made her bladder release with fear.

Too weak to move, Sabrina sat on the hardwood floor, soaked in a puddle of her own urine, entirely broken down. Slowly, she laid back, pulled her arms and legs in tight, and attempted to conserve what little body heat she had left.

Every time she molted, Sabrina reminisced on her childhood, a time before she had wings, before they first sprouted from her back. Now she recalled another memory, one from almost nine years ago: the day after Sabrina turned fourteen.

Gradually, her mind slipped away.

Sabrina stood staring at herself in a three-way mirror. The white, backless ball gown she wore was the most beautiful thing she'd ever seen, straight out of a Golden Age Hollywood love story, but she didn't want it. She didn't want any of this and wished the scowl on her face was enough to sway her father's mind.

"But I don't want to go," she whined.

"Sabrina, you know that every four years we fairy-kind must make a pilgrimage to Europe, and this year is very special. You are fourteen now. Your wings have finally matured and—"

"I don't want to talk about them," she groaned, turning away from her father's judging eyes. "Everyone's always talking about them and wanting to see them now... it's embarrassing."

"Never be ashamed of your wings, Sabrina," he said sternly, his own stretched out from his back. "Yours are glorious, just like your mothers: large and bright, a true myriad of colors."

"Dad!" she screeched with embarrassment, twisting the bracelet on her wrist round and round.

"What?"

Sabrina looked at her father's wings through the reflection of the mirror; they were smaller than hers, clear—totally unremarkable, like all male fairies'. With a sneer, she shifted her gaze back to her own; it felt like they had doubled in size overnight. *How am I supposed to hide these now?*

"I really don't want to go," she repeated. "Everyone will be staring at me. I don't want people staring at me."

"The unveiling is our tradition, Sabrina. All fairy-kind fathers celebrate their daughters in such a way."

Sabrina felt her cheeks heat. "Not all fathers are you, Dad. Not all fathers do it in front of everyone! Everyone!"

"True." He smiled and nodded. "Yet such an honor is only yours, Sabrina, Princess of the Water Kingdom."

"But I don't want to be a princess," Sabrina said, her wings fluttering. She wanted to fly away, but the dress weighed her down.

"But you are one—"

"Dad, please!" Sabrina cried. "I just want my freedom."

"It's past time you accepted the facts, Sabrina. Your days of floating about with the butterflies and singing with the birds are over. The unveiling is the beginning of the rest of your life, and it starts now."

Pulling at the dress, in an attempt to take it off, Sabrina shouted, "You make me hate my wings! Sometimes, I wish they would just fall off and never come back!"

She awoke later to the sound of footfalls rapidly approaching the room. She had no idea who it was but imagined it must have been him. *Kintner's here to finally kill me.* Her heart seized and a sour taste bloomed in her mouth just as a key unlocked the door. Sabrina scrambled across the floor and dove behind the desk. *Mira*, Sabrina thought, *if only she was able to protect me now.*

When the door opened, Sabrina saw the silhouette of someone other than Kintner. Backlit from the hallway's amber-tinted lights, she could see this was the narrow form of a taller, stronger young man.

"Hello?" she called out softly.

"Get out from behind the table, miss," A feminine voice said.

"Oh my God, please help me," Sabrina begged. "Please, help me! That sick bastard has me trapped in here and he's going to kill me."

Sabrina crossed the room toward the young guard; she felt her luck had finally changed, but when she reached the statuesque woman, she was stopped by a cold metal baton.

"Hold it right there, miss."

Sabrina looked up at the woman's eyes, but with her hat pulled tight over her face, all she could see were her lips—a deep shadow masked her identity.

"You're not leaving," the security guard stated, a second before shoving Sabrina backward.

"Look at me. I'm hurt. I'm bleeding. He's going to kill me."

"You must be mistaken."

"He's a murderer!" Sabrina whined.

"Here, take this." The woman offered her a white robe.

"Aren't you listening to me? He's going to kill me!"

The guard tossed the robe into Sabrina's lap and began to leave. "I... I have my orders."

"Please, please, help me," Sabrina whimpered one last time.

"For once in your life, Sabrina, help yourself."

The guard promptly shut the door and locked it behind her. Un-bunching the robe, she slipped it on. Sabrina had been naked so long she had almost grown accustomed to it, but the warmth of the robe was a welcome relief. Hands stuffed into the pockets, she was surprised when her fingers brushed against the shape of something thoroughly unexpected: a cell phone.

She dropped back into the office chair behind her and held the cell phone like it was treasure, its screen's glow illuminated her face a golden hue.

"Holy mother..."

Sabrina wanted to scream with excitement, but she was also wary. Why had the woman given this to her? Clearly no one had accidentally left a phone in a bathrobe. She walked back to the door where she spotted something glistening on the floor: two puddles of liquid where the guard had just stood.

"Mira? Mira is that you?"

Sabrina called through the space between the door and its frame, but quickly stopped. She didn't want to press her luck. Now that she had the phone in her hand, she didn't want to draw more attention. After a dash across the office to her hiding place behind the desk, Sabrina dialed the only phone number she could think of.

"Pick up, Moselle."

When her friend did not answer, she held her breath and pressed redial. Again, the line rang and rang with no answer. *Where the hell is she?*

Chapter Thirty-Nine

Means to an End

Jackson held his finger above the speed dial for Moselle on his cell phone. He had waited nearly all day outside Cade's town house apartment; the vampire was not there.

Moselle had told him that he might find a key at the bottom of an old pipe, to the left of the stairs to his home. Sure enough the pipe was right where she had said it would be, just hidden by a year or more of overgrowth and weeds. To fetch the key from the bottom was as easy; however, to place the key in the door and turn it—that was the hard part.

Jackson really didn't want to enter Cade's home uninvited, let alone unaccompanied. The thought of what he might find unsettled him so much so that Jackson had picked up a large branch from a tree across the road and carried it just for security. He wanted to give Moselle another hour or so to rest, so he put his cell phone away and went inside.

The first thing Jackson noticed was the lack of light. The windows were boarded up from the inside. With the setting sun at his back, Jackson left the door ajar so he could see into the room. Not even two steps into the house and Cade's lineage was painfully apparent. Opposite the front door, on a wall that would have been the back to a dining room, hung the largest Confederate flag Jackson had ever seen. By the time he reached it he had decided it was an actual Civil War era flag, obvious not only by the age damage, but also by the holes that were no doubt made by bullets.

The hardwood floors creaked under Jackson's feet as he moved through the front room to the back. He flipped every light switch he could find, but none turned on any lights. In fact, everything was dark; not the lamps, the digital wall clock, or the television came on.

When he reached the back room, he stopped and stared in amazement. The room that should have been an eat-in kitchen had been transformed into an armory. Weapons from the past several generations were stacked, racked, stored, and displayed in every inch of the room. Intrigued, Jackson began to question the contents of the four wooden barrels he had passed in the front room's entryway.

"Sweet freaking pack rat," Jackson said aloud to clear the tension. "Smells horrible in here."

An oil lamp sat on a small, makeshift table in the center of the room. Once lit by a long match from a box also on the table, Jackson recoiled in fear. The box at the base of the table had the letters T.N.T. lightly painted on the side in red.

"Careful where you extinguish that match, buddy."

"Cade?" Jackson jumped.

Cade stood at the front door to the town home, the setting sun at his back.

"I waited all day for you to come home."

"All day?" Cade raised an eyebrow as he walked toward Jackson. "You know we detest the sunlight, correct?"

"Oh yeah, you all burst into flames... right?"

"No, common misconception," Cade said, snatching the still burning match and then the stick from Jackson's hands. "More like dry up."

"Oh."

"Vampires have incredible vision. I remember my rebirth, my first day as a vampire. I thought I was going blind; everything looked so fuzzy. Turned out I just had to learn how to refocus my eyes to their new focal length."

"Cool."

"Darn right spectacular... until you open your eyes in the daylight. Everything awash with bright, white light that burns. I tell you, it's impossible for vampires to see when the sun is up, and if exposed to such intense light for any length of time, we'll go permanently blind." Cade pointed at his eyes.

"Sorta like when you go to the theater to see a movie during a sunny day and when you come out you can't see anything."

Cade sighed. "I wouldn't know, my friend, but if you say so."

Cade walked out of the kitchen, toward the front door.

"Doesn't your landlord get suspicious of all this? I mean the boarded windows, the lack of light?"

"Not at all, 'tis the benefits of an undead landlord, my friend."

"Right."

"Now, mind giving me a hand with something, Jacks?" Cade pointed out the door.

"Yeah, sure."

"Just need you to help me pull something inside."

Jackson followed Cade to the front door where the vampire hesitated. Before Jackson fully opened the door, Cade took a step back.

"The red sun of dusk and dawn creates quite the glare."

Jackson understood what he was getting at, but the vampire's signature smirk made him wonder what he was up to. Jackson was confronted by a scantily dressed young woman sitting on the top stair, who'd flopped over and lay with her arms under her head as if she were fast asleep. At first glance Jackson thought that it was Sabrina, but he quickly realized he was wrong; this was someone else, and she was not well at all.

"What the fuck is this? She's bleeding! Fuck, Cade, you bit this girl!" Jackson grumbled as he watched blood pool around her collarbone.

"If she's hurt, you best bring her in."

Jackson wrapped the woman's loose limbs around his shoulders then hoisted her up into his arms. She was surprisingly light, he thought, even after he realized how skinny she was by the touch of her ribs against his chest.

"Sit her on that barrel a moment. She's waking up," Cade instructed.

Cade moved across the room to Jackson's side with such effortless grace and speed it almost felt as if he had blinked from one side of the room to the other.

"Who is she? How badly is she hurt?" Jackson asked with a grimace as the smell of perfume and cigarette smoke hit him.

"Sally, a waitress from the bar I was holed up in most of the day. She drove me home and I reckon she's done worse damage to herself than I did with a little bite or two."

"Yeah, well, why did you have to bite her then?"

"Are you serious? Look at her: those lips, those pert breasts," Cade said, as he pushed a strap of her tank top down to reveal her left breast.

"Stop! You can't just use her like this," Jackson demanded.

"Sure I can."

"It's wrong—"

With a raised voice, he reminded Jackson, "Look, you're in my home now." It quickly became obvious to Jackson that Cade had kept his patience until now.

"I just..."

As they argued, the young woman's head rolled from side to side, her blonde hair swinging. Eyes fluttering, she mumbled, "Where am I?"

"Sweetie, you're at my home. You passed out when we pulled up."

"Oh, wow," she said, hanging her head between her wobbly legs. "Must've been that crazy shit we snorted back at the bar. I feel all light and floaty."

"Just rest a moment. I need to talk to my friend here."

Cade led Jackson away from her, back toward the kitchen, "Now, I'm guessing you came here to find me so we can rescue Sabrina and Mira."

Cade's fingers felt like icicles wrapped around Jackson's wrist; the sensation was so intense it made it hard to concentrate on what the vampire said.

"Listen here, Jacks, because I've got news for you: Kintner isn't human."

"Pretty darling? You said you had more blow here, or did you lie just to get me home with you? I'm not gonna fuck both you and your friend, you know!" Sally whined from the other room.

"Sweetie, I have what you need, and you have what I want. There's nothing more to worry about." Cade bared his teeth.

"What do you mean, 'not human'?" Jackson cut it.

"Thrasher, the windigo I told you about, he has tracked this guy through the generations. I told you before he's some sort of shaman or warlock. I don't know really." Cade shook his head. "I don't buy into all that Indian god mumbo jumbo, but I do know he's powerful. He's too damn powerful for me alone."

Cade turned and began to walk away but Jackson grabbed his arm.

"We go together, bring all these weapons with us this time."

Cade laughed and then turned back to Jackson.

"You? Okay, take your pick of any weapon here. Go to his home, try and confront him. I'll bury your corpse when I find it—if I find it."

"That's it? You've given up?"

"Do *not* imply cowardice where there is none, breather." Cade's accent flared up as he spoke. "I have a plan, but first I need to speak with an old friend."

Cade pulled his arm free and then walked back to the woman who still sat in the front room.

"I bet I'm not the first man to tell you that you are sitting on a powder keg, sweetie."

"It'll blow your mind." She giggled.

"I bet it will."

Cade took her hand, helped her from her seat, and escorted her to the basement door.

"Take anything you want, Jacks, but don't touch the locked cabinet. That beauty is all mine."

"Fine."

"And, hey, shut the door when you leave. I really do prefer to eat alone."

Left to stare at the assortment of weapons, one more foreign to him than the next, Jackson sighed. Cavalry swords, powder-muskets, Vietnam-era assault rifles—they all might as well have been alien weaponry scavenged from a spaceship. Jackson had no idea how to use any of them with any proficiency. When his ears caught the hint of a scream from the basement, he knew he'd passed his welcome in the vampire's home.

Jackson stared at the speed dial on his phone as he marched out the door. It was time to call.

Eyes on the vehicle he had borrowed from Moselle this time—a late '70s muscle car that had been kept in near mint condition—elevated his mood slightly. *These cars must be like clothes to her: no more than material items to store when out of style.*

Jackson's finger hovered another moment over the highlighted number before he pressed the call button and settled into the bucket seat. His frayed nerves and lack of a decent meal made his stomach upset as he waited, but all that went away when he heard her voice.

"Moselle, I'm coming home."

Chapter Forty

Call Backs

The sound of Jackson's voice made Moselle's skin tingle. She hadn't been able to control her thoughts since he'd left. The entire time she should have rested her mind and healed her body, she had focused on Jackson and her desire.

"Moselle, I'm coming home." He sounded exhausted.

"Are you well, my love?"

"Yes, I'm fine."

She smiled. "I am pleased to hear."

Moselle yawned, an act that was more a force of habit from her living life, years ago, than a physical necessity now.

"Did you find Cade?"

"Yes, but I don't think he'll help us."

"What did he say?" She peeled strips of linen from her chest while she walked to her bathroom.

"Something about Kintner being some sort of an Indian shaman and that he's way too powerful," Jackson explained over the sound of the car's engine. "He said something about an old friend of his. I don't know. Maybe he thinks two vampires are better than one."

"An old friend of his?"

"Oh, and Cade wasn't alone. He was..." Jackson paused.

"Was what?"

"Feeding."

Moselle could sense her boyfriend's frustration, and it made her want him home all the more.

"If Cade is meant to aid us, then he will. Worry about it no more, Jackson. Just return to me now."

"I'm sorry, I should have asked earlier. Are you okay? How are your wounds?"

Moselle looked over her shoulder into the mirror, to the spot the knife had carved open her flesh. Her caramel skin had returned, its faultless appearance reflected back.

"All better."

"Oh, good. That's great."

"Come home, my love. I yearn so badly to be with you."

When they hung up, just the thought of his warmth made her melt.

"Lady Moselle," one of her guards called from outside her bedroom door.

"Yes? Enter."

The tall man had come only to ask if she was well. After she swiftly dismissed him, the guard left and took the closest basket to the door.

"Thank you. That one has grown very close to full tonight." She nodded in appreciation.

She knew her guards would protect her no matter what. They would lay their lives down for her; all she had to do was stay safe within the confines of her home. However, if the wraiths came, would her guards stand a chance against them?

As Moselle unraveled the last strips of linen that constricted her arms and legs, she replayed the recent events again. She had lost count of how many times Jackson had proved himself to her. *He did not know the risks, and still he offered himself to me when I needed to heal.*

In all her years, she had never met a man who would give his own life for a woman who had no life left to give back. Moselle pictured the look on his face when he had carried her to the car, the knife lodged in her back. *He was terrified I would die.*

Moselle had known many people, human and otherworldly, since her resurrection years ago, and now she began to realize that she had never cared about anyone as much as she did Jackson. She could not lose him now. *Jackson, I love you.*

Jackson exhaled, as he stepped from the car. He had taken a deep breath to steel his nerves when he approached the main gates of Moselle's home and had nearly forgotten to release it when he spotted her waiting for him. A clap of thunder from an oncoming storm stole his voice, but the look she gave him was worth more than words. Moselle had something devious in mind; he could tell by the way her hips were swung out to the side.

"Good thing my cell has GPS. I would've gotten lost."

"You do not need electronic devices to guide you back to my arms. Higher powers would have led you back."

Moselle unwrapped her arms and rolled her shoulders back, dropping the shiny silk robe she wore to the stone porch. Jackson had seen a lot of things that day, but the sight of Moselle, tall and strong, in the smallest black lace bra and panty set he could imagine made everything worth it.

"Holy sh—" He caught himself. "Moselle, you look amazing... ly unhurt."

"Once I heard the deep concern in my lover's voice when he called, I figured he would want to inspect my body for wounds the very moment he arrived." She bowed dramatically.

"Flawless, Moselle, absolutely flawless," he declared.

"I thought you might like it."

His hand on the small of her back, he leaned in for a brief kiss, and when they pulled apart, a half-dozen guards stood with their heads bowed out of respect to their master.

"You're okay?" he asked again, as he peered over her shoulder in search of her wound.

"Care to inspect me more closely upstairs?" Moselle purred, as she latched her hands onto his waist so she could pull him into an embrace.

"Of course..." Jackson paused as his stomach growled.

She lifted her robe up to her hand with the heel of her foot, wrapped it around her body once more, and ordered her guards to prepare a meal of steak and fresh mushrooms for Jackson.

"Let us hurry. We can make love to the sound of the storm as it strikes."

Moselle broke into a sprint, Jackson barely kept up.

"Maybe I should get a shower first."

She stopped and her face lit up. "You're brilliant, Jackson!"

Moselle's hair whipped around her body and nearly into his face as she turned abruptly. They raced back down the stairs and across the great room, Jackson looking over her shoulder, curious where he was being led. For such a huge house, he had only seen a small portion of it: the upstairs bedrooms, kitchen, TV room, and den.

Through a set of large double doors, into a long, tunnel-shaped hallway, Jackson caught the scent of chlorine in the distance. *Is it possible*, he wondered, *that Moselle has an indoor pool?*

As they drew near the end of the tunnel, he heard the sound of water. A flash of lightning lit up the room as he stepped into it. The space was remarkable; it took up at least one-third of the size of her home, easily fitting the Olympic-sized swimming pool.

"We could light the torches, but that would take too long."

"This room is—"

"A fully skylighted bathhouse with a pool and three spa tubs." Moselle opened her arms wide to officially present the room to Jackson.

"Unbelievable."

"I know, it's grand. I love it." She squeezed his hand.

Moselle escorted Jackson to the nearest tub and instructed him to undress and get in while she retrieved a bottle of wine from one of her guards who had followed them.

Quickly settled into the warm water, Jackson's tired body welcomed the heat—he sighed and tilted his head back, watching as Moselle crossed the room back to him, dropping her robe and then her bra and panties.

Moselle stepped into the water and firmly straddled Jackson's legs. A flash of lightning from the skylight above eclipsed her, its brightness blinding him for a split second. When he reopened his eyes, she had leaned into him, her copious black hair spilled down his chest.

Another large branch of lightning filled the night sky, painting the room a pale yellow just long enough to give him a clear view of her naked body. By the time the thunder crashed, she had already mounted his hardness with an open-mouthed shudder that ended when she placed her lips on his.

"Mmm, Moselle, that feels good, but we really should discuss what we're going to do to find Sabrina and Mira." Jackson ran his fingertips down her spine as he spoke.

"We will. Afterward," she replied, while pawing the thick muscles of his chest.

"So..." He paused to catch his breath. "You're really all healed?"

"I know your eyes have worked my body over thrice since you have returned, my dear. Have you seen a scar, a scratch, or even a blemish?"

"Not one."

"Good," Moselle whispered before she kissed him again. "Can you hear that? The heavens have opened up for us tonight."

The faint sound of trickling rain had transformed into a steady drumbeat on the skylight. The sound itself grew louder and louder as Jackson looked up and into the empty black night.

"Kiss me, Jackson."

A roll of thunder so loud it shook the house followed another bright flash of lighting and during its boom, Moselle let loose a growl-filled moan like that of an angered wild beast.

"Damn, Moselle."

Moselle increased the tempo to match that of the intense storm outside, and Jackson kept up with her, thrust for thrust until she screamed his name, and her body quaked atop his.

"I feel... alive when I have you inside me," she said, her eyelids aflutter.

A high-pitched chime from a wireless house phone, accompanied by a flashing green light, finally stole his attention, and when Jackson looked over her shoulder at it, Moselle snatched up the bottle of wine next to her and threw it across the room, knocking the phone off its stand.

Shocked, Jackson stared at the small phone where it rested against the wall, until something moved it. As if the shadows themselves were alive, something writhed and struck at the phone.

The pale shadow moved slowly, its cylindrical shape overlapping the darker grey wall behind it. Jackson was unsure if what he saw was real or just his imagination, so he ignored it. Eyes back on Moselle, he watched her pour a handful of water down her chest and moved his hands up from where they gripped her waist to caress her glistening breasts.

Another flash of lightning lit the room and when it did Jackson, spotted what struck the phone: it was a large, pale brown snake.

"There's a snake in here."

"I know," she huffed, near release again.

"No, I mean there's a big freaking snake over there all coiled up with your phone."

"Focus on me, my love."

Jackson tried, but the phone rang again, like the snake was signaling him. Unaware of what he was doing, Jackson dropped his hands from Moselle's breasts.

"Jackson!" Moselle snapped. "Such a stupid interruption should not be tolerated."

"Sorry, it's just weird. That snake grabbed the phone the moment it hit the ground like it was, I don't know, some sort of tasty mouse."

When the phone rang again, Moselle twisted herself around and leaned back so her hand could rest on the cool tile floor. She snapped her fingers a few times and, to Jackson's stunned disbelief, the snake slithered across the room still entangled with the small phone. When close enough, Moselle snatched the snake from the ground, and she turned back to face Jackson.

"You see?" Moselle dangled the snake over his chest until the phone was free from its constricting grip.

"What the hell, Moselle! Careful with that thing," he warned.

As Jackson recoiled from the snake's flicking tail, the phone bounced off his sternum into Moselle's open hand.

"Not venomous," she proclaimed then tossed it back to the floor.

"Who called?"

"The number is unfamiliar." Moselle sharply pressed the off button. "A solicitor, no doubt."

"As long as it wasn't important."

"Now, Jackson, my love, would you care to finish?" Moselle said, rocking her hips.

"Not before you do."

Chapter Forty-One

The Tide

Sabrina had tried to reach Moselle and Cade for over an hour with no luck. As she searched the phone for an indication of exactly how much of a charge it had left, she came to a sickening realization. This was not just some office worker's phone; this was actually Alexander Kintner's phone—his email and private photos contained inside it. A spike of fear caused her to fumble the thing. Sabrina knew how she felt when she could not find her phone; she searched everywhere for it, even places she knew it couldn't be. *It's only a matter of time before Kintner comes here looking for this*, she thought as she picked it back up, *and when he does, he'll know I used it to call for help. He'll kill me for sure then.*

Sabrina dialed Moselle one last time, her hands shaking so badly she nearly dropped the phone again. This was her last chance—Sabrina could feel it in her soul.

"Greetings."

She laughed and cried at the same time. "Moselle!"

"Sabrina? Where in the heavens are you?"

"Kintner's offices, his lab I guess."

"Are you okay?"

"Fuck no!" She sniffed and ran the back of her hand across the dried blood on her upper lip. "Christ, Moselle, he wants my wings and he's going to kill me to get them!"

"I thought you were about to shed."

"I was, I mean I did, and I think it, like... freaked him out pretty bad." Sabrina began to shake all over uncontrollably. "I think it's the only reason I'm alive right now."

"He has no idea they will grow back soon, does he?"

"No. Shit, Moss, I think Mira is here too. I mean, I think she gave me this cell phone. I-I'm not sure." Sabrina shuddered. "Where the hell were you? I've called you—"

"Relax, Sabrina, my dear, please." Moselle's voice soothed her, but it did not change the fact that she was in a dire situation. "Are you badly hurt?"

"Yes, no, I guess not..." She began to cry harder.

"Sabrina, is there anything you can do to escape?"

"No."

"Then distract him, do whatever you need to do to keep Alexander Kintner from harming you long enough for us to come to your aid. You can do *that*, right, my friend?"

"I don't know."

"Sabrina, no matter what he is or claims to be, he is still a man, and all men have one very simple weakness."

A sound from the hallway made Sabrina abruptly end the call and shut the phone off. Her time had run out.

Moselle looked across the hot tub at Jackson. Sabrina was alive, but for how long? As much as Moselle wished she could stay, soak in the spa, rest safely in her home, have more much-desired sex with Jackson, she knew she was going to have to act. She had prayed that Cade would take care of this crisis, but it seemed even the cunning vampire needed help.

Moselle returned to an ominous thought. *If even a hint of this madness reaches the Assembly, the wraiths will be dispatched, and everyone involved will perish—a simple solution to a complex problem. Thoth, enlighten me, what should I do?*

Earlier, Moselle had considered asking Jackson to flee, to live out his remaining years in exile with her, but she knew his answer would be no. He was too honorable for that.

"Jackson, Sabrina is being held at Kintner's labs. He wanted to take her wings however they shed before he could."

"Jesus."

"She is hurt. To what degree, I am not sure, but her life is still in jeopardy."

"We've got to go save her." Jackson stood.

"Wait, please. There are things you should know."

"Moselle, I've been thinking about this all wrong. We don't have to go in there guns blazing. We can sneak in and grab her and sneak out."

After another loud sigh, she asked him to detail his plan.

"It's easy; I just need your computer," he explained, an ever-watchful eye out for other snakes. "Oh, and do you have a business outfit of some sort in your closet?"

"I do."

"Great. All I need to do is pull up video of one of those newscasts we saw the other day when Kintner was at his facility. In the background, I bet you can see guards and administration."

"I do not understand, my love," Moselle said, as she motioned for him to sit back down.

"I need to see their security badges, so I can design us some fakes real quick. Then we walk right in the front door, find Sabrina, and walk back out with her."

"You think it will be that easy?"

Jackson looked ponderously about a moment—seemingly everywhere but at her—before he said, "Moselle, how did you get that snake to come to you earlier?"

Moselle stared silently at Jackson a moment, she preferred not to answer him, but did anyway.

"They are attracted to me." She reached behind herself without looking away from Jackson.

The snake, which had brought her the phone on the floor earlier, slithered right to her outstretched arm and coiled around her hand from wrist to elbow.

"All those snakes earlier in your bedroom... why not tell me then?"

"It's not something I am proud of." She dropped her eyes in shame.

"Why are they attracted to you?"

"You can't just be stolen from death; there is a cost. When that cost is not properly paid, there are repercussions. This is my curse."

"Curse? You mean you're cursed?"

"Great Isis protect me," Moselle whispered as she sank down into the water. "Yes, I am."

Moselle was mortified to admit to such a shame, but to her surprise Jackson found it all amusing.

"The mummy's curse, huh? Funny, Moselle, but seriously what do you have? Some sort of perfume that is like cat nip for snakes?"

"I would never joke about such a burden," she snipped, insulted.

"Are you serious? You're really cursed? Wait a minute..." Jackson paused. "Is that the only curse you have?"

Moselle watched Jackson step out of the tub and when he did, he slipped on the slick tile and fell to his seat with a thud nearly as loud as the thunder that had rocked the room earlier.

"No. Not the only one."

"My ass! What the hell?" Jackson pulled a piece of molted snakeskin from his heel.

"Sometimes people get a little clumsy around me. Don't they, my love?"

Jackson stood cautiously with his hand pressed firmly to brace his sore back.

"You're serious," Jackson said in wonderment.

Moselle nodded. "You are sure your plan will work? I don't want to take any unnecessary risks. There are dangers here you are yet unaware of."

"As long as we stay smart and calm, we should be okay."

"Should?" she repeated, looking into his eyes.

"Yeah."

"Jackson, please sit." Moselle guided him back into the tub. "Listen, my love, I have another idea. We could leave now, go to South America or Africa. I know of places where we could hide and be free of this all. Cade will save her."

"South America?"

"Yes, I lived there for many years with my parents before we settled here."

"If you want to run, you can. If that's how you really feel, fine, but I need to at least try to help Sabrina. I owe her as much for leaving her behind."

Moselle held quiet and still a moment, calculating the risk and reward. No matter what she added to the equation, she came up with the same answer.

"You are a brave man," she said, taking his hand and pressing it to her chest. "We will do what we must to right this horrible wrong. Just know this, Jackson: with all my soul, I love you."

Jackson smiled. "I love you too, Moselle."

"If you did not, I would tell my snakes to bite you," she smiled devilishly as she said.

"I bet," he nodded, standing to go. "We better hurry."

"Jackson—" Moselle's eyes drank in the lines of his abdominal muscles as they moved down. "Allow me a moment to call

Cade?" She pointed at the phone. "He needs to know what we do."

"Of course. Then we'll get started."

"Yes... but first"—she took his manhood tight in hand with several strokes—"before we start, we need to finish... again."

Chapter Forty-Two

Menagerie

Cade stood at the open gates to Alexander Kintner's home. Kintner had threatened to destroy him if he came back and he took the threat seriously; that's why he had returned well-prepared.

To his left, were Thrasher and two of his windigo friends—an uneasy alliance, but necessary against this common foe. Cade found it funny that the shape-shifters fell into such a stereotype: rough and tough bikers who grunted their words and had such poor hygiene it was both visually and olfactorily offensive. It was always a shock to Cade that vampires had such a bad image in the human media. He, unlike his new friends, at least brushed his teeth after his latest meal.

"What's in the bag, bloodsucker?" Barton grumbled.

"A Barrett M82 Special Application Scoped Rifle."

"That's quite a sniper rifle; a buddy of mine had one when we fought in Desert Storm. Tell me something vamp where did you learn to use such a weapon?"

"Been in just about every major conflict this world has seen since the American Civil War," Cade said.

"What the hell is it with your people and war?" Barton grumbled.

"War's the best time to feed," Thrasher answered for him.

"Did you all know that European vampires didn't come to America until the beginning of the Civil War? The population of this country was too small, and the lands were virtually unknown at the time. Few clan elders would even risk such a trip by boat back then," Cade explained.

"Enough. I only care about one thing... You think you can hit him?" Thrasher asked softly.

"Once things get rocking, I plan on picking off Kintner from here. There's no way he can stop a bullet when it's traveling at his forehead at 2700 fps. He'll never see it coming."

"I'd rather tear off his arms myself," Rex said with a raspy cough.

"I pray you're right, Cade."

Thrasher held still, his only visible movement the slow rise and fall of his arms crossed at his chest as he breathed. Cade knew the windigo's concentration was on the multitude of people below them; he could've been trying to count them all the way he was so intently staring.

"Quite the roving mass of hostiles between us and Kintner's home, huh, Thrasher?" Cade asked.

"I see them, but they're not our *true* enemy, vampire."

"You say that now. Wait until they start shooting at you."

"These people are victims—innocents, no different than those Kintner has hurt in the past. All of them, ensnared in a butterfly effect of evil," Thrasher grumbled.

"Poetic."

"Down there, I see the loved ones Alexander Kintner has taken from us," Thrasher continued. "I see my wife and kids, Barton's mother, Rex's brother, and now I see Clayton—all dead."

"You sure you're ready for this?" Cade had begun to doubt Thrasher's commitment to the plan.

"So many lost souls. I considered doing the math; just how many lives do you think each of these people have touched?"

"I knew you were counting." Cade smirked.

"No, vampire, that would only prevent me from doing what needs to be done."

"Which is?" Cade pressed.

"Which is massacring them one and all."

"Sounds like you'll be busy then. I guess you'll have to *end* me later."

"Yes, first things first," Thrasher agreed, cracking his knuckles.

Cade chuckled. If only Dunyasha could see him now—side by side with the kind of creatures she raised him to hate, his weapon pointed past them instead of at them. Even at Thrasher's implied threat, Cade felt no fear. The slumber called and all he wanted to do was sleep, but first he intended to kill Alexander Kintner, save Sabrina, and take his just reward.

"Okay, boys, suit up and stick to the plan," Thrasher ordered.

The three men took off their heavy leather jackets and prepared for their transformations.

"Oh, about that plan, I have one tiny revision." Cade cleared his throat before he shouted as loud as he could. "Gayte!"

Thrasher grabbed a hold of Cade's collar and shoved the undead man, not even half his size, hard to the grass.

"What the fuck was that? You know what's at stake."

Before Cade could answer, the ground began to shake as though an earthquake had begun. As the ground vibrated, Cade grinned. Unable to hold their footing, each of the beast men toppled like dominoes.

"Friend," a deep voice emanated from the shattered rocks and shifted dirt.

At Cade's feet, the dirt, grass, and rock formed an inhuman mouth. Slowly, a nose and eyes emerged from the earth and, when the quake stopped, a head the size of a boulder had sprung forth. The dust rose in the form of a thick cloud and made good cover, so Thrasher instructed his men to shift.

"Gayte, thank you for coming to my aid, old friend," Cade said, his voice full of southern charm.

"Friend." When the mouth moved, dirt and grey pebbles spilled out.

Thrasher had circled the vampire while he was distracted, but when he saw the large face of stone, he stopped dead in his tracks. The windigo inhaled deeply through his snout, after which he proclaimed, "Ancient earth spirit."

"You thought they were all gone, didn't you?" Cade teased.

Thrasher looked astounded, "Forever melded into the earth's mantle..."

"What the hell is that thing, Thrasher?" Rex crept up on all fours, his human guise shed.

"The Earth's core, Thrasher. You know that's their heaven, their Valhalla," Cade interrupted Rex. "The many becoming the one, all elemental spirits have their version of it. All strive for peace and—"

"Omnipotence," Thrasher finished.

Cade nodded.

"Spirit of earth, why haven't you merged like your brethren?" Thrasher asked, as he knelt before the giant stone head.

"He's not ready yet," Cade answered. "Right, Gayte?"

"Not time," Gayte answered. "Save water."

"Yes, let's save the water spirit," Cade said with a nod.

Gayte receded back underground, leaving little hint of his existence past the crack of earth and a cloud of dust. The windigos stalked the area like cats, their noses up to sniff the air, their curiosity piqued.

"How would you know such an admirable being, vampire?" Thrasher looked pained by his own question.

"Let's just say we shared a grave for many years."

The earthquake grew in intensity as Gayte moved away from them, toward Kintner's army of mind-slaves. Gayte, traveled underground. He merged and separated with the rock and soil of the land at a steady pace.

"Watch what he does when he reaches the enemy. I've only seen him do this once before; it's a real treat."

As Alexander Kintner approached the room, he had left Sabrina in, he grasped his head and screamed in pain—a wave of cries from his subjects hitting him.

Gayte rose up again, adding the rock and soil nearby to his composition. Now he surged like an unstoppable tidal wave. The earth spirit stood thirty feet tall and was still growing.

Bodies flew through the air like rag dolls. Gayte released a growl like a lion, his breath made of the gasses trapped in the soil. Those lucky enough to avoid his initial strike screamed and ran for their lives, but their efforts were wasted, as the very ground under their feet was the foe they tried to escape.

"Thing of beauty, ain't it?"

"What's your new plan, vampire?" Thrasher asked, as Gayte crushed a man under his oversized stony hand.

"You know, back in Virginia when I was a boy, my father had a pair of old coonhounds. When we went hunting for quail, he would release them into the bushes to flush the birds out. That's when I got my timing down. My father couldn't hit the side of a barn, but I could bring down three or four birds every time. Bang, bang, bang!"

"Here, I thought you bloodsuckers were hatched, not born," Barton quipped.

Cade huffed with frustration. "Gayte and I will take care of the fodder out here. You all go inside and flush the man out.

Kill him if you can, but if you get him outside, I can get a clear shot."

The windigos raced off into the ruckus and when they were just out of earshot, Cade said what his father always did, "Get them quail, boys! Good dogs."

A cloud of unsettled dirt floated about Kintner's front yard, but Cade paid it little mind. He had learned to shoot through the smoke of muskets and cannon fire a long time ago. He rested his rifle on a stone rise that Gayte had left behind. Quick to aim, he squeezed the trigger over and over again. He kept track in his head, looking forward to telling his kill count to Jackson.

It had been a few minutes, long enough, he thought, for the windigos to use their bear-faced snouts to sniff out Kintner—or perhaps long enough that Kintner had slain them all. Gayte had done his part and turned to Cade for recognition. The earth spirit had grown so large his expressions were easy to read. Gayte was having fun; Cade had known he would.

When Cade's cell rang, it startled him. Phone pinned to his ear by a shoulder, he answered, unsurprised by the sweet voice on the other end.

"Miss Moselle, you sound well. How are your wounds?"

"All healed, thank you."

"Your suitor no doubt came home crying that I would not help him." Cade shook his head.

"He did."

"Yet you know me better than that." Cade loaded his rifle.

"I do."

There was a pause after her words, and Cade fired into the sky just so Moselle would hear the sound of his rifle.

"So, what may I do for you?"

"I know where Sabrina is, and no doubt her abductor is not far. She's no longer at his home; she's currently being held inside Kintner's main corporate laboratory."

"Oh, really?"

"She called me not long ago. Cade, Sabrina's hurt. She's... bleeding."

Sabrina had torn him from torpor because she needed his help and he had failed her once already. She couldn't turn to her family for many reasons, but the main one was his fault. Any harm that befell her was his burden to shoulder.

"Give me the address."

As soon as Cade had the information, he ended the call, broke down his rifle carefully, and stowed it in its bag. The air had become sour; a mixture of too many scents overwhelmed his keen sense of smell. There was blood in the mix, lots of it, but it was all tainted with Kintner's drugs. Cade had not thought of it before this very moment, but more was at stake than just Sabrina's life. If DUST tainted blood, then his entire kind's food supply would be ruined.

Taking one last glance at Kintner's home, Cade saw only an empty enemy fortification in need of destruction.

"Gayte," he yelled. "Level it!"

Chapter Forty-Three

Corporate Casual

Moselle strutted like a runway model, one foot planted firmly before the other, her high heels clicking like the hammer of a revolver. She may not have fully agreed with Jackson's plan, but once set into motion, she played her part to the fullest.

To get access into Kintner Co. was not a problem; Jackson's identification badges, although fresh off Moselle's laser printer, were flawless. The pair posed as an Eastern European investor and the security guard appointed to her for the length of her stay. Jackson pretended to be just another working stiff, stuck on a bad assignment; he smiled and traded jokes with the three front desk guards, drawing their attention to Moselle, who stunned in her navy blue attire—something she referred to as a peak lapel pantsuit.

"First day on the job and they make me pick up this icy broad at the airport," Jackson chuckled, pointing over his shoulder at Moselle.

"Tough draw."

"I've had to drive Miss Yugoslavia here all over. Thank God we're finally back at HQ. All I have to do is escort her to the big boss and I'm done."

"Who is she?" one of the guards inquired.

"Foreign investor."

Jackson turned his back to Moselle again.

"Man is this rich euro bitch stacked, or what?" he snickered.

"Is Kintner really meeting with her for business—or pleasure?" the youngest of the three guards, a man a few years younger than Jackson, joked.

"If I had Kintner's money, my business would be pleasure, know what I mean?" Jackson slapped the desk with his open hand as he laughed.

On cue, Moselle bent over to wipe some dirt off the toe of her high-heeled shoe. Slowly, she gave the front desk guards a good long look at her supple cleavage.

"Look at those! What'd I say? Stacked!" Jackson let out with a grunt.

Moselle suddenly looked up, in an effort to catch the guards as they gazed inappropriately, and when she caught them, the jaw of the oldest of the guards, a man who had remained silent through the conversation, fell open.

"We're shit-fucked," he grumbled.

Moselle stomped her foot in anger while she unleashed a long string of ancient Egyptian.

"Great, now you made her mad! Kintner's going to can all our asses if this lady ain't in a good mood when she enters his office. I mean three hundred million Euros is a lot of money!"

"Damn, man, sorry!"

"I better get her up to Kintner before she calls her homeland, and we have World War Three on our fucking hands!"

The guards waved them past and unlocked the elevator that had access to every floor.

"Kintner's main office is on the twentieth floor," the oldest guard said. "Elevator will take you right up."

"His office is on twenty, but he's currently on ten," the youngest guard explained.

Jackson placed his hand on the small of Moselle's back and swiftly led her onto the elevator.

"Magnificent, Jackson. Your acting skills are on par with—"

"Moss, cameras," he interrupted.

"Cameras?" She shrugged.

"Security is no doubt watching us."

"Oh, well then..."

Moselle turned to Jackson and yelled at him again. Hands raised in defense, he cringed.

"What?"

"I just called you a sun-rotten swine corpse."

Ding. The elevator door opened onto the grand entry for the twentieth floor, with high ceilings and dramatic lighting. Unlike the first floor, which simply displayed Kintner Co. in big letters, the top floor had a giant logo above the front desk.

A bit aggressive for a corporate logo, Jackson thought. The image, a profile of a wolf, was red in color and runic in design. Its pattern was broken into three jagged pieces, the focus of which was its hunched shoulders. *Aggressive, but effective, nonetheless.*

Once more the pair was greeted at a front desk by a secretary, who doubled as security by the looks of her. Although seated, Jackson could tell this square-jawed, blonde woman was tall and strong.

"May I help you?" She spoke with a thick Slovak accent as she stood.

"I'm escorting Miss Zhanna Poroshina to see Alexander Kintner."

"Poroshina? I haven't seen her name in the books. Does she have an appointment?"

Moselle strutted to the side of the front desk and placed her briefcase on the table. As Jackson explained that she was a foreign investor who just flew to Los Angeles to speak directly with Alexander Kintner, Moselle opened her briefcase just a hair and reached in. In her hand, pinched by its neck, was a three-foot long red, orange, and white striped snake. After a nod between them, Moselle tossed the snake to the floor behind a decorative plastic tree, closed her briefcase quietly, and opened a compact she had in her pocket; it was the signal Jackson was waiting for.

While he spoke, Jackson moved back toward Moselle, drawing the secretary's line of sight directly to the snake as it slithered about. When the woman's eyes found the serpent, she screamed like a child.

"What?" Jackson played dumb.

"Snake!"

"Whoa, how did that get in here?" Jackson acted surprised. "Is that one of those highly venomous snakes? The ones that can kill you in under a minute?"

"I got to... I um, I-I need to..." the lady stuttered as she stared, eyes locked on the snake.

"I guess we'll leave. Tell Mr. Kintner I tried to get his investor here, but—"

"No, no, no. Mr. Kintner is not in his office at the moment. His waiting room is over there. Please have a s-seat." She pointed before jumping back a few feet.

"Works for me." Jackson smiled.

"I'll be right back."

Jackson led Moselle to the waiting area outside of Kintner's office and took a seat until the secretary ran off. When she vanished around the corner, both he and Moselle sighed with relief.

"Darling, this is not going to work."

"Relax."

"That woman, she looked at me rather oddly. I fear our fraudulence may have been discovered."

"First things first, please relax. Second thing, fraudulence?" Jackson shook his head while he spoke. "Who says fraudulence?"

"My father does."

"Well... last, you're probably right. We should split up now and try to cover more ground as fast as possible. Sabrina said she was in an office, right? Well, I'll check his office here. Let the security cameras watch you go off to the bathroom, wait a moment, then check the offices at the other end of the hall like you're lost."

"Anything to see this to a fast and positive end."

As they parted ways Jackson whispered a word under his breath. "*Nakatomi.*"

"Excuse me?"

"Nothing," he said, with a wave. "Just some old movie that's been stuck in my head since we pulled up to this place. I'll tell you all about it later."

Chapter Forty-Four

Hide and Seek

The click-clack of Moselle's heels echoed in the empty hallway of Kintner Co.'s twentieth floor. She had no idea where to go or what to look for, so she just followed the direction of the hall.

Moselle had never put herself in such danger before and the potential repercussions filled her head. At the same time, she had not felt so alive in years. She had forgotten how much fear invigorated her soul.

Besides, the wraiths scared her more than Kintner did. She knew if they were dispatched, there would be no way to stop them. Not even her father, with all his power and influence, could reason with such entities.

The thought caused a tingle to run down her spine just a moment before her nose caught the salty scent of the ocean. It was an aroma she associated with Mira.

"Mira!" she called out hesitantly.

With no response, she followed her keen sense of smell to the end of the hallway, where there was only one egress, a staircase down. A small puddle of water sat at the doorway; it was a mere capful of fluid, but to Moselle's nose it might as well have been a great lake.

"Mira, my friend, where are you?"

Jackson was surprised to find Alexander Kintner's office unlocked; a simple turn of the handle and he had gained access to the private space of one of the most powerful men in the world and the very man who held two of his new friends hostage.

A large, stained-glass chandelier hung from the tall ceiling and illuminated the room. At first glance, Kintner's office seemed just like any other CEO's Jackson could imagine. It was spacious, with a large window out of which was a great view, no doubt the best in the whole building. Large, cherry wood furniture filled the perimeter of the room with Kintner's desk dead center. As Jackson approached it, the shadows that covered the bookcases that flanked the room moved aside and revealed objects from the past. *Kintner must've spent hundreds of thousands of dollars on the artifacts in his collection*, Jackson thought as he walked toward the bookcase on his right.

Arrowheads, bead necklaces, and old, brittle pottery lined the lower shelves while stone-carved figurines cluttered the top ones. The last time Jackson had seen such items was Moselle's home. While Jackson reached for one of the crystal idols that glimmered brighter than the rest, he heard the distant ding of the elevator.

Jackson turned to dash out of the room and tipped one of the idols off the shelf with the cuff of his shirt. The tiny thing's rattle echoed in his ears as it fell over the ledge.

"No!" He turned back and dove for the idol like a wide receiver over the end zone.

Jackson's hands stretched to their limit, the idol brushed his fingertips, bobbled to the left and then crashed against the wood of Kintner's desk. The damage, a gash in the otherwise flawless cherry wood, filled his vision as he laid there, but Jackson knew he had to move. He jumped to his feet and rushed toward the doors.

As he backed slowly out of the office, he heard the sounds of a man's heavy breathing behind him. "What the hell is going on here?"

Startled, Jackson turned fast on his heel, only to end up eye to eye with Alexander Kintner.

"Disturbance. Snakes," Jackson blurted out the first thing he thought of.

"What?" Kintner asked again, inhaling deep as he passed Jackson.

"The receptionist reported a snake up here. I was sent up to find it, sir."

As he rubbed his head, Kintner groaned. "You're dismissed. If I see the snake, I'll stomp it myself."

"Sir."

"Clear the floor, I need a few moments to myself, undisturbed."

"Sir," he replied as he walked calmly away.

Jackson quickened his pace as he exited the waiting room. He told himself that as soon as he reached the front desk, he would sprint, find Moselle, and tell her that he had actually stood less than a foot from Alexander and still held his composure. Only three steps from his goal, he was overcome by the roar of Alexander Kintner's irate voice.

"Stop!"

Jackson thought he might douse his pants with the contents of his bladder.

"Undoubtedly there's something amiss here. Turn around."

His eyes down, Jackson's greatest fear was that Kintner would recognize him from the other night.

"Sir?"

"Drop it. I know you don't work here."

"I'm new, sir," Jackson lied as the sweat that had begun to form on his brow dripped from his forehead to his fake security shirt. "Tonight's my first night."

"You're a little small for one of those cannibals and not pretty enough to be a vampire. Could it be possible a mere human would mistake me for a fool?" Kintner's voice was loud and clear. "I have lived a hundred lives for your one, I cannot be so easily tricked, boy!"

Alexander released a gale force wind that blew the leather chairs across the room at Jackson. No stranger to dodging hits, Jackson avoided being smashed by the furniture, but that was not all that Kintner had under his power. Suddenly, the front desk rumbled from the ground and titled toward Jackson.

"Shit!"

Jackson vaulted the front desk like he leapt over the wall between shift changes in a hockey game and he felt good about his success until thrown to the ground hard by another gust of strong wind. Jackson rolled over to his side when a lamp was tossed at him, and was surprisingly, eye to eye with the snake Moselle had brought in. He snatched the serpent by the tail and swung it over his head like a bola as he rose to his feet.

"Eat snake!" Jackson released the reptile at Kintner Co.'s CEO.

Hand up, the snake hit something invisible before it struck him. Not the result he hoped for, but Jackson seized the moment of distraction and fled.

Kintner laughed out loud. "Where do you think you are running to, vermin? This is my building—my second home. There's no place to hide here that I couldn't find you."

Jackson sprinted away in desperation; he ran faster than he ever had before. He ran for his life.

As he turned down a side hallway, there was an explosion—a collision of wooden furniture against the stone wall behind him. Jackson yelled and leapt forward, while Alexander Kintner threw office furniture at him like they were snowballs.

The sound of laughter made Jackson turn, but it wasn't the creepy smile that scared his heart into his stomach; it was the fact that the man was flying. Kintner flew like he was skiing downhill... and directly at him.

"The coyote always catches the rabbit, no matter how fast it scampers away!"

"But he never catches the roadrunner, asshole!" Jackson quipped over his shoulder.

A metal waste can slammed into Jackson's shoulder and spun him around fully. His balance lost, he fell to the seat of his khakis, the impact with the floor jarred his back, but he popped right up and started to run again. The end of the hallway was near, a staircase to his left; all he had to do was reach it, kick open the door, and jump down to the next landing—get away at any cost.

With one last glance back, Jackson saw that his pursuer had abruptly stopped. Kintner now stood still, silent.

Jackson was confused. He had not escaped yet, so why, after such effort, would Kintner give up chase? Jackson slowed himself so to get a better look at him, and out of the blue the man began to stir. Arms lifted chest height, Kintner moved his hands around in a motion that seemed like some sort of Tai Chi. Entranced a moment, Jackson watched as Kintner raised his hand up in the form of a gun. *This can't be good*, he thought. Jackson looked to the staircase, then back at the man—a split second after he decided to make his move for the stairs, he saw Kintner had lowered the thumb "trigger," and he was struck by something. Jackson felt suddenly woozy. The hard blow twisted him square to his enemy.

"What the hell?" Blood soaked his sleeve. "What hit me?"

Jackson looked up in time to see Kintner's thumb close down again, and this time he spotted the projectile an instant before it made impact. A virtually invisible spike, no wider than a pencil but the length of a yardstick, struck his shoulder. The translucent shard pinned him to the wall as his body jerked with unbearable pain.

Jackson's scream was incoherent, but his growl of pain ended with the word, "Fuck!"

Kintner launched two more spikes at Jackson, one skewered his other shoulder, the second the meat of his right leg. In agony, Jackson let loose with another scream that nearly deafened himself.

"Now, rabbit, do you understand your place on the food chain?" Kintner asked as he walked down the hallway toward Jackson. "Do you understand my power? Do you see how nothing you can do can stop me?"

"Hurts," Jackson grunted. "Oh God, it hurts."

"Good!" Kintner screamed in his face.

"What are you?"

"'What are you,' the flea asks the dog? I'm the end of the human race! What are you?"

Jackson mustered what little strength he had left to kick at Kintner's leg with his left foot, a strike that landed hard enough to buckle the man.

"I'm..." Jackson wanted to say something heroically witty, but before he could get anything out, Kintner gored him again, this time through his left leg.

"You're a distraction. That's what I bet you are. The persistent vampire sent you, didn't he? He destroyed my home, and he thinks he has killed all my followers, but he's wrong—dead wrong."

"I—"

"You're going to bleed out. Let's see if your master can resist a taste of your blood when he finds you... that is, if he's fortunate enough to make it this far."

Jackson closed his eyes; the room had become too blurry for him to discern shapes. He felt cold, numb, peaceful. *I tried, Sabrina... I tried.*

Chapter Forty-Five

Decision

On the tenth floor, Mira's scent dissipated. Moselle looked back up the staircase behind her. *Could she have backtracked?* she wondered. *Where am I being led?*

Kintner Co.'s headquarters were large, and the lack of employees at night left the building with an abandoned feel. Moselle knew how her father did business; he worked his employees hard, all night if need be. Kintner was on the brink of a full-scale drug release; there had to be people at work in this building at night.

When Moselle opened the door to the east wing of the tenth floor, she finally heard the buzz she searched for. As she stepped cautiously into the hallway, she knew a hive of worker bees were not far away, but where was their queen?

Braced against the wall, Moselle removed her shoes, her stocking-covered feet returned softly to the floor. Moselle's movement was much quieter now that her heels were off—in fact, she made almost no noise as she glided down the hall toward the drone of the workers.

Light from two large windows on opposite sides of the hallway seemed to wash away the dreariness of the colorless décor. As she approached the edge of the light, she could see into the large rooms on either side of her. Dozens of workers, all dressed in sterile white gowns moved around, scurrying about like ants as they ferried things across the room. *This must be it,* she thought, *this must be where they make DUST, or at least the part of it they do not want the general public to know about.*

Moselle wanted a better view, but a security camera above prevented her from moving further into the hallway. Curious, Moselle inched up past the edge of the glass where she hid. She knew there was a risk of being spotted by either the camera, or the workers she looked at, but she had to know if Mira was in there. Moselle began to count the white coats; she reached fifty before she stopped. Rattled, when it appeared that one of the workers looked straight at her, she ducked back behind the window.

"Mira, are you near?" she called out lightly. "Sabrina, can you hear me?"

There was no response. Frozen in place, she stared down the hallway. She knew she was going to have to walk this gauntlet of light, windows, and cameras, directly into the view of all those workers if she wanted to continue her search, but her body did not want to acquiesce.

A female security guard walked by, and Moselle's nose twitched. She knew that scent.

"Mira!" she shouted.

Moselle dashed shoeless across the hall. All she thought about was reaching Mira before she vanished. One turn of the hall led to another with no sign of Mira, until a puddle of water spanned the distance between a water fountain and the women's bathroom door.

The bathroom lights were triggered when Moselle swung open the door, which meant that, if Mira had entered the room first, she did so in some form invisible to the sensors: a mist or puddle of water. Moselle ran the length of the bathroom in a frantic search, but Mira was not there.

"By the great Goddess Ma'at, was that you, Mira, or have my eyes been plagued with mirages?"

Moselle splashed cool water onto her dry hands as she resolved to turn back, find Jackson, and finally tell him about the wraiths. *Then he would agree to flee this land now and forever.*

"A human's lifetime of love with Jackson is all I ask. If we escape this night unharmed, I will take him into the deepest desert and worship him as a king until the day he dies, and on that day, I will burn myself along with his body. So swear I."

In spite of her intentions a sliver of light under a closed doorway further down the hallway caught her attention. Drawn straight to it, Moselle placed her hand on the door and jiggled the locked handle.

A set of footfalls, too heavy to be female echoed in Moselle's ears. She had to hide quickly. The door to the room across from her stood open, so she dashed into the darkness of the office and turned to peer out into the hall. Had she been alive, she would have held her breath.

The footfalls belonged to none other than Alexander Kintner and when he stopped in front of the door she had just tried to open, Moselle knew her intuition had been spot-on; there *was* something important in that room.

Chapter Forty-Six

Self-Worth

Sabrina had made a vital decision since she last saw her jailer. She had decided to fight.

She had searched the office until she found a few things that sparked an idea. Hidden under a pile of papers, in the only drawer of the desk that was not locked, was an old bottle of wine. Next to it was a rusty corkscrew with a splintered wooden handle and blacksmith-molded metal. Sabrina snatched both up and hid them under the desk while she continued to hunt.

Stored in a closet was an extra suit with the Armani price tags still on it. With the clothes tossed under the desk, she continued her search. For the first time that day, she felt like more than a prisoner; she felt normal and, further, she felt in control.

On her hands and knees, she crawled behind another desk where more paperwork sat. Behind it on the floor, she found two things: a long red ribbon and a plastic men's comb. She snatched up both.

A plan now in her head, Sabrina stared out the window at the streets below. They were lifeless, not a soul around. *Moselle should be here by now*, she thought. *Cade should have kicked the door in and whisked me away long ago. Perhaps Kintner stopped them... Perhaps he... killed them.*

Kintner's cell phone in hand, she briefly contemplated a call to Cade, but the fear of rejection—the thought of her friends ignoring her cry for help—stopped her. The guard—Mira, whoever it was, was right; it was time to help herself. Sabrina slammed the phone down on the desk over and over until she demolished the tiny plastic device.

Blood spilled from the fresh cuts on her palm, but Sabrina did not cry; she laughed, taking great joy in the destruction of Kintner's property. Not only that, but unlike the times she had broken the camera in her dreams, Sabrina actually felt better. After she wiped her hand off on the stark white robe, she spun around in a circle, in search of other items in the room that she could destroy.

Sabrina started with the large laser-jet printer off the back desk. She scooped it up and smashed it against the wall in one fluid motion. The thrill made her shriek; her hands clawed at everything they could find and snatch. Paper, staplers, pencils, and books were all thrown around as she circled the room. Sabrina created enough racket to wake the dead, but no one came.

She paused a moment to catch her breath and stood silently near the door. She realized something was off by the way the stapler she had thrown had come to rest on its nose, balanced in an impossible way. When she kicked it, her foot collided with something unseen.

"What the hell?"

Out of an invisible case, spilled an old laptop, it's tiny green light catching her eye. Curious, Sabrina withdrew the laptop and opened it.

To her sickened surprise, what greeted her in 1920 by 1080 resolution was an image of her from almost a year and a half ago. It was of her unconscious in the passenger seat of a high-priced sports car. As hard as she tried, she could not recall who she had been out with that night; of course, the driver had been cropped out of the photo. Not a second later, that photo vanished and a new one took its place. It was a shot of her in a tight black dress, the circles around her eyes matching her clothes—sunken in and dark, dog-tired from a rough night of partying. One of the dress's straps was down, her nipple exposed. She remembered this photo well and the one that followed it. It was of her as she got in a car; the paparazzi had snapped a shot of her dress as it rode up. She would never forget TMZ's remark: "I see London, I see France, would someone get this pop-tart some underpants!"

Mesmerized, Sabrina stopped her search for things to break. Quiet returned to the room as she knelt beside the computer, head tilting to the side as she watched the slideshow. She had not seen most of the images in months, not since the night Mira helped her put away the past and begin to move forward; she felt oddly compelled to watch.

Sabrina began to realize that the pictures were not of her, or at least, she felt she was no longer that woman. The young woman in the pictures was lost; she felt small in a world far too big for her. Alone, that pathetic mess screamed for attention and took it from anyone who would give it. In retrospect, Sabrina was disgusted with herself... and yet something more occurred to her as the last image faded and the slideshow began anew. *There are thousands of photos of me on the Internet, and Kintner chose these... he chose these horrible ones for a reason. I may have to alter my plan a little.*

She closed the laptop; her fit was done; it was time to switch emotional gears. Sabrina uncorked the wine bottle and smirked when it popped loudly. Nose to the bottle, she took a deep sniff. For a moment she thought it smelled like urine, but then she remembered her accident.

"I must look like a real fucking mess," she whispered to herself.

She patted her face and felt how swollen her lip was, but there was no way for her to tell how bad her hair looked or even how much makeup she still had on.

It was time to clean up.

First, she worked to untangle her hair with the comb she had found earlier. With a mouthful of wine, she came up with another idea. Sabrina allowed the bloodstained robe to fall to her feet after she untied the belt. Once naked, she raised the wine bottle up and poured its contents over her body. The wine cascaded down her curves, rinsed off the blood and urine, and replaced their scents with one of its own. When the bottle chugged empty, she placed it on the corner of his desk.

"Much better," she smelled the air as she patted dry with the robe.

Dressed in the white shirt that came with the change of clothes in the modest office closet, Sabrina set up a scene to greet Kintner with when he returned. *All I need to do is distract him for a moment, and if there's one thing I know how to do, it's distract men.*

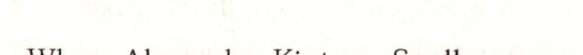

When Alexander Kintner finally opened the door to his secondary office, Moselle spotted Sabrina: half-naked, bruised, and bloody. Although elated to see her friend alive, Moselle knew that Sabrina needed help, more help than she alone could provide. As Kintner entered the room, Moselle realized: *This could be the end for Sabrina.*

Osiris, please bless my friend.

Chapter Forty-Seven

Shock and Awe

It was obvious to Sabrina that Alexander Kintner was surprised. She had seen the look on many a man's face before-shock and awe, she liked to call it. She sat up straight on the desk, her legs spread wide, with just a man's unbuttoned dress shirt on. She gave the impression that she belonged in a pornographic movie, not at all the picture of a captured woman.

"What have you done to my office?" Alexander asked.

"Your office?" she played dumb. "Oh, then it must've been your laptop, I found, Alexander. I saw the slideshow. I saw myself on your little screen there... and it made me think."

Seemingly confused by the disarray before him, he looked at her strangely. "You found my laptop?"

"Yes, you have quite the Sabrina London gallery," she stated. "I see you have even found some topless and upskirt shots too. Did you search for them all yourself?"

"What is this?" Kintner took another small step into the room, where his foot kicked a toppled over pen cup.

"You like me, don't you? It's okay," Sabrina replied, her voice husky. "You know, I think there's something other than my wings I can probably interest you in."

Alexander rubbed his temples. The images of his home being destroyed as seen by his mind-slaves, the fairy's actions, the destruction of his secondary office—it was all too much.

Alexander had viewed Sabrina's photos earlier in the evening, and the flirty fairy was right: there were other features of her body he was interested in, but none of them would supply him with the ingredients he needed for DUST.

Still, Alexander squinted his tired eyes, looked past the destruction she had caused, and focused entirely on her body. The way she sat on his desk and leaned forward on her hands as they rested between her legs—the way her arms ever so slightly squeezed her breasts together—she looked no different than the photos he had of her.

"This night, my prized fairy, has become a truly peculiar one," he stated as he stepped closer. "Who knew there were still so many new experiences to be had?"

"Why don't you tell me all about it... later?" she said, twirling the ribbon in her hair.

"Later?"

"After you fuck me. You do want to *fuck* me, don't you?" Sabrina enunciated the word with her upper lip raised. "You can if you want to."

"Such foul language should not spill from such a pretty face." He took her chin in his hand and pinched it. "Albeit a bit roughed up one at the moment."

He stared into Sabrina's eyes, trying to read them, to determine what treachery was in store for him, but she didn't falter. Sabrina's gaze was as solid as his.

"Give me your warmth," she said, then licked her lips.

"Captives always seem to offer their abductors the promise of sexual favors."

As Alexander moved away from her to shut the door and switch on the lights, he summoned a layer of dense air over his back from the floor to a foot below the ceiling—just as Sabrina tried to bring the wine bottle down on the crown of his head.

Sabrina shrieked for help, but Alexander extended the dense air around him into a large fist and slammed it into her stomach so hard it knocked her off her feet and into the clutter of broken office equipment.

"Do you truly think I'm new at this, fairy? Do you think I could amass such wealth or be on the brink of world domination if I was fool enough to fall victim to some spoiled whore's charm?"

"Better men have." She coughed.

Arms at his sides, Alexander pushed the air around the room faster and faster until it swirled around him like a vortex. The office supplies, broken equipment, and trash rose up from the floor and got caught in the vortex, turning once-useless objects into weapons.

"There is no *better* man."

Sabrina would have marveled at his show of magical power if it were not directed against her. Still hurt, she wheezed from the shot to the gut. Bent over at the waist, arms wrapped around herself, she glared angrily at Kintner until something blunt, cold, and metal struck her in the temple.

"Stop..." she groaned.

Before she could identify what had hit her, something else struck her leg, and then a small paperweight breezed by her face, just missing her nose.

"What the hell!"

Face covered, Sabrina tried to move in Kintner's direction, but she could only take baby steps. She reached out to him, her thoughts on how she would strangle him if she could only grasp his neck or claw his eyes out with her fingers—anything to stop him. But she was still too far away.

"I can do this all day, Sabrina." Kintner waved his arm, and a small waste basket struck her in the chest.

Sabrina yelped in pain when a pencil stabbed her leg, the lead point piercing her skin like an arrowhead.

"Stop!"

"Why?"

"S-so cold."

The air was bitter enough to make her shiver—or was the chill she felt the result of the adrenaline leaking from her body? She had no idea; she just knew it was bad. Her new wings would never spawn unless she warmed up.

"What's that, Miss London? You need to borrow my stapler?" Kintner laughed as he pelted her in the face again.

Dazed, Sabrina closed her eyes, and for a split second, everything seemed calm. Quiet enough to think, her mind received the message that her body wanted to give in and rest, but that was no longer an option.

Chapter Forty-Eight

Fight or Flight

Cade coasted into the parking lot across the street from Kintner Co. on his Honda CBR600RR sport motorcycle. He had refinished it flat black, so the bike didn't reflect the shine from the parking lot's lights and kept him all the more camouflaged; what he needed right now was the utmost secrecy.

After he parked the bike, he unpacked his rifle and rested its long barrel on the bike's seat. The cool wind rustled the trees on the small island of grass to his left. He could smell the night; it had a brisk aroma to it, one that smelled like freshly dug earth. Cade rubbed his eyes with the back of his hand; he tried his best to shake off the sensation that grew within him. No, it was not the night he smelled; it was torpor-the slumber-that called him.

Cade hated feeling as if he were the only vampire above ground, and he knew he could not resist it for much longer.

While he leaned toward the rifle's scope, he heard the sound of vehicles racing his way. *Security?* he wondered. *How could they have spotted me so soon?*

Two vans screeched around the corner of the parking lot behind him. The scent of burning rubber filled the air, but his nostrils picked up a second odor: one he had thought he had left behind fifteen minutes ago.

"Vampire, die," the driver muttered as he stepped from the van.

"Oh, I see, you all followed me here. Careful, or I might think you guys are getting sweet on me."

"Destroy him," the driver of the other vehicle yelled as six people piled out the back.

"Hey, tell Kintner he needs to instruct his soldiers to bathe once in a while." Cade smirked. "The smell of you all is killing me."

With both vans empty, Cade faced a dozen men, all wielding weapons that ranged from baseball bats to butcher knives. He had no fear; he could overcome them all, but it would take time he did not have to waste. As he sidestepped away from his cycle to take the fight to a better location, he spotted the last man to exit the van, and it was at that moment he realized he was in dire trouble.

Not since World War II had Cade seen what this last man carried: a vintage flamethrower.

"Shit," he said flatly as the tip of the weapon ignited.

Cade kept his eye on the flamethrower as he faced the first of Kintner's men. Fast on his feet, he ducked one man's wild punches then stepped to his side, wrapped his arm around the man's neck, and broke his spine as he pulled him backward over his hip.

"Who's next?" One by one, the men attacked him.

Cade unbuckled the fastener that held his old bowie knife, and cut down two more men, their blood coating the ground before him. He wanted nothing more than to drop to the pavement and lap it up, but it was tainted with DUST, and as long as that man stood at the back ranks with the flamethrower, Cade knew he could not drop his guard.

"Burn the vampire."

Cade dove behind the back of the closest van as a cone of fire blew out at him. Although shielded by the metal of the old Ford Econovan, Cade could feel the heat on his porcelain-like skin, and it was the warmest his body had felt in over a hundred and fifty years.

Face blank, like all the rest of Kintner's mind-slaves, the man with the flamethrower stood at the opposite side of the van. Cade peered cautiously at him wondering why he'd stopped his attack. A shout snapped Cade's eyes to the side; one of the men he thought he had killed had stood back up, his guts had all but spilled out to the ground, but the eviscerated man pointed, and the flamethrower ignited with another burst of flames.

Cade jumped into the rear of the open van and saw a shiny opportunity dangling from the steering column. He scampered through the van on his hands and knees. Knife in hand, Cade slammed the blade down hard on the gas pedal, piercing and pinning the entire thing to the floor. He popped his head up and peeked through the windshield as he turned the key in the ignition.

Engine on and gears shifted, the van lurched forward its speed increasing as it rolled toward the man with the flamethrower. Cade gazed into the mind-controlled man's soulless eyes as he opened fire.

Flames poured over the van and through the open side windows. Crouched on the floor, Cade crawled through the length of the vehicle, the heat from the fire becoming so intense that he swore the hair on the back of his head would burn off.

Upon reaching the back door, Cade spilled himself onto the pavement with a thud a second before the van collided with the man who operated the flamethrower. He watched in awe as the van continued forward with the man wedged underneath its chassis. Sparks from the gasoline filled canister on the man's back jumped out several feet like embers from a giant sparkler.

Cade knew what would happen next and didn't care to be around for it. Back on his feet, he sprinted through the crowd of Kintner's slaves to his bike, he tucked his rifle under his arm and kick-started the thing. The moment the engine turned over, he released the clutch and shot off like a rocket. Handlebar cocked to the side, he raced away from the scene just moments before the sparks ignited the flamethrower's gas tank.

One small explosion filled his ears a moment before a much larger one erupted. The force of the van's breached gas tank launched the vehicle twenty feet into the sky while a shrapnel-filled shock wave blew through the night air. Kintner's men were instantly toppled, killed or fatally injured.

Unable to maintain control of his bike, Cade ditched it in a thick bush that sat atop one of the many parking lot islands. The impact threw him over the handlebars to the cold, black pavement where he landed hard on his back.

A moment passed and Cade just stared up at the night sky. His whole body ached, but all he could think was how his enemy no doubt heard or at least saw the explosion. The last thing any sniper wanted was to have his location determined by the enemy; Cade knew with all certainty that Kintner would be all the more difficult a target now.

Alexander bared his teeth, grinning slowly as he looked past Sabrina's shoulder at the bright light of the explosion. He surmised the vampire's undead life was finally at an end. Not only had he removed another thorn from his side, but he had also been presented with a reward. Alexander had killed many opponents in his life, but to kill a man and take his woman was a true warlord's accomplishment, a prized moment he would not turn away from.

Alexander brought the winds in his office to an abrupt stop, and Sabrina spilled forward, lifelessly into his arms. He brushed his hand across her puffy red cheek and carefully removed a few wayward strands of hair that had gotten caught in her eyelashes.

"You were planning to hit me with that bottle all along, weren't you? What else did you have in store for me, Sabrina London?" He ran his hand down the small of her back until he felt something foreign. Under the tail of the dress shirt that covered her, he found his old corkscrew taped to her back. He tore the rusty tool free from the tape and threw it to the floor.

"I just—" she mumbled.

"You just don't want to die? Isn't that right? Isn't that what you were going to say?" He released her to the floor.

On her knees, Sabrina crumpled into a pile. "Please don't kill me."

"'Please don't kill me,'" he mocked with a pat to the top of her head.

Alexander turned his back to Sabrina to collect his thoughts. So much had just happened—the fight outside, the fight inside—it all left his already tired mind dangerously split.

Regardless of the chaos that surrounded him, in Alexander's mind he had won some battles: first, the lowly human downstairs was no doubt dead by now. Second, the persistent vampire outside was most likely burned to ashes, a distant memory now. Lastly, the wingless fairy was battered and broken at his feet.

Alexander enjoyed that Sabrina was defeated, but his victory was absent its spoils: her beautiful wings. He might as well toy with her a bit before he killed her; it would make him feel better.

"Sabrina, I have worked several hundred years to find, prepare, and deliver a solution to the human problem. You might think my goal is the enslavement of mankind, but it's not. My goal is their utter extinction."

"You're insane." Sabrina wheezed.

"Oh." Alexander's voice rose with excitement. "Well then, here's something you might find of interest. Fairy wings are not the only special ingredient in my miracle cure. You see, you need a vice to overcome a vice, and I found, through my feud with those bothersome windigos, that the consumption of human flesh creates quite the impossible addiction to overcome."

Chapter Forty-Nine

Not Much Left

"Why are you telling me all this?"

"Because it's time for you to die, my poor wingless fairy."

Delay him, distract him. Damn it, Sabrina, do something. Don't give up. With your wings, you could escape. Get your wings. Sabrina closed her eyes as Kintner reached to pick her up off the floor. All she could see inside her mind was the one thing she wanted most, the exact thing he had wanted: her wings.

"I'm cold, hurt, and tired," she whined. "I just don't care anymore—"

Kintner guffawed, "Would you care if I told you your friends, the human and the vampire, are both dead now? There's no rescue for you, sweetie."

"Dead?"

Sabrina thought she had nothing left to give, but she was wrong. She felt one more stab of pain. Human and vampire could only mean Jackson and Cade, and the thought of Kintner hurting them brought forth a reserve of strength she didn't know she had. *I can do this. Concentrate on your wings. Fuck, if only I had something to calm my nerves*, she thought.

"Look behind you, out the window. You'll see fire and smoke. There smolders the remains of your former lover the vampire."

Sabrina got to her feet slowly, lifted her head and rolled back her shoulders before sauntering through the rubble on the floor to stand at the window beside him. She saw what Kintner was talking about: a vivid orange blaze glowed in the distance. Sabrina felt her heart break. Cade, the man she loved, must have been destroyed. A ball of emotions formed in her stomach, but she held them back; now was not the time to cry.

"Your rescue has been thwarted. I even dealt with the boy personally. A pity the vampire did not make it into the building. I had set a trap for him if he made it that far. Your lover would have found his human ally atop a pool of his own blood. The vampire's desires to kill me, to save you—they would have fallen aside as his hunger took over. You see, I had two of my men ready. They would have ended the lives of the boy and the vampire at once. A quick death to both. Well... quicker for the boy. The poor thing has no doubt bled to death by now."

"You bastard."

———⟨∞⟩———

Moselle, who had watched everything to this point frozen with fear, gasped; fortunately for her, with no air in her lungs, the impulse was silent. She had heard Kintner's words from across the hallway. *He means Jackson.* The fear that had held her back instantly washed away, and she jumped to her feet and sprinted in the direction of the staircase. Accustomed to a leisurely lifestyle, her body was not used to running at such a pace... or at all. She had already taxed her body to overexertion twice that day. Without having properly rehydrated herself, Moselle felt weak, her skin dry and stiff.

At the elevator before the stairs, she returned to the twentieth floor. The doors opened to the sight of broken and splintered furniture; the ground was littered with it as far as she could see. The destruction only heightened the urgency to find her lover.

"Jackson!" she screamed.

The debris trail led Moselle to the upper lobby. The spot was entirely destroyed, furniture demolished, potted plants upturned, the soil spilled to the floor, several florescent lights even dangled from above, knocked free of their housing.

Moselle tried to stand still, to figure where to go next, but her body shook. Her nerves frayed; she had not felt like this since she was alive.

"What do I do?" she said softly to herself, and then yelled. "What do I do?"

The scream cleared her energy. She felt like she was stable upon the ground again and not in the midst of a hard side to side sway.

The destruction took shape in her mind's eye and began to paint a picture for her. *If this is where the fight started, it must lead in the opposite direction, past the elevators.*

As she passed the first elevator, the front desk woman stepped through the open doors of the second.

"You, you're not supposed to be here!"

Without acknowledging her, Moselle lashed out and struck the women's neck with her right hand like a viper, squeezing with such pressure her captive was powerless to move. A purple aura so dark it was almost black seeped from Moselle's body. The woman clawed at Moselle's hand, tried to speak, to cry for help, but could only release the tiniest wheeze.

Slowly, the purple aura that lined Moselle's body began to intensify, attaching itself to the living woman.

"What are... you doing to me—" the woman managed to croak.

The purple energy soaked into the other woman's flesh, and in a matter of seconds, the front desk woman's eyelids widened, and her eyes bulged. Moselle watched the woman convulse, her teeth gritting as she was gripped by pain likely worse than the woman had ever endured.

"Stop!" she shrieked.

Just as the aura had formed around Moselle moments before, it grew out of the woman's body now. Yellow in color, this aura glowed bright and sparkled with energy.

"I'm deeply sorry for your family's loss," Moselle whispered. "May your soul find rest in the afterlife."

Moselle siphoned the energy from the woman into her own body through her hand and the process of rejuvenation began instantly. Quickly, her skin, which had grown dry and hard over the last few hours, regained its normally supple and dewy quality. While her strength surged, Moselle released the dying woman, with a toss that flung her into the open elevator with such force that the bones in her spine snapped upon impact with the wall.

Unchanged in her goal, Moselle moved on, the debris coming to an end after a bend in the hall. There she finally discovered Jackson.

Moselle ran to him in silence. It felt like it took longer than it should have to reach him. With each step, the grimness of her lover's wounds became more apparent. Unable to contain the swell of emotions, Moselle collapsed to the ground, her knees in the copious blood that pooled under his body.

"Jackson," she cried. "Jackson. Jackson. Jackson."

Chapter Fifty

One Bullet

With his rifle braced against his shoulder, Cade peered through the scope at the windows of Kintner Co. He had no idea if this was the side of the building Alexander would be on, or if the man was stupid enough to glance out at the fire from the explosion, but he swore, through all the other scents, he could smell Sabrina. He panned from right to left then descended another level; still, Cade saw nothing out of the ordinary until he spotted a blonde woman on the tenth floor. He adjusted the scope until he realized that it was not just any blonde; it was Sabrina.

"I would recognize those curves anywhere," he snickered. "Now let's see who is in there with you."

Cade shifted the rifle side to side with precise movements and tried to investigate the office as best he could. At first it appeared empty, and Cade considered how to signal her, but quickly decided against it. *Could be a trap.*

Lucky for him, the explosion had popped the bulbs of the two lights nearby; he had just enough shadows to move about undetected, but for how long? Not long at all, he guessed. Fire engines would arrive soon, police as well. It was time to act.

Alexander Kintner moved in behind Sabrina as she stood by the window. "My patience for this night is gone. I now know that if I'm to have any satisfaction, it will be by taking it forcefully."

At the back of her neck, he bundled her hair and placed it over her shoulder. Sabrina tensed up at first, repulsed by his touch, but when she felt his hands around her neck, she told herself over and over to relax; this was the only way. She needed him as much as he needed her.

"Before I end this, please tell me what happened to your"—he paused briefly—"glorious wings?"

"Don't you know?" Sabrina replied softly, her eyes averted from the blaze across the street.

"No."

"They molted."

Once his hands were removed from her neck, he peeled off the unbuttoned dress shirt that hung on her.

"You can't be serious." It was clear from his tone that he did not believe her.

"All your research and you didn't know we do that?"

Sabrina peeked over her shoulder to see his response. When she realized he stared intently at her naked back, she arched it, pronouncing her butt.

"I had no idea," he said tracing his fingertip over her back, where her wings once sat. "I finally procure the component I need to progress my creation to completion—"

"And my wings shed," she finished. "I know of others."

"What did you just say?" Kintner looked up from her back.

"I know other fairy-kind. I can help you catch them, you know, so you can complete your project."

"You would turn traitor against your own kind?"

"My own kind cast me out. They don't want me and at this point... I would do anything," she whispered.

Unexpectedly, Kintner slammed her face first into the window, then pinned her in place by her shoulders.

"Who do you know?" he yelled. "Who, fairy? Whose lives would you trade for your own?"

She pressed herself off the glass just enough to turn her bruised forehead to the side and scream back in his face, "My parents! Asshole! My fucking parents!"

"You'd betray your own parents?" Kintner asked. "You surprise me, Sabrina. After all my research about you, I never would have guessed it. Well, perhaps you're just as the media says, a spoiled rotten child."

"Research? You call staring at half-naked pictures of me all day research? Pal, I saw the file log. That slideshow was on its like five-hundredth loop!" Sabrina stabbed him with sharp words when she knew his guard was down.

"You have no idea what you are talking about."

"No? Cause, I'm guessing guys your age have to look at naughty pictures over and over—"

"Shut your mouth!"

"What's the matter, Alex? Embarrassed you can't get it up? I hear there's a drug for that."

Unable to push her chest off the cool glass to turn around and physically confront him, Sabrina did the next best thing and pushed her buttocks out hard into his groin.

"Come to think of it, this isn't the first time you had me bent over and just like last time all you could think about was my wings. Guess I was wrong about you."

"You fucking whore, I'll kill you."

"Go ahead, kill me already," she screamed back. "You're sure as hell not man enough to fuck me!"

She was close; she could feel it. Sabrina had started to sweat; her back tingled and itched. She was very close.

From below, Cade watched as his rage grew. No stranger to the brutality of man, Cade knew if he did not act soon, his sweet sunshine would be further harmed—even killed.

Years of experience reinforced his thoughts. He knew he would only get one shot: one bullet to end this mess; a single metal slug to prevent the bigger catastrophe that would come if the wraiths were dispatched. Kintner's head bobbed back and forth, side to side, a difficult target that would require more time than Cade had to spend.

Cade waited for his shot; he could see the blood trickle from a new wound on Sabrina's head after Alexander Kintner slammed her into the glass. If her naked body pressed against the large window wasn't a big enough distraction, the blood only made it worse. *What's really happening up there?* he wondered. *What's being said? Why aren't you fighting him, Sabrina?*

When the sirens came closer, Cade moved his aim down to Sabrina's chest. From this range he could put a bullet through Sabrina that would most likely terminate his primary target. It was a tactic he had employed before, but never with such dire consequences.

"Come on, sweetheart, move to the side or something; give me the shot, before I have to take one we'll both regret."

The room had grown suddenly quiet. The only sound was that of the jingle of Alexander Kintner's belt being unbuckled by his shaky hands. Sabrina thought this might be her opportunity to move, run for the door, even fight, but she still couldn't push her chest off the glass.

Kintner was using his powers to hold her in place. She felt it now, like hands pressed flat to her back and shoulders. It did not matter though. Just a few more minutes she told herself—

just a bit more warmth and her new wings would pop. She just had to stay alive a few more minutes.

The sound of his pants dropping to the floor was followed by the touch of his fingers gently around her waist. His hands were hot, and although he was her enemy, their presence on her skin felt fantastic.

"All mine," was all he said.

"Yes, all yours." She rolled her eyes as she spoke. "I want your hands all over me; touch my arms, my stomach, my... my back."

Sabrina spread her legs and rose to the tips of her toes. Her enticement worked, Kintner was filled with a rush of desire, she could tell by the way he forcefully gripped her waist. She was in control now—the balance of power had shifted, and he hadn't even realized it.

His touch should have nauseated her, but this was not the first time a stranger had taken advantage of her. All those drunken nights spent in the clubs—Sabrina had danced and hopped from partner to partner, hooked up with unfamiliar men—it had made her cold inside. It was Sabrina's job to smile, to act happy; being fake was just another part of her everyday life. *You can do this, Sabrina. Your wings will save you.*

Kintner pawed at her stomach before he moved his hands up to her chest. Unable to cup her breasts because he had her pressed so tightly to the glass, he had no option but to release her so he could have at her.

"Yes, Alexander," she fake moaned. "Squeeze my tits."

"Hold still, fairy!"

When Alexander's hands released their kneading grip on her breasts, she knew the inevitable was next and just about preferred death to the alternative.

"Wait," she interrupted, her head turned to look at him. "Aren't you afraid your employees will hear us?" She grasped at a flimsy excuse to prolong the inevitable. "What will they think?"

"It's late," he huffed. "Skeleton crew."

Once again, Sabrina felt Kintner position himself to enter her from behind, but before he could, she involuntarily shuddered.

"What is this?"

Two pools of color grew on her back like ink blots on a napkin, changing in shape and detail as they did.

"Touch it." Sabrina gritted her teeth through a sensation that made her heart flutter.

Kintner reached up and placed his hand on her hot back. Slick with sweat, he brushed his palm in a circular motion across her flesh until the touch of a slight indentation caused him to gasp.

"Y-your wings?"

Kintner stepped back, his feet still tethered together by his dropped pants.

As Sabrina stood upright, her wings slowly emerged from the core of her body.

"Unbelievable. To think, I was going to kill you only moments ago. Had I not played along with your pathetic efforts to seduce me, I'd be staring at your broken corpse lying on my floor right now."

Sabrina barely heard him—to unfurl newborn wings was a nearly orgasmic experience. The tingle that normally crawled across her skin with the release of her wings electrified her limbs, made her stand on the tips of her toes and spread open her hands until every finger was out so far, they almost bent back. Fresh energy, like the sound of radio static, crackled around Sabrina's body as her wings grew and grew from her back, their rainbow-colored light increased exponentially brighter with every inch.

"Their glow... so intense," Alexander shouted over the noise.

Sabrina pivoted carefully; she wanted to face her adversary. What she saw was not an unfamiliar sight. He was just another man, desperate to own her, his pants around his ankles, his life in ruins. The sight diminished him and for the first time since she had seen him at Moselle's father's club, Sabrina no longer feared Alexander Kintner.

"I-I've never seen fairy wings grow so large." He smiled.

Sabrina could see it in his eyes: in his mind, he had already cultivated her wings.

"Still want to kill me?"

He hesitated to answer, clearly awestruck by the beauty of her wings and the shimmer they cast across her nude body. With as little as one flap, Sabrina was airborne. Once afloat the movement of her wings was minimal; they moved just enough to maintain her hover a foot off the ground.

Kintner picked up his pants. "I saw them shed... you said they shed, or was that all a trick?"

"You sure don't know much about us, do you?" Her nose crinkled as she spoke.

"A predator only needs to know how to kill."

"Oh really?" Sabrina giggled at him. "You don't look like a predator anymore to me. You're just a sad little man who lost his—"

"You have no idea what I am!" Kintner shouted over her. "Come here and let me show you—"

"Thanks, but I'm outta here."

The heat that radiated from Sabrina's wings had grown so intense that it began to melt the large window at her back. When she floated back a foot, her wings came in contact with the already weakened glass and burned a hole in it instantly. With a gust of wind and the sudden shift in air pressure, Sabrina's entire body was sucked out the window into the night sky.

Cade watched from the scope of his rifle. The pitch of the sirens told him how close the emergency vehicles were. It would be only seconds before they pulled into the parking lot. He had to leave now; there was no choice if he didn't want to confront them.

One last time, Cade aimed at his target and against his better judgment, he rushed his shot. *Boom.* The bullet drowned out all the other sounds in the parking lot as it raced from the muzzle of his rifle. In through the hole Sabrina had floated out, the bullet struck Kintner in the left arm.

Despite the fact that the projectile tore through its target's flesh and muscle, both shredded beyond repair, it missed its precise mark. Cade growled like a tiger, hungry for a kill and angry that his prey escaped.

Cade knew he needed to find some elevation for a better shot, so he got on his motorcycle and sped toward the building across the street, a commercial bank. After he parked his bike in the shadows he watched until the last police car zoomed by to the scene of the explosion. His people had firm rules about killing humans; there were a few professions all vampires knew to steer clear of and firemen and policemen were at the top of the list. Their murders were too high profile and threatened the discovery of his kind. Yet, even with those rules in the back of his mind, he considered slaughtering them all, since he knew it would be only a matter of seconds before one of the emergency crew spotted the impossible: a naked glowing woman who hovered high in the sky alongside the Kintner Co. building. A single report on the radio from one of these policemen would mean the end for them all.

"Gotta move. No time to waste," he whispered to himself.

Cade scrambled up a fire ladder to the flat roof of the two-story bank. Once again, he set up his long-barreled rifle and took aim. While he adjusted the scope's focal plane, he spotted movement outside the front door of the building; it was Moselle, and she carried Jackson's lifeless body in her arms.

Chapter Fifty-One

No Looking Back

Moselle knew Jackson was dying. Breath barely passed his lips; his pulse was faint—nearly impossible to sense. The fifteen buckets of snakes they had deposited outside the front door of the building had given her the results she had hoped for. The main entrance was evacuated; the guards were dead. To leave Kintner Co. was as easy as a stroll out the door, but Jackson should have been at her side, not dying in her arms.

Moselle had to find her lover some help; she had to save his life. Nothing else mattered—not DUST, not Kintner, not the wraiths. In that moment, Jackson was everything.

She heard a scream behind her; one of the security guards she had encountered early in the night had not yet succumbed to the snake bite. As she continued her slow escape, she heard him yell again, this time deciphering his word.

"Stop!"

Stop was the last thing she would do. A gunshot echoed in the night as the guard tried his best to steady his hands. Moselle did not flinch.

Cade had put a bullet in the guard's brain, splitting the man's head in two. He may have missed his shot at Kintner a moment ago, but he was determined that was the last bullet he wasted tonight.

The police between Cade and Kintner Co. quickly tracked the origin of the shot. With weapons drawn they sprang into action. Ducked down behind a ledge on the roof, Cade held still a moment while he determined what to do; alas, the decision was already made for him. He stood up with a shout and fired off the sniper rifle from his hip just to hold everyone's attention. While up, he took one last glance at Sabrina and then dove to the ground to avoid a hail of bullets. Even with his enhanced eyesight, all he could see was the bright light of her wings as she floated near the building. *What the hell are you doing? Fly away, Sabrina.*

Sabrina laughed at Kintner while he buttoned up his pants with one hand. Instead of a quick escape from her enemy, she mocked him, and her overconfidence gave him enough time to summon his mastery of the elements. Inside the office, she watched a hand made entirely of condensed air formed and then reached out to her. Snagged out of the sky, the fingers wrapped around her waist and ribcage with such intense pressure it made her exhale.

Sabrina struggled and with what little energy she had regained, she tried to pry the nearly invisible fingers off her or at least flutter her wings hard enough to fly free, but she was trapped. Like the slingshot ride at her favorite theme park, she was suddenly yanked back into the building by Kintner's powers.

As Sabrina felt the force wrap tighter around her body, her heart seized. She could be crushed at any moment; she knew it. She had already cried, begged, and whined for help today. No more—not now.

Anger built inside Sabrina like she had never known. This one man had filled her last few days with so much trauma that her once-beautiful world had turned to ash. *Embarrassed, imprisoned, beaten, and nearly raped—it ends here.*

"Off me!" she grumbled, as she twisted her arms, in an effort to free them from where they were pinned to her body.

"You challenged me to get you." Kintner's voice grew louder until he was screaming. "Well, I got you now!"

With a broad wave of his magical arm, he slammed Sabrina face-first into the closet door. The impact should have knocked her out, but the closet door was soft, unlike the glass or concrete walls that surrounded it. Still, she dropped to the floor like a rag doll and her body crumpled.

"Your wings are mine."

Chapter Fifty-Two

Ashes to Ashes

Alexander Kintner unlocked the top drawer of his desk and retrieved a long fish-scaling knife, the very weapon he had used to de-wing and subsequently kill many fairy-kind in the past.

"It's past time I take this."

With little effort, he snatched the bracelet off her wrist and carried it up to his hand atop a small gust of air.

As he approached Sabrina, deciding which to slice first, her throat or her wings, she moved. Slowly, this woman he had written off as frail and hopeless pushed herself up off the ground.

"You want my wings, Kintner," she screamed, spitting out an eyetooth as she did. "Take them!"

The already-powerful glow from her wings intensified, their shine so bright that Alexander had to raise his hands to protect his eyes. The man who had killed so many of her kind had no clue it was already far too late for him. The concentrated radiance had begun to burn all that it touched with the exception of its source.

"Take them!" Sabrina screamed again. "Take them!"

Alexander felt the skin on the back of his hand burn and bubble. His clothes sizzled until thick, white vapors rose up to his nostrils. For the first time in many years, Alexander Kintner knew he had been beaten. As he turned to flee, he attempted to summon his powers to protect his exit, but something stole away his concentration.

Alexander did not hear the gunshot or feel the impact of the slug; all he saw was a puff of red mist over his left eye, a chunk of something he thought looked like orange pulp splattered to the ground. When he reached up to his face with a smoldering hand, he understood better what had happened—the sniper had managed to hit his mark.

It was then that a flash of light as bright as a nuclear bomb washed away everything Alexander saw. White light filled his vision; there was no sound, no smell—just the taste of ash in his mouth before all sensations disappeared.

The noiseless flash lit the parking lot below, all the way across the street to where Cade was positioned. The illumination was so bright that everyone who faced it was momentarily blinded. Since Cade had ducked down for protection his eyes were spared.

Carefully, he peeked from the second-story building at the law enforcement officers below. Most of them were muddled with confusion or blinded by the flash; the sight relieved him of much of his stress. Cade wouldn't have to break any more rules before he returned to slumber, and that was fine by him.

A sparkle of colorful light, like the pop of a distant firework caught his eye. Sabrina was flying away from the building—she was finally safe.

Cade jumped off the bank's roof and he landed only feet from his motorcycle, where, with a quick hop, he was seated, key in the ignition.

"Huzzah!" he cried out as he sped off toward Moselle.

Chapter Fifty-Three

Aftermath

Sabrina puffed on the end of a newly lit cigarette as she pulled the soft, pink covers of her bed over her bare chest. A smile decorated her face; she felt amazing, despite the half a dozen bandages that covered her body and being minus an eye tooth.

Her eyes clapped onto Cade's lean, muscular buttocks as he walked around the bed; he had gone to the kitchen to retrieve them another bottle of wine. The way he strutted made her giggle, but then again, everything made her laugh today; it was a good day.

"Hurry up! I want to do it again!"

"Do what again?" Cade inquired from the doorway as he swiftly jumped into his jeans.

"Make love."

"Make love," Cade chuckled. "Since when did we graduate from fucking to love making?"

"A few hours ago. Now hurry up, butter buns!"

"I never thought the day would come that you and I were a couple again."

Sabrina hoped that was the case, she could not imagine a reason why Cade would leave her again, not after what had happened.

The past four days were a jumbled mess in her head; Sabrina was happy to just have a moment to relax and enjoy. With Cade's encouragement, she had accepted that it would no doubt take time to sort everything out; Mira was gone, Alexander Kintner was dead, Jackson was—

"Maybe we should go back to the hospital," Sabrina said as she took a half-eaten lollipop from where it rested on her end table.

"Sweetie, you just got back from there three hours ago. We've been at this for four days straight. You need a break."

"I know, I just feel like there's something that needs my direct attention," Sabrina replied, looking at a small, framed photo of her and Mira that she kept at her bedside. "I want to go looking for Mira again tomorrow."

Sabrina's cell phone rang loudly.

"Get that for me, babe?" she shouted.

Mira—just hearing her name made him sad. Cade feared Sabrina's friend was lost. He hadn't told Sabrina yet, but later that night, the night of Kintner's death, he had returned to search for her.

Cade saw the red glow on the skyline from miles away and followed it to the source. No number of firemen would put out this inferno; Kintner's headquarters would burn to the ground.

From across the street, Cade could smell their flesh on the ashes, a different aroma than human skin. Thrasher and his friends had fulfilled their quest. Somehow, they survived the demolition of Kintner's home, only to no doubt slip into his headquarters and finally destroy all that remained of the man's drugs and research records.

Cade found it poetic; Thrasher and his gang had chosen to end their curse, to be cleansed with the flames. They died to protect the world, human and otherworldly alike. Thanks to the windigo, there would be no risk of discovery in this high-profile story. By morning, all traces of Alexander Kintner and his company would be gone.

Cade stared at the fire and sniffed the air one last time. *No water elemental could survive such a blaze. Mira must be gone.*

Cade snatched Sabrina's phone from where it danced across the kitchen table and then playfully, annunciated, "Good evening."

"Cade, it's Moselle," she whispered.

"Lady Moselle, is everything well?" Cade asked, hearing a series of loud beeps from the other end of the phone line. "Has Jackson's condition changed?"

"Cade, I-I need your help." Moselle's normally confident voice wavered. "Something unexpected has occurred. Please come to the hospital right away."

The call ended abruptly, and Cade stood in silence until Sabrina shouted from the bedroom.

"Who was it? Was it my father?"

"Huh?" Cade was unsure how to answer.

"Who was it?" Sabrina repeated.

"Just another reporter," he lied.

"Oh, well, please leave the phone on in case Moselle calls."

"Yeah... I will," Cade said as he did the opposite. "We need more champagne. I'm going to dash out and get us some."

"I could've sworn we had another bottle of Dom in the cabinet."

Cade held the bottle she spoke of in his left hand. It was a good year; he recalled it well. The champagne would have had a delightful taste, but he was too curious to not explore Moselle's request.

"None there; I'm afraid," he lied again.

"Okay, well, hurry back!"

"Of course." Cade retrieved his jacket from the living room floor.

"Oh... and Cade..." Sabrina called out to him again, but he did not reply. "Cade?"

He did not stop. He walked out of her apartment, took a deep breath, turned around, and locked the door behind himself.

"Goodbye, my sweet sunshine."

THE END

The story continues in
TWO POLLUTED BLACK-HEART ROMANCES
- Book Two of the Water Kingdom Series.

About the Author

Kevin James Breaux is an award-winning author and artist. He has written ten books and devoted many years of his life to crafting short stories and novels. He has held active memberships in many writing associations, including the SFWA, ITW and Paranormal Romance Guild. Breaux is always enthusiastic about the challenge writing presents. He lives by the motto "Write Makes Might!"© and sees each new page as an opportunity to improve and advance.

He refers to himself as a creative being and loves to see his ideas become tangible. You can explore his projects on the following social media sites and his website.

Website: www.kevinbreaux.com
Facebook: www.facebook.com/KevinJamesBreauxAuthor
Twitter: @author_kjb
Instagram: @author_kjb
e-mail: kevin@kevinbreaux.com

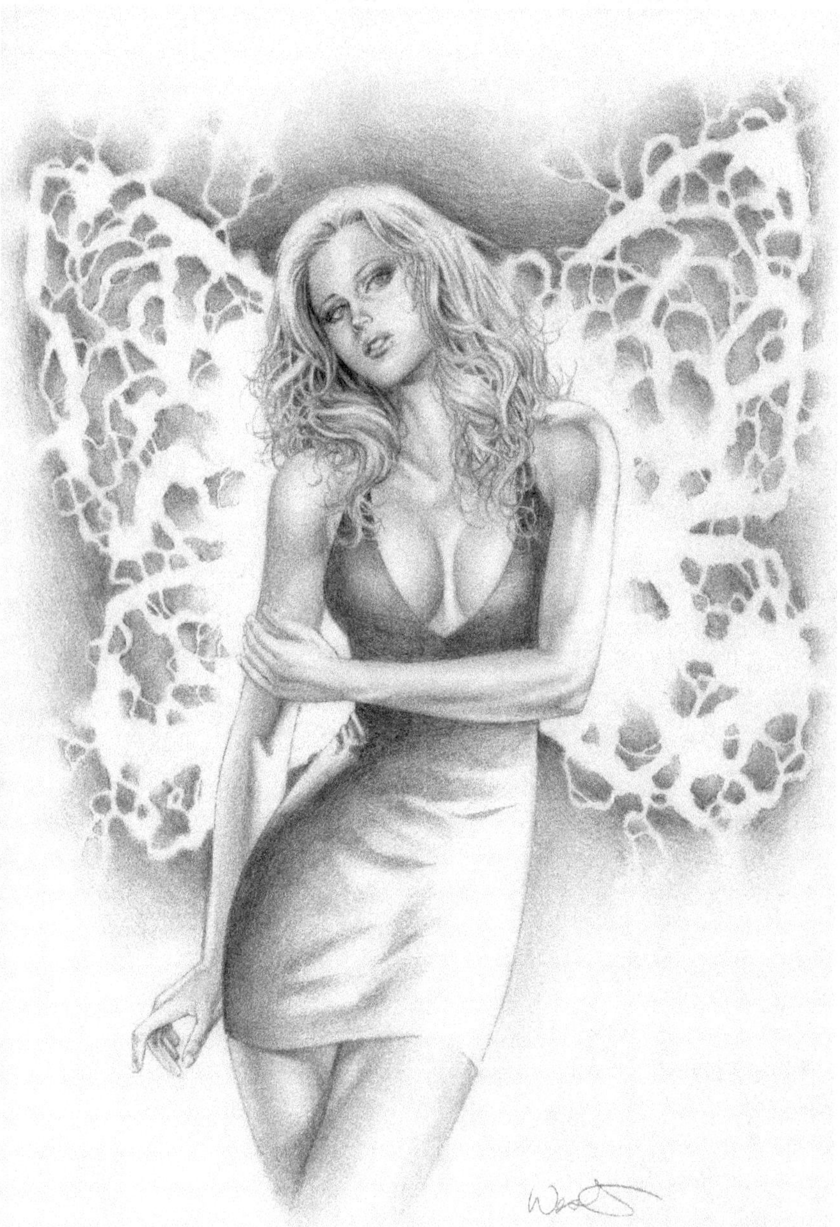